TO HELL OR SLIGO

By
Angus Cactus

Copyright © 2016 Senan Gilsenan
All rights reserved.
(Revised edition 2017)

ACKNOWLEDGEMENT

I would like to acknowledge and thank both Tessa Gilsenan and Mik Hartshawn for their excellent contribution in the editing process.

DEDICATION

This book is dedicated to my sister Bernadette, who envisaged this book, and who I am sure would have loved reading it, if only she had been able to live a little bit longer.

She is featured in this story, along with her husband Jimmy, our father Paddy, our mother Margaret, and Guinness, her loyal Yorkshire terrier. Sadly, they have all passed away, but my ambition is that they live on in these pages.

This is a work of both fact and fiction. What I mean is that some of this story happened and some of it did not. To honour the dead, their names have been kept the same, and to honour the living, most of their names have been changed.

There is so much love in this book; I really hope it comes across.

PREFACE

There is a thin line between truth and fiction, and you won't find it here in this tall story told about a ripping yarn in which fact and fiction are inseparable because both are equally absurd.
PT Barnum said that when faced with the mundane reality of the truth, 'always print the legend.'
I have always been amazed at the lengths that Sligonians will go to embellish a story when telling it. These stories grow legs and achieve a life of their own as they are retold again and again by different folk who each add a new abstract layer to the original truth. In the end, the story becomes so much prettier than the truth.
This book is to honour the art of Sligonian story telling. Within this very story which I tell into Hell or Sligo, lays some real Sligonian stories which were related to me, all apparently true, and more than likely half made up. Now I have added by own layer of embellishment and mixed them into a fictional story which includes real people mixed in with a range of fictional characters. To protect the living, I have changed many of their names, and to honour the dead, I have kept their names the same.

A tall tale about buried gold brings an unhinged set of characters to a mad town and pits them against even stranger locals.
I don't know whether Sligonians still tell stories about 'blow-in' newcomers living off the fruits of gold buried by their ancestors, or even whether there are new versions of this story. These were always my favourite tall stories along with those anecdotal stories which featured nefarious outsiders being unexpectedly thwarted by brave or obstinate locals. Of course, this all had to go into the storyline.
To Hell or Sligo is also homage to three of my favourite comedy film plots. Those being: In Bruges, Pineapple Express, and the Ealing comedy, The Lady Killers.
At **http://anguscactus.wix.com/author**, you'll find extras that might be helpful or interesting to have when reading *To hell or Sligo*. Photos of places featured in the novel, explanations of concepts and ideas referred to in the storyline, and other background information.

CHAPTER INDEX

Introduction .... *vi*
1   *Lord Louis* *1*
2   *Belfast* *4*
3   *The plan, the dream, & the team* *10*
4   *Clancy & Walsh ESQ. (Thursday)* *12*
5   *Letterkenny   (Friday)* *17*
6   *Sligo Town   (Friday)* *20*
7   *The Bective Hotel   (Friday)* *23*
8   *The Barman   (Friday)* *27*
9   *The Bogmen   (Friday)* *36*
10 *Séamus Tooley* *42*
11 *The Happy Huong   (Friday)* *44*
12 *The Other Gun Club   (Friday)* *51*
13 *Hazelwood   (Friday)* *55*
14 *Colleen's 21st (Friday)* *63*
15 *After-Party   (Friday)* *67*
16 *The Troubles   (Friday)* *73*
17 *Saturday Morning* *77*
18 *Maeve   (Saturday)* *84*
19 *Two Car Tail   (Saturday)* *89*
20 *The Road To Ballintrillick (Saturday)* *91*
21 *Cheeseburger Express (Saturday)* *94*
22 *Eileen's Pub   (Saturday)* *97*
23 *Sligo Sunday* *105*
24 *Amelia   (Sunday)* *112*
25 *Doorly Park   (Sunday)* *115*
26 *Taxi for Huong   (Sunday)* *120*
27 *Streedagh   (Sunday)* *124*
28 *Prisoner of War   (Sunday)* *132*
29 *Buffalo Soldier   (Sunday)* *136*
30 *Diarmuid & Grainne's Cave   (Sunday)* *140*
31 *The Car Pool   (Sunday)* *147*
32 *Missing Person   (Sunday)* *150*
33 *Switchboard Terrorist (Sunday)* *152*
34 *Mullaghmore   (Sunday)* *158*
35 *Desperate Measures   (Sunday)* *159*
36 *Special Detectives   (Sunday)* *161*
37 *All in the Prep   (Sunday)* *162*
38 *The Knife   (Sunday)* *163*

39	*Raghly Point (Sunday)*	*165*
40	*Geniff Horseshoe (Sunday)*	*173*
41	*The Refuge (Sunday)*	*179*
42	*Maxie (Sunday)*	*184*
43	*Gun (Sunday)*	*186*
44	*Reunion (Sunday)*	*188*
45	*Mickey (Sunday)*	*190*
46	*Aftermath (Sunday)*	*194*
47	*The Next Day (Monday)*	*200*
48	*The Right Thing (Monday)*	*204*
49	*Repercussions*	*219*

Introduction

There is something peculiarly Irish about the concept of buried gold. Maybe the source of this lies within its ancient legends; perhaps all those leprechauns had to bury their pots of gold somewhere. No better place than in County Sligo and Sligo Town, where generations have told stories about 'blow-ins' bringing in foreign gold and burying it here in secret locations.

These stories are never told with the notion of anyone finding it. Instead, the stories are used to explain how certain people came to acquire unknown sources of wealth and income. Surely they were living off the proceeds of some golden stash which was buried long ago by their ancestors.

You see, the term blow-in is derogatory. A verb and a preposition used to denote that you may never be really accepted in Sligo unless you went many generations deep. The Sligonians have always been suspicious of outsiders, and ready if necessary to defend their bit of turf. Possibly when the English coined the expression, 'To hell or Connaught', they really meant Sligo.

The first foreigners to bring in their own gold were literally 'blows-ins'. The Spanish Armada met a fate worse than Drake off the coast of Sligo Bay. They were dispersed by violent storms and blown onto the rocks at Streedagh. Many galleons floundered there; the wrecks of their keels are still visible in the sand at low tide.

The locals weren't too hospitable to the survivors. Many were hacked to death on the beaches, whilst others hid and tried to integrate with the local populace. Only a few made it back to Spain. Much of the flotsam was washed up on the shores or recovered from the shallow wrecks. Strangely no gold, despite the fact that these ships were laden with as much of the stuff deemed necessary to support a Spanish army of mercenaries abroad for at least two years.

In Sligo, it was rumoured that the gold had been buried. Perhaps it was intended to be squandered by future generations of black Irish which was the name given to the descendants of the Spanish and their local brides.

Those stocks of buried gold were replenished in the closing months of the Second World War. German U-Boats were very familiar with the west coast of Ireland. Shipments of arms had been delivered to Connaught with the intention of creating a thorn in the side of the British up north. When this Irish cause became futile, the German's developed one of their own. The Nazi elite knowing that the war was practically over intended to spirit away many tons of gold and precious cargoes to be buried on distant beaches. Much of it made its way to Chile and Argentina, but the U-Boats allegedly surfaced off the coast of Sligo too. Those buried crates of gold which were intended to rebuild the party following the war were now consigned as treasure for a later generation. That generation was rumoured to be the sons, daughters and grandchildren of the U-boatmen.

In the late 70s, much like the rest of the world, Sligo had terrible unemployment. Despite this, West Germany was doing well, and a number of German manufacturing firms had set up subsidiary factories in County Sligo; one of them was purpose built in Hazelwood on the banks of Lough Gill. As a teenager, I heard the local rumours about the German 'blow-ins' who managed these. Apparently they were all the offspring of the same U-boat commander. Anyway, that was the way the story was told.

Then in the early 80s, a new story about buried gold arrived in town. This is the story I am going to tell you. Except that it didn't begin in Sligo; it began in Belfast. However, before my story takes you there, I have to briefly take you back to the beginning. That was the beginning of my young romance with Enya. A few years earlier, our first date together was to become profound for both me and rest of the British Isles.

1   Lord Louis

Grange, Co. Sligo, Monday morning, Aug 27, 1979

Meanwhile, 20 miles north of Sligo, nothing was happening. To be more exact, I was sitting on Enya's bed and trying to work out how to penetrate her protective shield which was in the form of a disco inspired blue jumpsuit with tight long sleeves and baggy leggings which tapered in tightly at the ankle. I had already worked out that the flap that ran down from the neck to the waist hid no zip or buttons. It was just a cunning tailor's ruse to hide the real target fastenings which Enya was now so protectively lying upon. I fiddled with the wide red sash belt wrapped tightly around her trim waist, but that had no give in it. It was like a fortress; the jumpsuit seemed to have no beginning or end. From its tight military collar down to its termination in a pair of bright red boots, it made Enya look a bit like Superman. If so, she was under the restraining power of krypton, because she was lying flat and rigid on the bed, which was in my limited experience, the universally adopted position amongst Sligo girls for retaining their virtue. Strangely enough, this posture also represented the Sligo code for access all areas. For a seventeen-year-old lad like me, it was a difficult quandary. In fact, most of my peer group would often rely on the reasoning powers of alcohol to work out this dichotomy. Sadly I was sober at the time and unable to work out just how far she was letting me go. With her tousled shoulder length dark hair and piercing blue eyes, she looked up at me from her pillow like that picture of Jane Russell lying in the hay. I think it was from 'The Outlaw' which was a film from way before my time. Nevertheless, that picture had served me well when my hormones were playing me up, and the page of the scrapbook that it was in was torn where it had stuck to the next one. This was a true testimony to its erotic appeal when every other source of eye candy was strictly unavailable to a catholic boy living in a catholic country in an age of non-enlightenment.

My biggest fear in life back then was getting a girl pregnant. I do not really recall why, except that it was shameful and known to be a game changer. I guess I didn't want my adolescence to end, and besides, as a father, I would have to one day explain about the birds and the bees to my child. Teaching my progeny everything I knew could represent a problem because I knew precious little about anything, and what I knew about sex could be written on the back of a stamp.

ANGUS CACTUS

I looked at my Super-Girl with needy eyes which pleaded with her to help me help her out of her clothes. She stared back at me with yet another undecipherable look which probably meant 'get on with it'.

Although this was our first date, we had worked together for a couple of months and we had begun to notice each other during our busy restaurant shifts. Fleeting eye contact had developed into full body contact. We would press up against each other as we tried to place our orders in the kitchen thinking that this was our little secret.

I would have asked her out to a discotheque but for two factors which stopped me. One was the fact that she lived 20 miles outside of town and I would need a lift to collect her. The second was nerves, which beset me when it came to matters of passion. At seventeen, I was inexperienced, a little shy, and convinced that male virginity was not a good thing.

I got a car when I was nearly 17 but had to wait for my birthday in order to legally drive. After that, legality went out the window. I taught myself to drive which must have been a traumatic experience for other road users. Four wheels and as many gears gave me the confidence to think that I could pass any test. Regardless of my confidence, the examiner grabbed hold of the steering wheel during my driving test, and following that insult, I asked him to step out of my car at least a mile from his office. This punishment didn't help change his mind. And as a result, I had to drive that car forever with a provisional license, leaving insurance in the lap of the Gods.

At seventeen, I just loved speed, and with my foot to the floor, I could take that Fiat 127 to over a hundred, which cut down commuting time substantially to the village of Grange, which was situated 20 miles north of the town of Sligo where I lived on the provincial west coast of Ireland.

The first day that I made that journey with Enya was on the morning of Monday 27th August 1979, and I was driving her home. The hotel where we worked together had been booked out for the last four days and we had had a very busy weekend. With the extra shifts involved, we had both worked exceptionally hard, and Enya had stayed over for the duration.

Last night had witnessed our first kiss, and now I was dropping her home. My appetite was only whetted. I hoped that some privacy together might help get me the main course. However, her mother seemed more intent on serving me tea; the Irish equivalent of the Native American peace pipe. I sipped politely and ate the offered scone, as well as passing her interrogation with flying colours.

Her father who was an ambulance driver was already at work, and I assumed that I would meet him at some later date. Anything was possible now that her mother had been won over with anecdotes and politeness.

This meant that the main defensive shield to Enya's bedroom was down; and once inside her daughter's room, I had intended to wreak havoc. But that didn't happen because her mother was soon knocking on the door and sounding distressed.

"Your father was on the phone Enya. He said that they have had an emergency up at Classiebawn castle. His ambulance was called out initially for a suicide, but that was some kind of confusion. It's Mountbatten. His boat has been blown to smithereens."

Not that I am an ambulance chaser, but her father was the driver, and I did want to meet him. A boat blown up at sea also offered the prospect of danger and excitement, and the two of us jumped back in the car and raced the few miles to the scene which was at the harbour in Mullaghmore. This small fishing village, just like Grange, was in the shadow of Benbulben Mountain which prominently stood out like the backbone of County Sligo. It was part of the Dartry mountain range, yet technically it wasn't a real mountain at all. It was merely the remnant of an ancient plateau that had been eaten and eroded by glaciers. These had since departed and left behind Benbulben's pronounced jagged features. The glaciers were reminiscent of the English rulers of this land that had shaped this country and its customs, but withdrawn once they had outstayed their welcome. Now only a few remnant Lords were left behind.

Mountbatten was one of these Lords but he was a well-respected man locally. Every year, he spent August in his castle near Mullaghmore. I had never met him before this day, and yet I still never got to see him alive. The bomb had killed him, along with his grandson and a local boat boy. I saw their bodies as they were carried to the ambulance, and yes, I also got to meet Enya's father.

This was the first time that the northern troubles had visited Sligo, and it wasn't to be the last. I looked out to sea and witnessed the floating debris from the explosion. Then I observed all around, checking the horizon and the surrounding shoreline. If the bomber had used a remote control, they were probably still there, watching and witnessing, just as I was. It made me wonder what kind of person indiscriminately takes lives so easily, and then my glance took in the painted slogan on the side of Benbulben. The white letters, 30ft tall faced in this direction. They said 'BRITS OUT', and that probably included Mountbatten. I reckoned they should have read, 'BLOW-INS OUT' because that was the real sentimentality applied to non-Sligonians who had no roots here. I looked back again taking in the suffering of the wounded and all of the carnage. This wasn't hell, it was Sligo.

2 Belfast

The St Agnes Social club in Andersonstown, Belfast. May 1983

It was a good pint of Guinness, perfectly pulled by a taciturn barman who wore the stock expression of indifference which came with all the employees of these republican social clubs.

This club was in the part of Andersonstown which bordered the lower Falls Road and fancied itself as a fierce Catholic no-go area. That meant it was off limits for the police, army, and the nearby protestant & loyalist communities. Thus, no British laws applied here or in any of the other illegal drinking clubs that flouted the strict licensing laws which closed every other licensed public bar on a Sunday.

The man who was going to drink this perfectly pulled pint was Mickey Kavanagh. He was a tall and heavy-set man in his mid-forties. He had a matching large head, fully serviced by a retainer of gingery brown hair, and despite his round friendly looking face, he didn't suffer fools easily.

You could even describe him as hulking. In his youth, he had been an amateur boxer, but perhaps a defensive stance had not been his strength. His large head now resembled a mountain rock in which all the sharp features had been rounded off.

His hair was brushed forward, almost touching hooded, cynical eyes. The same blue eyes that held a small glint that could easily be transfigured into a smile, because it was a large jolly heart which drove him, and a spirit of mirth which radiated from within. A generous nature and a convivial persona all helped to make his bulldog features appear more attractive.

He hated drinking alone and wasn't a great fan of drinking here either. This place suffered from damp and also from an underlying oppressive attitude of aggression subdued only by a hidden pecking order of hard men.

The damp walls had been masked over by poorly decorated panel boards, but the smell of mildew remained. The aggression had been masked over by poorly orchestrated background music, a mix of ceili and nationalist folk songs, with the occasional rousing rebel song thrown in the mix. The amp was practically blown and the sound was fuzzy and thus kept low in the background.

Kav as he was known to everyone, including his mother, liked to stay in the background too. He wasn't frightened of anyone here, except maybe a few heavy hitters that he sat far away from. His credentials were good here. He was a volunteer with the provisional IRA. The emphasis, however, lay with the word volunteer.

After ten years of service and loyalty to the cause and to Belfast command, he was no longer on the payroll. This was a bone of contention for him. He had leanings towards active service with an ambition to run his own unit. However, he was unlikely to be allowed to pick his own cell, when command wouldn't even assign him to active service or put him on the payroll. They didn't see him as reliable, and nor was he proven as a good earner. His loyalty was never in doubt, but his conviction to ruthlessness was, and that was not uncommon to old republican soldiers who had seen and lived through too much.

The cause took second place to his conviction to alcohol. Even now, he was here purely for a Guinness. In this Presbyterian controlled city of Belfast, these illegal drinking clubs were the only place you could get a drink on a Sunday.

Kav found a small table in the midst of a thriving social section of the room. Although he kept himself to himself, his active mind and smart intellect couldn't manage to play along and he unconsciously listened to the broad range of conversations taking place amongst the different social pairings around him.

One conversation he was listening to intrigued him. On a nearby table sat two young men in their early twenties. One of whom he had been acquainted with for some years, but the other one looked really out of place here. He had bleached white hair cut in a mullet style that betrayed a stronger interest in the music scene than the republican one. His accent kept slipping too. Kav inclined his head slightly to listen more closely, and he noted the west Belfast brogue seemed put on in order to fit in here.

Kav wondered where he was from and whether he was an Englishman. With his thin druggie appearance and the long white plaits in the back of his hair, he certainly wasn't a soldier or a policeman. In fact, he looked too far gone to even be a reconnaissance agent. Some of those spotters were hard to tell, but they never had dilated pupils the size of saucers, and nor did they ramble on delivering a diatribe of inconsequential spiel.

However the more Kav listened to the thin young man, the more he got drawn into the story that he was re-telling to his friend. Seemingly, it was about a Vietnamese man and a Chinaman who had buried a large horde of gold down south. He had mentioned Sligo a few times, so Kav assumed that it was buried somewhere in that county. The story about how the gold had arrived in the area was even more bizarre. Someone was a fighting Buddhist monk who had either stolen or taken his temple's gold and somehow spirited it over to Ireland.

It was a tall story; that was for sure, but the depth of detail he managed to overhear lent it some credibility. Apparently, this young man knew all of this because his girlfriend worked for one of the Asians, but nobody knew where their gold was actually buried.

Kav took a long sup of his drink and eyed up the young man trying to determine his trustworthiness. He even went for a walk past his table to get a closer look at him. If he would have gone to the toilets, Kav would probably have followed him there, but despite the blond youngster's obvious thirst here tonight, he hadn't gone to relieve himself once. Perhaps that was a wise move coming from a 'quare fellow' like him whose accent kept slipping.

Sure the guy looked like a space cadet, and would have even stood out in a David Bowie concert. Nonetheless, there was a glimpse of intellect portrayed in his conversation which suggested that he was by no means simple or stupid. His descriptive words inspired much imagination and Kav saw himself gazing down at a buried crate of gold bullion and coins, and he sensed a road-map to his future forming in the back of his mind.

This was serendipity which he was here to witness. A portion of that gold would gain him kudos as an earner when he handed it over to Belfast command. Following that, he could put together his own active service team and probably go down in the annals of republican history.

He just had to find it or extort it from the Asians, but first, he would have to speak with Dillon, the young Sligonian's friend. Judging by his body language, he was less enamoured with the story, and Kav wanted to know why. It was probably better that he speak with him another time when he was sober and Dillon was alone.

Shane departed the St Agnes social club in Andersonstown almost crippled by the need to urinate. He had been too scared to go inside, envisaging kidnap followed by torture. In truth, he had little to fear apart from someone taking a dislike to his appearance.

The source of his paranoia was the copious amount of cannabis which he had smoked earlier in the evening and the unsettling effect of the few magic mushrooms he had taken as a substitute for speed. Eight was the magic number. They gave you a buzz and a strong desire for alcohol. Anymore and the shadows began to come alive.

The extra mushroom he had eaten for luck had decided to provide a little altered-perception instead. Dillon's gaunt features were now extra pronounced, his hair a brighter shade of copper, and his gangly legs seemed even thinner and longer. He appeared taller and his stride seemed exceptionally long and difficult for Shane to keep up as they headed in the direction of the bus zone.

In the no-go nationalist areas of Belfast, only black taxis were available as public transport and neither of them wanted to take one. Dillon was just trying to save some money, and Shane was wary of getting into the back seat of any provisional IRA courier service.

Dillon was drunk enough to cut Shane some slack, but he point blank refused to stand guard for him whilst he took a slash against a wall. Disrespectful behaviour like that was punished in these parts, and any clandestine behaviour invited the soldiers in the fortified high-rise viewing platforms to target you.

Getting closer to the non partisan main city centre, they hopped on a bus which took them back to the Holy Land. Their mutual friends Sean and Caitlin lived in a flat in Jerusalem Street which was one of the many biblically named side-streets which bordered Queen's University.

There was a certain relief at reaching the house where they were staying; Shane, mostly because he had missed his closer friends who had declined to come along, and Dillon, perhaps because his flat was on the first floor. He didn't invite Shane up and had climbed the stairs by the time Sean had opened up the three mortise locks, night latch, and two chains that secured his ground floor apartment.

"Ah, our intrepid explorer to the wild and lesser visited nationalists clubs has returned," said Sean impersonating David Attenborough.

Sean was a couple of years older than him, of similar height but stockier, and had a thick mop of the darkest black hair. His image showed the battle-lines drawn between his carefree image of a stoned biker and his more formal business persona of a retail manager down south.

"Tell me; how is your armed struggle progressing?"

"Very funny," replied Shane. "You should have come, it was good craic."

"Hmm."

The jury was definitely out on this one. Sean was canny enough to realise that frequenting these unlicensed clubs could only lead to trouble."

"You do realise that I am a Catholic," said Shane defensively.

"I am also aware that you grew up in London, and only last week you visited a loyalist drinking hole in the Shankill road."

"Billy said it was safe."

"And Billy thinks he is Bob Marley's cousin. Don't be so naive Shane.

You are playing with fire just to get a Sunday pint, and in the meantime, you are missing all the craic here."

"What have I missed," said Shane dismissively. "A few hot knives?"

"Maybe, but you are just in time for the next one, young Gilshey."

Sean was leading Shane through to the kitchen as they spoke. As he walked passed him, he nodded at Billy who lay comatose on the floor. "He has the lungs of an Englishman just like you."

"I am more Irish than you Sean," replied Shane with hurt feelings. "I just went to school over there, and now I live here, but I can trace my family back to the Tuatha de Danaan. Your's came over with the Normans."

"Methinks you can only trace your heritage to Orpington."

"Now you are pissing me off," said Shane at the mention of the quiet Kentish suburb where he had studied.

"Don't get irate, just soak your lungs with some of this," said Sean, handing Shane the cut plastic bottle full of smoke, trapped by his thumb at the top, and his outstretched palm at the bottom.

Shane inhaled with one mighty gasp and then consumed the rest of the smoke in three smaller breaths. He tried to talk to settle his earlier point, but wafts of smoke came out of his mouth as he tried to speak causing him to start coughing.

Meanwhile, Sean had taken the empty open-ended two-litre plastic coke bottle off him and was holding it in his mouth. With his two free hands, he took the two red hot pieces of cutlery. Two table knives that had been resting over the burning ring of the gas hob, onto one of which he asked Shane to drop a small knob of cannabis resin, near its tip. Sean sandwiched it with the other hot knife, and captured the copious amount of smoke produced within the two-litre bottle, which still held by his mouth, hovered overhead.

He consumed every last trace of the smoke in one mighty breath and held it in until his eyes seemed bloodshot and ready to pop. Only then did he exhale, and without coughing, managed to taunt Shane as the retired smoke came out. "Now these are the lungs of an Irishman."

"Where's Caitlin?"asked Shane.

"She's in the bedroom, probably sleeping. She is getting up early tomorrow to see us off."

"That will be 5am."

"That is what a good girlfriend will do for you."

"I have a good girlfriend," said Shane defensively.

"Allegedly."

"For chrissake, we have been dating for three and a half years"

"And never once have you brought her up to see Caitlin."

"She doesn't like it up here."

"More like she doesn't want to spend time with us."

"This is not really her thing Sean. She is into sports, running, and the great outdoors kind of thing."

"Oh what fun you can have running around a circular track," said Sean derogatorily.

"She is serious about athletics. She nearly earned a place on the Irish national team."

"Just so long as she looks after and takes care of my best friend," said Sean protectively placing his arm around the shoulders of his younger companion.

3   The plan, the dream, & the team

It wasn't hard for him to find Dillon's address in Jerusalem Street. He had asked around in the right circles and been directed straight here.

Micky Kavanagh had known Dillon since he was a youngster. He had been a volunteer in the Republican Youth, and later on had become a runner and a messenger for the Provos. Then as he had got older, the messages had got more violent, and Dillon no longer had the stomach for it anymore.

It wasn't that he was a coward; it was just that weed had got a grip on him, and the lad liked to smoke and drink himself to oblivion. Now he preferred to play the devout republican by turning up at the nationalist clubs on a Sunday when he was really just looking for a venue that remained open for a drink.

Dillon showed the prerequisite degree of respect for the older republican, for whom as a teenager, he had once run messages. However, he did show a little resentment at being disturbed on his doorstep, and more than a little surprised to be answering questions about Shane.

"I don't know him that well; he is more a friend of the guy that lives downstairs."

"Well is he in now?"

"No, he is at work"

"So I will come back after five"

"No you misunderstand, he works down in Sligo. He won't be back till next weekend."

"Ah," said Kav showing frustrated disappointment."

"Well, what do you know about where I can find him in Sligo?"

"He is a barman in some hotel on the River."

"The river?"

"I have no idea, but he mentions it a lot."

"Anything else?"

"Like what?"

"Anything about a Chinese or Vietnamese friend?"

"His girlfriend works in a local Vietnamese restaurant if that helps."

"It does. Thank you, Dillon."

He had heard enough, and as far as he was concerned, the hit was on.

He was probably going to kidnap either the Vietnamese or the Chinese businessman and extort the gold from the other. If they were truly inscrutable about giving it up, he was going to have to become a bit more ruthless, although he was not too fond of the idea of hurting a man who wasn't his enemy.

Kav had lost his patience with the indiscriminate violence being dished out by the younger zealots. With retrospective consideration, he now disagreed with the mainland bombing campaign of the past decades. Personally, he only favoured causing collateral damage, and getting money through fraud, robbery and extortion. It was views like this that had helped sideline his paramilitary career, but hopefully, it was going to be a crate of gold which jump started it again.

He was also going to need assistance, and there was really only one candidate he would consider using, and that was his best friend, Aden. Despite their age difference of eleven years, they were like birds of a feather with a similar mindset and a shared sense of humour. The younger man wasn't his protégé; he was his soul mate.

Kidnappings in his experience could often be long and drawn out, and Kav could think of no one else that he would prefer to spend that time with. What's more, Aden had lived in Sligo when he was younger. That local knowledge would be invaluable.

4 Clancy & Walsh ESQ. (Thursday)

Aden Clancy was a handsome man, with an athletic build and neatly groomed black hair. He was both trim and of average height. His most notable feature being his thick dark eyebrows which covered almost black, edgy eyes. He had a boyish look, always on the alert for a new stimulus or opportunity, and his facial expressions could be quickly transformed by his mercurial mind, flitting from a happy disposition to amorous intent, or they could exude the threat of potential violence. There was no disguising the intelligent mind which controlled his demeanour, sometimes carefree, sometimes distrustful, but often racked by inner turmoil.

It was no surprise that Kav needed his help. Sometimes he felt like he was that man's rudder, giving him direction, and steering him away from the emotional rocks which had crippled him in the past. Those rocks being that bitch he had recently divorced, and the heartless bureaucrats that commanded the Provisionals.

Nonetheless, he looked forward to an adventure in Sligo with his best friend. The only problem was that he was going to have to meet him there. He had personal business to deal with first, and that was why he had travelled to Donegal.

His girlfriend Sheila had a father just recently passed away in Letterkenny. That town was in Donegal which was subject to the southern State's law. Things were done differently there, and because they had no evidence of a will on record, the estate of her father had gone into probate. After Sheila had attended his funeral, she had visited a local solicitor who was assuming responsibility for her father's estate and probate. He had agreed to first conduct a legal search for a will, and if found, he had agreed to surrender the case to the relevant solicitors and only charge a prearranged minimal fee. Except the scenario that was envisaged had come to pass, and he had not held up his end of the agreement.

The man's name was Kevin Walsh, and Aden was visiting his law practice in Letterkenny. Aden's appointment was for midday on Thursday, and he had only recently arrived by coach from Belfast. He would stay locally tonight and then head on down to Sligo tomorrow morning.

The appointment had been arranged a few days back by Sheila, her purpose being to let Aden represent her, his own purpose being to apply some coercion to make this stubborn Donegal jackass concede. Aden was foregoing anonymity, therefore, it was crucial that he applied subtle intimidation rather than overt.

Aden was a gifted mimic and actor, and right now he was playing the role of the threatening enforcer. He had seen first-hand how others used the tools of intimidation and he was employing some of those now.

The right voice was crucial, and Aden could adapt his west Belfast accent, slowing it down and emphasising certain words that carried gravity. He certainly had Walsh's attention, because he seemed to have induced a nervous tick in this waspish man with the long thin face.

"Here is a letter to confirm her earlier phone call authorising you to deal with me as her agent."

"And you are?"

"It says in the letter."

"Mr. Aden Clancy, of course, but I mean what is your relationship to my client here?"

"That is private between us."

"Is it business or personal, is what I am trying to ask you?"

"Business, in this case."

"I see, and are you a practising solicitor?"

"Don't get smart with me; you already know that I am not."

"You see, she has a brother in England and a step brother in Glasgow who are also making claims on the estate. I am not comfortable dealing with a partner of one of the siblings when I represent the others as well. They will have to agree amongst themselves who will take charge of probate, and that responsibility usually goes to the oldest child, which is her full brother."

"I am not her partner, I am a business associate, and those brothers of hers won't even talk to each other."

"Business associate; what does that even mean? I am really not comfortable talking to you about this."

"And what does the estate comprise of?"

"A couple of bank accounts and the farm which he owned locally."

"And payment arrears from a UK pension, I am told."

"How do you know about that?"

"Because as Sheila explained to you over the phone, there is a will which her father lodged with a solicitor in Belfast. She has instructed them to be taking over the legal proceedings here."

"Yes Mr. Clancy, I am aware of this and they have contacted me."

"So you haven't handed over a damn thing yet."

"Because there are contributing factors here."

"Like what?"

"Well for a start," Walsh supplied a fake look of disappointment, "That will is very old, and it goes against the interest of her brothers who are also my clients. They may wish to contest it. Secondly, there is the matter of the unresolved fees of mine. Until those are settled, I cannot release my interest in the estate."

"It doesn't matter how old the will is, it still supersedes probate, and besides, her old man disowned his own sons a long time ago."

"Allegedly, and that still leaves the factor of my fees. If they were to be settled, I would, of course, relinquish my hold on her father's estate."

"You mean the ransom."

"I don't know what you mean by that, and I am not sure I like your tone."

"Let's keep this business-like. There is no need to make this personal. You are asking for nearly two thousand punts, yet you told my client that if there was a will lodged with another solicitor, you would only charge her between fifty and one hundred. Now you have either forgotten that, or you are lying to me. But I don't think a man like you forgets that much."

Aden lowered his voice and adopted a much more threatening tone. "So if you want to lie to me, I will take that as an invitation to take this on to a more personal level. So now let me tell you; when I get personal with a man, I like to befriend him. That means I want to know where he lives and who he lives with. Then when I meet his family, I want to get to know them and befriend them too. That is how I like to get personal, but if you prefer, we can just keep our relationship on a business footing."

"Are you threatening a solicitor? That is not a wise thing to do."

"No, but judging by your tone, I think I might be getting personal with you."

"I am allowed by law to record this conversation. It's Mr. Aden Clancy, isn't it? I have to warn you, that threatening and coercing a solicitor are criminal acts and forbid me from further discourse with you."

Aden looked completely unfazed by the solicitor's warning, and by the fact that he was now being recorded. "You asked me earlier about my credentials as a business associate. Well, you can ask around, and you will find out that I work in the field of personal persuasion. I persuade people to do the right thing often against their own better judgement."

"I don't care what your business is, you can't threaten me, and you don't scare me," said Walsh.

"So it looks like you and me are going to become friends. Give my regards to your lovely wife and children" -standing up to leave, but then turning briefly to face him- "No don't worry about that, I will tell them myself."

Once the Belfast man had left his office, Kevin Walsh took a little while to compose himself. However, the nerves were soon replaced by fury and seething anger.

"Fionnula!" he shouted at his desk intercom system. "Get me the local Garda station."

"You won't get to speak to anyone of any consequence at this time of day. They will be out having their lunch," she replied over the intercom.

His legal assistant could often be as contrary as him, but it was her condescending tone which irritated him most. She always seemed at variance with him, and always finding a contradictory solution to the one he proposed. Walsh realising that she was probably right in this case, now began to doubt the effectiveness of bringing the guards into this. What's more, he had a better idea, and he wasn't going to share this with Fionnula because she would probably find fault immediately. His cunning new strategy was to fight fire with fire.

He span through the contacts on his desk mounted Rolodex as if he was spinning the cylinder on a revolver. He had the same intent on his mind, and finding the details for Brendan O'Leary was tantamount to putting one in the chamber.

He dialled his number and got through to the man, but he seemed unwilling or unable to help, and Walsh's request was met with negativity and reticence.

"I have done you more than a few favours over the years and now you owe me one at least," said Walsh growing more assertive as he sensed weakness.

"I know that Kevin, but what you are asking could pose some problems for me."

"Listen, I am not asking you to shoot the bastard, but the fecker threatened my family as well as myself," said Walsh, his voice growing louder and higher pitched as the profanities began to leak out of his mouth.

Walsh had a rare kind of Tourette's syndrome which induced increased profanity and swearing only when he was confident and angry. His stammer would only reappear when he was nervous.

"I want you to grow some balls Brendan. Either way, he needs a talking to. If he is connected, you can feckin call him off, and if he is telling fibs, then you can beat the crap out of him. You can at least send a man to my house to protect my family or Jayzus, do I have to do that myself. What kind of feckin useless paramilitary are you? Don't piss me off by telling me about your problems."

ANGUS CACTUS

"Kevin," shouted the other man down the receiver. "Calm down, will you? I know your condition is playing you up right now, but you really should not let it get the better of you."

"Will you feck off, ya righteous salubrious bast'rd," screamed back Kevin in near tantrum.

"I am just saying that using language like this could get you in hot water with other members of the Irish Republican Army. I am cutting you some slack here Kevin, but you need to calm down. Then I can tell you what I can do for you."

There was a pause, and then a quieter response, "Okay, I'm listening."

"Kevin, for reasons that I cannot go into over the phone, I am not allowed to deal with direct interventions like this, but I can refer this to some guys that can. But! And it is important that you take this into consideration first. I need you to fully appreciate that these are dangerous waters that you are rowing in, and these men that I can send to you, may have a price for their involvement."

"You're a robbing bast'rd O'Leary; after all the favours I have done for you. How much do you want?"

"For the love of goodness, will you calm down Kevin. We are not talking money here. We are talking commitment and involvement instead."

"It's free," Walsh exclaimed with passion and release. "Ah, why didn't you say so, Brendan. Apologies for my language, tell them, boys, they're most welcome."

5   Letterkenny   (Friday)

Letterkenny was only a 25-mile drive and a border crossing away from the city of Londonderry. However names can be contentious, and over half of its population preferred to refer to it as just Derry. Two residents who subscribed to that preference had just made this journey. They were now standing outside Stanton & Walsh solicitors which was positioned next to a nearby shopper's car park in Market Street.

It was 9.30am on Friday morning, but the solicitors weren't opening until 10, and so Charles McCreadie had gone to pay for an extra hour's parking. Their advertisement banner in the Golden Pages local business directory had said 'available' parking.

McCreadie smiled at the implied deception, but his smile was often lost under his thick bushy moustache that curled down into his chin and joined a trail of whiskers that led back to his long sideburns. He was one of the 'black' Irish with matching thick black curly hair and brown eyes and a slightly darker complexion. Turning to the younger man who was to be his colleague today, he decided to share his thoughts.

"Snakes; All of them! They couldn't represent the truth without making a plea bargain with deception."

"Who are you talking about?" asked Terence Brady demonstrating a lack of interest rather than curiosity.

"Solicitors. They are never straight with you. Always withholding that little crucial piece of information."

"I have never needed to use one myself," said Brady dismissively.

The men weren't really friends. They were just a couple of soldiers allocated to a search and destroy mission looking for a rogue Provo that was operating outside of his jurisdiction. McCreadie was to take the lead, and Brady would do his best to follow, despite his lack of faith in McCreadie's credentials and abilities. Although Brady was the younger of the two, what he lacked in experience when compared to the company of this seasoned veteran, he made up for in his willing tendency towards violence and raw aggression.

However this part was the client consultation, and it was obvious to both of them that McCreadie should do most of the talking. It involved intercepting their client, Kevin Walsh before he went into his office. Therefore, they passed the time smoking whilst waiting at the front entrance for their man. It was raining which was pretty usual weather for mid-May on the west coast.

ANGUS CACTUS

Walsh saw them first. Two rough looking men wearing black leather jackets loitering at his firms entrance. Both were stocky, but the younger one was leaner and taller and had a mean looking long face. It was kind of angular, but with his intense stare through non-blinking eyes and cropped hair, combed forward, he gave off a very menacing presence.

These men made Walsh feel uncomfortable enough to stop in his tracks and consider leaving, but the older one seemed to recognise his face and called out to him.

"Are you Kevin Walsh?"

"I..I…am…yes," he said with real effort. "If..if..the Guards directed you here…looking f..for legal representation, we do n..n.not do c..criminal law."

"No Mister Walsh, we were directed here by Brendan O'Leary."

The man talking to him, despite his rough appearance had a more engaging persona and his confident demeanour put the solicitor at ease rather than intimidating him further. Walsh became less aware of his own stammer.

"Do you work f..for Brendan?"

"He actually works for us now," replied McCreadie. "There have been some changes and his branch of the Officials is now affiliated to the Irish National Liberation Army. That is why we have taken on your problem for you."

"I.N.L.A; Thi..is is a big surprise. You h..have a reputation for violence. I am not sure that..that I need the INLA on my side at all."

Kevin Walsh's stammer had returned with full intensity and this fact was not lost on the two paramilitaries.

"Your man Clancy is a known Belfast Provo. We will be making sure that he doesn't bother you anymore," said Brady in way of introduction.

"Thank you gentle..men," he said glancing quickly at Brady and then deciding never to stare back at him again. "Will you be placing a g..guard on my home?"

"Babysitting your family is not our kind of thing," said McCreadie. "We intend to eliminate the problem at its roots. This is just a courtesy call."

"So you've found him?"

"Not yet. But we will find him. He is in our backyard now."

In any small provincial towns in the west of Ireland, strangers always stood out. The locals always noticed newcomers, and they often liked to gossip about them. Everyone needs somewhere to sleep, and this one weakness always gave a stranger away. Whether it was at a relation's, an

TO HELL OR SLIGO

ex-girlfriend's, or a guest house, people talked, and McCreadie and Brady listened.

It was a Letterkenny barmaid who had taken quite a fancy to Aden Clancy who talked, not directly to them at first, but her boyfriend did. An address where he was staying was supplied and it was a guest house which was literally a few streets from Stanton & Walsh, and easy for them to find.

"This guy is pretty predictable," Brady pointed out.

"More like Lazy," said McCreadie looking at the bus & train terminus across the road.

"Perhaps he thinks it is safer down here."

"He is like a Thomson Gazelle who has just got off the train in Lion country."

"Who is Thompson Gasell, is he another Provo?"

Chuck McCreadie looked Brady squarely in the eye trying to work out if the younger man was making fun of him. He wasn't, and McCreadie shook his head, wondering at what age his new colleague had stopped going to school.

"Yes, he was a Provo that I shot back in the Creggan and buried at sea," said McCreadie, making fun of him.

"I don't like boats or rough water," said Brady in reply.

McCreadie looked back at Brady again trying to get a measure of the man.

"What?" asked Brady irritated by his stare.

"Nothing! Listen, if this man Clancy is still here, we need him alive to answer our questions, but let him think that we are ready to kill him, okay?"

With the order of play sorted out between them, they entered the building, and whilst McCreadie talked with the owner, Brady quietly slipped upstairs. He found Clancy's room empty, and meanwhile McCreadie found out from the owner that they had missed him by two hours.

The proprietor looked most disturbed as Brady jogged down the stairs. In return, Terry Brady gave her a withering stare which was enough to keep her silent. Joining McCreadie at the entrance, he showed him a scrap of paper.

"I found this on the floor beside the bedside phone. It's an address he has written down. The BECTIVE HOTEL, BRIDGE STREET, SLIGO. I reckon this is where he has gone."

6 Sligo Town   (Friday)

Aden Clancy was a teenager when his family moved to Sligo. His father was a skilled mechanical fitter, and a local factory which had just been built had not only offered him a job but offered him a way out of Belfast where it was hard for a skilled catholic artisan to find work.

Aden switched schools and changed worlds because it was nothing like back home in Belfast. Sligo was lost in another time and a place where shops parcelled up your goods with paper and string and sent money to the office along Victorian pipes by compressed air.

Sligo was a provincial town with a population of around 16,000. It was the capital of a rural county which was part insane. Even the locals avoided the shepherds and farmers when they came to town for market on Thursdays.

Aden had tried to fit in with his new peer group at school. They were welcoming enough because the local kids had the courage of fighters but no cause to expend it on. Teenagers here were restless and felt that they were missing out on the revolution in youth culture that was happening elsewhere. Aden with his cosmopolitan city background could oblige them somewhat, and in return, he was made to feel welcome.

Nonetheless, both he and his family were always made to feel a bit isolated from others and strangers in a strange land. They were seen as blow-ins, outsiders that had moved here, not to be fully trusted, and no matter how long they lived here, they would never be Sligonians.

It was the insular attitude that they hated about Sligo, other than that they were fond of town and of the beautiful countryside that surrounded it. Regardless, after two years they left and returned to Belfast, and just like his parents, he was left with mixed feelings about Sligo Town.

It had been a long time since he had last been here, and memories from his childhood were rekindled as the coach travelled around the town's one-way system. The Bus Éireann coach was a direct connection from Letterkenny and as it threaded through the back streets to ease the restrictions of the town's main thoroughfares, he caught a glimpse of the tall spire of the cathedral. Of course, this made it a city, or that was what his father had told him anyway. He couldn't even remember if it was a Protestant or Catholic cathedral.

TO HELL OR SLIGO

Compared to Belfast, there were very few Protestants in town, and they kept a low profile despite the fact that much of the local wealth was still centred in their community. He learnt at school, that this town had had a chequered history. Its buildings and infrastructure dated back to a time when British law applied here, and a Protestant ascendancy ran the place. Before that, it had been a garrison town which policed an unruly and rebellious county. It protected a port whose greatest export was Irishmen, women, and children being sent to the west. Centuries back they were bonded servants being sent to work in the Caribbean. Later on, they were economic migrants seeking a better life in the cities of America.

Despite the vast number of emigrants passing through its ports, the incoming ships, the cathedral city status, and the mixed population, the town remained insular and cut off from its neighbours. Even its new housing estates held each other in suspicion and judged the older estates such as the 'Hill' to be populated by savages. Newcomers to the town were held in the greatest suspicion, and gossip often turned into tall tales. Sometimes they were coming here to dig up and live off the proceeds of the county's stashes of buried gold.

The Bus Éireann coach terminated at the bus and rail station beside the massive Great Southern hotel. As it pulled in, Aden could see his good friend Michael Kavanagh was waiting for him in the pickup zone sitting in a white saloon car. They were fond of staking each other out, like kittens learning to hunt. So Aden employed some stealth as he approached the car from its off-road side and jumped in the front seat.

"Jaysus," shrieked Kav as his friend appeared in the seat beside him. "I wasn't expecting you to jump in like that. I saw you on the bus; I was just daydreaming."

"I thought you were coming down in your own car."

"It is best not to use northern registrations down here. They draw too much unwanted attention."

Aden nodded in agreement but his attention rested on the broken driver side window and all the pieces of shattered glass in the driver's foot well.

"I see you are still having difficulty breaking into cars."

"I was in a rush, that's all. I have no problems in that department."

Aden nodded again and smiled— he knew better.

"So was it difficult finding out where this barman worked?"

"Dillon said it was on the river, and that left only two to check out. The hotel is called the Bective, and Shane does works there."

"So have you spoken to him yet?"

"No, I thought I would wait till you got here, and then we could go down and sink a few pints together while we checked him out."

"That sounds like a good plan. Are we driving there now?"

"No, this car has got issues, the clutch is playing up. I think it needs a service."

"Christ Kav, can't you even steal a car that works."

7   The Bective Hotel   (Friday)

The walk to the Bective took them past the only other hotel beside the river. The Silver Swan; which was the first place which Kav had checked out.

"It's a bit posh in there, our place is a bit more rustic and much friendlier".

The two friends had taken the river walk that linked the two bridges. The Bective lay ahead of them on the other side of the river. It was a family run hotel situated beside the fast flowing river Garavogue. A flat roofed three-story building, like a large cube, painted cream and brown with balconies facing out onto the river. It stood like a gatekeeper protecting the town's lesser bridge. A bakery and a labour exchange guarded the other side.

Upon reaching the street entrance, they had a problem getting in the door. It wasn't a mechanical fault; it was more a question of anger management. A man walking his Alsatian had preceded them, and a very small and aggressive Yorkshire terrier was repeatedly running at the door's glass panel and head butting it. Every one of his teeth was on show, and his incessant growling was almost blood curdling. A fair-haired woman in her sixties was struggling to control him, and was trying to verbally calm him down, but it was plain to see that he was too far gone and the mutt's blood boiled even more at the sight of the two Belfast men waiting patiently outside.

"He reminds me of someone you were once married to."

"Now don't start on her case Aden, we are back on talking terms and aiming to be friends again."

Kav had waited long enough and pushed the door open. As the dog launched at his trousers leg in attack mode, he caught him with one hand, and then picked him up and handed him back to the woman.

"Guinness!" she exclaimed calling out his name in shame. "I am so sorry, but he gets carried away when he sees certain dogs.

"No problem Ma'am. Is Shane working today?"

"Yes, he is in the long bar; sorry again about the dog.

And it was a very long bar, maybe 80ft or more, and the two took a seat up at the bar counter which ran half the length of the room. There

ANGUS CACTUS

were a moderate amount of customers in the place, a few were sitting at the counter, a priest and probably his housekeeper sitting in a corner, and a large group of women were commanding a nest of tables over by the fireplace.

Aden, who fancied himself as a bit of a Ladies' man, gave them a wide berth. They were a bit too austere and plain looking for him. However, he did spy a fairly decent girl at the end of the bar, and another attractive woman dressed in business attire sitting alone at a table. He made a point of introducing himself and saying hello to her, but when she declined his offer of a drink, he re-joined his friend who was sitting at the counter.

Kav had picked the seats at the end nearest to the entrance because the till was located there. He always found this a good place to strike up a conversation with a barman. However on this occasion, he was mistaken. The Guinness pumps were at the other end of the bar and when he came to take payment, the guy was so distracted that he just deposited their change and walked away.

It was definitely the same fella that he had seen in the republican club in Andersonstown, although his demeanour was different. Less intoxicated, but more erratic. This guy didn't stand still. He was either making sandwiches or pots of tea, taking deliveries, or serving in the other smaller bar. He seemed to make bartending a half empty bar look like hard work.

Then when he did take a break, it was to sit down the other end of the bar talking to a girl who appeared to be his girlfriend. They seemed like a nice couple, at least up until the point that a 2nd prettier girlfriend walked in and then proceeded to call him over and start kissing him. She was standing practically beside Aden, and he couldn't help but watch and admire her bottom as she leaned across the counter.

She told the barman that she was going to change her clothes in his room and that someone was double-parked waiting for her outside. Then before leaving the room with a jaunty step, she turned briefly to look at Aden and smiled at him.

"This one is definitely his girl," said Aden watching her walk away, with an overly keen interest.

Meanwhile, Kav, who was studying the first girl who now sat glaring at her love rival, remarked to his friend, "Could he possibly have two girlfriends on the go?"

"That one could be his sister," said Aden referring to the first girl.

"I doubt it unless his sister likes looking at his ass."

"I don't know what either of them see in him."

"Well, he is either cursed or is a lucky man, depending on whether his

TO HELL OR SLIGO

pint is half full or half empty."

Aden considered his words. His friend Kav was a bit of a Guinness philosopher rather than a Guinness patriot. However, he did manage to often find some wisdom lurking at the bottom of his glass.

The barman, who was now down at her end of the bar, was looking admonished and stressed whilst talking to the seated girl. She looked pretty upset with him, and he looked like he was seeking some opportunity to get away from her. Kav sought to provide this, and raised his empty glass in the air and called another couple of pints.

This time, the barman didn't run off after giving them their drinks, and Kav seized the opportunity to break the ice.

"Is that your girl, the one that kissed you?"

"Certainly is," said Shane with a satisfied smile.

"Lovely looker; lucky man so you are, and you have another one on the go as well."

"Who Maureen? no way, she just thinks that she is my girlfriend."

"Why would she think that?" asked Kav who seemed genuinely intrigued.

"Well, she kind of asked me out, and I kind of said yes."

"You shouldn't mess a lady around, son," said Aden.

"I didn't. It was the way she asked. I got confused, and she took the wrong meaning. We are both going to the same place later on, and I thought she wanted a lift rather than to go out with me. Look! it's all pretty complicated."

"Where you going?" enquired Kav trying to draw him out.

"Just to a birthday party up the Dublin road."

"Pierce Road," said Clancy showing off his local knowledge.

"Aye, Jury's hotel."

"That's pretty swanky. Your friend must have rich parents."

"He's a Sergeant in the Garda. Do they pay well? I don't really know, but it is his daughter's 21st and so I guess he wants her to have a nice party."

"So which girlfriend are you going to take?" asked Kav.

"Neither; I am going with some friends coming down from Belfast."

Both Kavanagh and Clancy were taken aback by that unexpected answer.

"Belfast?"

"Look, I am sorry, but I have to go and prepare the snug bar for the gun club"

"The gun club?" asked Kav.

"Well, it maybe the other gun club. You know the 'Stickies'. I get mixed up a bit; they do alternative Fridays."

"Stickies; do you mean OIRA?" asked Aden.

"Who the hell is OIRA?"

"The Officials," replied both Aden and Kav in unison.

"Oh yes, the official IRA, that's them! But as I said; it may be the actual gun club meeting tonight. I have got to go; I will be back in a few minutes. Keep an eye on the bar for me would you please?"

"Sure; no problem," said Kav.

"Oh and don't be talking to those Ladies over there. They don't like men. They usually keep them in chastity and use them as servants."

"What?" said Aden with a quizzical look on his face.

"Well, I noticed that you like to chat up the Ladies. I just wanted to warn you; to give you the heads up, so to speak."

Kav was looking completely bewildered by the young barman's comments, but he waited for him to leave before expressing himself.

"What the bleedin' Jaysus is going on in that young man's head, or in this crazy place? What's he even mean by gun club anyway? Are people allowed to carry guns down here?"

"No, he probably means a shooting or a hunting club."

"Isn't that the same thing?" Kavanagh's face looked almost contorted with culture shock. "If I'd known guns were legal in Sligo, I would have brought along my Armalite."

"My dad had a shotgun when I was young, and my uncle had a rifle," replied Aden as if this explained everything. "It is all legal if you pass the police checks."

"And what do they check for?"

"IRA membership in your family, and such."

"Well that's your application fucked right away," said Kavanagh already laughing at his own comment.

"Kav; what if it really is the Stickies meeting here tonight. Are we safe?"

"Well, they don't know us from Adam."

"But they may be suspicious of our Belfast accents."

"Look! There is no 'red' IRA meeting here tonight," stated Kav with some authority. "That boy is on drugs. He's got some warped imagination for sure. I mean look at those ladies over there. Do they look like they keep their menfolk as slaves?"

8 The Barman (Friday)

The pretty girl, who they had seen kiss Shane earlier, had just reappeared and was wearing a change of clothes. This outfit which was a tight black skirt and white blouse was much simpler and formal than the trendy clothes she had worn earlier.

She approached the counter and stood just behind them seeking to get their attention.

"Hello again, I am Enya. Will you tell Shane the barman that I am off to work now, but I will hopefully see him later?"

"I can certainly oblige you on that front, sweetheart," said Kav in a friendly tone whilst his trained eye studied the girl intensely.

Meanwhile, Aden was studying the girl's shapely ass which along with her very pointy breasts, helped to accentuate her hourglass figure. His gaze was interrupted by Kavanagh's foot kicking him in the shin, but he said nothing in reply until the girl left the bar.

"What did you do that for?"

"Perhaps your salacious stares were frightening off the lass. We may need her for leverage in case this space cadet of a barman doesn't tell us where to find this Vietnamese or Chinaman."

His words were almost prescient in predicting the re-emergence of Shane through the adjoining swing door. Kavanagh was quick to notice that it led to a large kitchen that was already bustling with chefs and catering staff preparing for the evening trade.

"Hey! Sunshine," Kav called out to get Shane's attention before he disappeared back through the portal he had just emerged from. "Your other girlfriend gave us a message for you."

He was carrying a tray of sandwiches along with his usual vacant expression which masked his daydreaming thoughts. Stopping on the spot, he looked up as if some hypnotist had just issued a seeded codeword.

"Which girlfriend?"

"The one with the shapely arse and pointy tits," said Clancy salivating at the memory.

"Enya? What did she say," said Shane staring questioningly at Clancy wondering whether to take offence from his last comment.

"She said that she was going to work but would probably meet up with you later," replied Kav. "She didn't say where she was working, though," he added as a seeded question that was fishing for an answer.

"That would be the Chinaman's restaurant in Gratton Street," offered up Shane in naive innocence.

"Chinaman!" said Aden Clancy repeating the word as if it answered the last clue in a crossword puzzle. "Would that be the man she mentioned who was double parked waiting for her?"

"The very same; he drove out to collect her all the way from the village of Grange, just to fill an emergency shift."

"At his restaurant," added Aden picking out the choice clues and offering them up to Kavanagh as tasty morsels.

"Do you have many Chinese fellows in town?" asked Kavanagh in response to Clancy's prompts.

"Nah, just him."

"What about Vietnamese; do you have any of them, fellas, locally?"

"Well we have the Vietnamese-Chinaman; does that count?"

"And where would you find that chap?"

"Are those our sandwiches?" came the imperious interruption from the middle aged woman who had just approached the counter.

"Yes Ma'am," said Shane. "Would you like to take them," he added as he held out the tray and proffered it to her.

"No, I would not," replied the dourly dressed woman sternly. "I think I would like you to carry them to my table and wait for further instruction from my sisters."

"Now listen here love," interceded Kav annoyed at her interruption. "We are talking important business with this young man. Perhaps you can go sit down and wait your turn."

"Wait? On YOU!" said the woman addressing Kavanagh harshly as if he were some peasant that worked in her fields. "I would have you know that I wait for no man, and definitely not for an uncouth northerner who doesn't yet know how to address a Lady."

"Don't get on you high horse Missus, we are trying to be civil," interceded Aden in the role of peacemaker.

The woman ignored him and turned once again to address Shane still holding out the tray of sandwiches.

"Please tell your other guests not to address me with either of those disrespectful titles and to mind their own business." She was speaking slightly louder and far more assertively now that she was addressing a man she recognised as her temporary servant.

Of course, Shane realised that it was only a rhetorical instruction, seeing as she had practically told the Belfast duo to shut up herself. His gaze lay with some of the others in her party who were leaving the sanctity of their private tables at the other end of the room and heading over in support of this woman who appeared to be their obvious leader.

"Yes Ma'am," he said feeling a strong urge to placate her before the others got involved. Then raising the counter flap, he joined her briefly on the other side before leading the way back to her table.

"And Bar-Boy" she bellowed after him. "I expect my bill to be adjusted for your delay, and for their rudeness." The woman glared with disdain at both the northerners as she spoke. Aden returned her stare with implied menace, whilst Kav just smiled back at her.

Shane walked past the other four women who stood like sentries guarding access to their nest of tables, and the comfortable bench seating beside the real coal fire.

He placed the tray down on the table but made sure to wipe it first with the cloth he carried.

"There is a mess on the floor that you need to clean up as well," said one of the younger women in an impertinent manner.

Shane examined the wet patch on the floor she was pointing to by her feet. "I will get a mop and clear that up for you, Miss."

"You have a cloth already. I would prefer that you cleaned it now using that and a little effort on your behalf."

The girl was about his age but wore handmade garments and no makeup. He looked her up and down and found her unmade-up appearance an anathema to his own cool 80's styling. Shane didn't want to follow her instructions at all but was embarrassed by all the aggressive stares that were directed at him from the group of eight women sitting in close proximity. Peer pressure and the obligation to concede that a customer was always right, persuaded him to oblige her.

"Excuse me," he said simply as he crouched down to squeeze under the table using his already damp cloth to mop up the spill. The young woman didn't excuse him but instead kept her feet firmly rooted to the spot forcing him to carefully clean the area around them. He noticed the splurge of egg mayonnaise and tomato being dripped close by from the same girl who was now picking at her sandwich disdainfully. He chose to ignore it but found himself rebuked once again when he stood up.

"You missed some mess down there," she pointed out with a lascivious cruel smile forming on her thin lips. Shane actually felt a little turned on by her assertive nature, and a little intimidated too. He didn't need to be asked again, but returned to his station and made sure to remove all trace of the spilt sandwich filling.

She didn't thank him, but instead the middle-aged leader of this bizarre female cult issued him with his next instructions. He was to fetch another round of hot drinks for everyone and return with some menus from the

adjoining restaurant so that they might choose their evening meal. In fact, Shane was quite glad to be dismissed, but now seemingly had to placate the two northerners who had watched the whole embarrassing scene. They intercepted him before he had a chance to return to safety on the other side of the counter. They had more questions for him to answer and now they too seemingly wanted to take advantage of his nervous disposition.
 "Why do you let those crazy lesbians treat you so disdainfully?" asked Aden, who was never one for mincing his words.
 "They are guests here, and we need their business. They have been staying for a couple of weeks."
 "Well don't let your fine girlfriend see you fawning over them. She might get ideas herself, and then you are going to be pussy whipped." Shane took exception to Aden Clancy's crude illustration, but let it go. There was something a little sinister about these two Ulstermen and he decided it was better not to push their buttons.
 "Why are they staying here for two weeks?" asked Kavanagh who was genuinely intrigued.
 "They have bought a farm somewhere out in the Cliffony area, near Ballintrillick. My understanding is that it has been unoccupied for quite some time. Most of them are staying here whilst a few others are busy employing their men folk to fix it up."
 "Why a farm? Are they farmers," he asked scornfully.
 "No; they are the 'Screamers'. They wanted to buy a secluded farm where they can set up a new commune."
 "What the hell is a screamer when it is at home?"
 "Like I told you before, they are a community of female supremacists that live without the benefits of the modern world and keep men as their slaves. They had an isolated refuge up in Donegal, but it was too barren for their liking. They reckon the border between County Sligo & Leitrim is more suitable for farming. It is more private and isolated as well which suits their purpose."
 "So who does the farm work?"
 "I guess that would be their long-suffering men folk," answered Aden under his breath as he stared intently over at the group of women.
 "I guess it takes all kinds to keep this world turning," said Kav, shaking his head in reflective resignation.
 "Like Chinamen, Vietnamese, and Stickies," said Aden hoping to prompt his friend.
 "Oh yeah," said Kav placing his hand on Shane's arm as if button-holding him for an important answer. "About this Vietnamese man; where

do we find him?

"Why are you so interested in the Vietnamese man," asked Shane genuinely interested.

"That's for us to know," said Aden in a menacing overtone.

"What he means," said Kav raising his hand to reprimand his friend, "Is that we are looking for a particular Vietnamese gentleman who used to be a monk."

"Well, that would be the Chinaman," answered Shane.

"What Chinaman? We are talking about a Vietnamese monk here," said a frustrated Kavanagh.

"He is the restaurateur who Enya is working for tonight."

"But I thought you said she worked for a Chinaman, not a Vietnamese?"

"Aren't they one and the same?"

"What No! What makes you think they are? They are two completely different countries. America fought one of them in a war," said Kav.

"Actually, America fought both of them in different wars."

"What; no! Shut up Aden; now you are confusing me."

"So this Vietnamese-Chinaman was previously a monk and now he lives in Sligo and owns a restaurant," said Kav, trying to ascertain if they really were one and the same person.

"Yes, how do you know this?" asked Shane with excited curiosity.

"Never you mind what or how we know things," said Aden again using his sinister voice.

"I'm just saying that I am surprised that news travels so far. I don't think he owns the restaurant, though. He probably just manages it."

"So who owns it then?"

"I heard that it was the Triad."

"The Triad?" exclaimed both Ulstermen in unison.

"Or maybe the Tongs. I get these organised crime syndicates mixed up"

"Are you making this all up?" Kavanagh asked Shane directly.

"Which part?"

"Any of it."

"Well I am not completely sure about the interests of the Tongs or the Triad, but my girlfriend Enya does work for him in his restaurant on Gratton Street."

"And the part about him being a monk?"

"Oh, that's definitely true. The man teaches Kung-fu classes at the Sports Complex out beyond Doorly Park. He is a 2nd Dan and apparently got his Shaolin grading from his temple master who was a 6th Dan."

"How do you know this?" asked Kavanagh in a conspiratorial manner.

"Sure, it is common knowledge in these parts. I've done a few of the Kung fu lessons myself but otherwise I am just repeating what I have been told."

"And what were you told about the Gold?" asked Aden Clancy mistaking his favourite threatening tone for a conspiratorial one. He got another kick in the shins from Kavanagh for messing up.

"What my friend is saying, Shane; if you do not mind me calling you by your first name," said Kav smiling disarmingly at the young barman. "Is that we heard a crazy rumour about a monk who escaped Vietnam with all this gold and we wondered if you had heard anything about this."

"Seeing as you is a barman as such," added Aden in explanation, "and get to hear all these rumours."

"Yeah, I do as such, but this is private stuff, and is kind of like secret."

"And what is his secret exactly?" asked Kav amazed at how easily he could coax a secret past Shane's lips.

"Well, he was told to remain behind and defend his Temple's gold and precious jewels from the Chinese who were invading from the North."

"Do you mean the North Vietnamese during the Vietnam War?" asked Kavanagh exasperated by Shane's lack of understanding concerning the difference between Vietnam and China.

"Them's the boys. So these northern Chinamen—"

"Vietnamese," corrected Kav.

"Yep, these Vietnamese were too strong for the monks to repel them. So a suicide squad elected to stay behind and fight to the death, so that some of the more junior fighting monks could sneak out under cover of darkness and escape with the temple's hoard of treasure."

"That treasure being mostly gold and I assume exceptionally heavy," said Aden pointing out logistics.

"They had a pack of mules and they took it up the river by boat and crossed into Cambodia. They were heading for Laos but then they got in a fight with some other fellows who were warring in Cambodia. I think they were Chinese."

"Were they perhaps the Khmer-Rouge who took over control of Cambodia after the American's bombed it," enquired Aden who was a keen student of wars and military history.

"Those are the same boys; the Kimer-Chinese or something."

"Christ! Forget the fuckin Chinese," exclaimed Kav in exasperation.

Both the other men looked at him in surprise, and then Shane continued with the story.

"So Li Han made it to Laos all by himself with most of the gold which he buried somewhere and then set about escaping to Ireland.

"So that's his name; Li Han," Kav asked in confirmation.

"Oh yes Li is the man for sure," continued Shane. "And he managed to bring his sweet mother along with him."

"Now hold up one minute," said Kavanagh once again taking hold of Shane by his arm. "Are you telling me that all the other monks were wiped out by the Khmer Rouge, but somehow his mother managed to fight her way out of Cambodia along with her son. Is she some kind of Kung Fu legend?"

"I don't think so, but she is a damn fine Chinese cook."

Kavanagh grimaced at the latest mention of the Chinese, but he decided to let it go unchallenged. Shane paused, noticing the man's facial contortion which he put down probably to indigestion. He continued the story by clarifying his earlier account.

"No, the mum didn't fight her way out. The Americans gave her a visa instead. She wasn't even with him at the Temple. He came back for her later and brought her to Dublin with him."

"Dublin?"

"Yes, they used to live there and had a restaurant there too. At least I think they managed it on behalf of the Tongs."

"Please Shane," said Kavanagh tightening his grip on Shane's arm. "Enough with the Tongs or the Triads. What did you hear happened to all that gold?"

"Well I heard that he went back for it, dug it up, and shipped it over to Sligo, or maybe Dublin; I am not clear on the details."

"So where do you think it is now?"

"Definitely buried somewhere in the county. Out by Lough Gill or maybe Benbulben."

"So you don't really know?" pointed out Kav in clarification.

"Of course not, why would I," he answered perplexed by the question. He also seemed agitated by the time as he kept glancing up at the wall-mounted clock. "Listen, gentlemen; it was nice talking with you but I have to get a move on. Those ladies want hot drinks and menus and I have to get ready for the handover to the next barman.

"Yeah, you better get a move on or you might upset them bunch of hairy witches over there," said Aden smiling whilst making a whipping gesture with his hand.

"Yes thank you for all your interesting stories, Shane. I hope we meet again sometime."

As they walked out onto the street, a man who was crossing their path on his way in looked up in surprise upon hearing the northern intonation of their Belfast accents.

"So where are we going now?" asked Aden.

Kav declined to answer until the other man had passed out of listening range. Then he back stepped to the glass door to watch the same man disappear into what he assumed was the front snug bar. Aden was already fully aware of what his friend was thinking.

"So that was a Stickie?"

"I think so," confirmed Kav who started walking across the bridge and in the direction of Gratton Street.

"A bit long in the tooth if you ask me. No wonder these boys never got their hands dirty. They probably all prefer playing bingo rather than busting heads."

"Appearances can be deceptive Aden," said Kav as he stood at the entrance to the river walk looking back across the bridge at the Bective Hotel.

"Let's take the scenic route alongside the river," said Aden.

"Does this head in the right direction for the restaurant?"

"There are three walkways that come off it, the second one takes you directly to Gratton Street," said Aden demonstrating his local knowledge. "It is not very big; we will find the restaurant easily."

"It looks pretty dark and dangerous down there," said Kav casting an eye over all the old derelict warehouses that were masked in darkness as the sun had already set.

"Sure this is Sligo, we have no enemies here."

"They are still a dangerous element," said Kav gesturing at the Bective hotel directly across the river."

"What; the hotel staff?"

"No you idiot, the hotel is fine. I was even thinking that we could stay there later. My concern lays with the Stickies; the Official IRA. They are not our friends."

"We don't even know that that is them. That barman has a hell of an imagination," said Aden making a crazy face in a mocking gesture. "They could be stamp collectors for all we know."

"All the same, I am glad we unearthed this little nest. This location might be of interest to the INLA."

"Ah Lord, you wouldn't talk with them fellers in the Irish Republican Socialist Party would ya?" Aden's expression was one of surprised contempt.

"Well, they do have a walk-in centre in the Divis flats on the Falls Road."

"Yeah, the Planet of the IRPS."

Both men laughed at local reference to the Belfast HQ of the Irish National Liberation Army.

"Them boys are nearly finished anyway. They can't keep from killing each other; those bloody monkeys," said Kav.

"Black bastards; all of them," agreed Aden. "The Officials; the INLA, and the Irish Republican Socialist Movement; The Ulster Freedom Fighters; The UDA; the UVF; the Brits, and even the Post Office."

"I know Aden, but remember that the enemy of my enemy is my friend," said Kav putting on his wisest face.

"You do realise that this little nugget of wisdom was first coined by a Sultan who ended up being killed by his enemy's enemy."

"Jaysus, I didn't know that Aden. You sure know your history, our fella. Besides, how did the post office get on your bad side?"

"Those feckers keep turning me down."

"I am not surprised. I wouldn't even like you knowing where I live."

The two men laughed in unison one more time.

9   The Bogmen   (Friday)

It was their decision not to follow the river walk between the two bridges in town which spared a most likely confrontation between the two members from the Irish National Liberation Army and the two volunteers from the Belfast Provisionals.

They would have crossed paths for certain near the derelict patch of old warehouses that bordered the River Garavogue. The stench of freshly slaughtered pigs from Denny's abattoir would have masked another scent of slaughter as the four gunmen with competing allegiances faced each other down.

However, Brady was averse to fast flowing water. The result of some trauma he'd had as a child; and so he declined to take the shortcut between the two hotels which sat on each bridge. Instead, they found a route from the plush Hotel Silver Swan along Stephen Street and past all the towns' banks.

McCreadie had visited the Allied Irish Bank on Stephen Street once before, but he had been wearing combat clothes and a balaclava on that hot summer day. He recalled the stench of sweat as they made their getaway in the cramped interior of a Ford Transit van.

"Look, there is Bridge Street ahead," said Brady keen to get a move on. As far as he was concerned, they had already wasted too much time on this Aden Clancy. They would find him, question him, and maybe clip him afterwards. That would solve the solicitor's problem, and it would also send a clear message to the Provos, to stay out of Sligo. It was their town. The whole damn south belonged to them. They just didn't know it yet.

As they turned into Bridge Street, the three storey building which was the Bective Hotel appeared prominently in view at the end of the road. The street was short but despite that it housed three pubs. Each one was busy with custom despite this being a midweek early evening. They had come to realise that this was par for Sligo.

They studied the hotel's location beside the bridge and the river. It was not the scenic view that they were taking in, but rather the other exit points on their mind.

"Do you think he might take flight out the back when he sees us?" asked Brady.

"He doesn't know who we are and so we have the advantage upon him. You go and nosey about upstairs. I will wait for you in the bar and keep my eyes peeled and ears to the ground," replied McCreadie.

As they walked through the main entrance, they were met by a vicious little Yorkie that seemed to know that they were up to no good. He was spinning around and almost choking on his own vitriol.

"Guinness," rebuked the kindly looking woman who introduced herself as the proprietor of the hotel. "I am so sorry. He has a tendency to get carried away."

"He is a little tearaway, like a little black and tan. I guess that is why you named him after my favourite pint. Is he a miniature?"

Brady couldn't understand if McCreadie was genuinely interested in small dogs, or whether he was just buttering up the owner.

"No; he's a toy Yorkshire terrier. He was my daughter's but he only follows me about now."

"Do you think I could have a quick word with one of your chefs? It is about a special dietary requirement for a dinner party I am organising."

"Of course, I will go and get one of them to come and talk to you," she said as she exited through one of the two doors to the left on route to the kitchens. He peeked inside to see where she had gone and noticed that there was a restaurant there which was fairly busy.

As soon as she had disappeared McCreadie told Brady to quickly head upstairs, whilst he himself made a low profile exit into the long bar on the right.

'Damn,' he thought, 'This place is empty' as he tried to find a concealed location down behind the pool table. Apart from the barman, there were only a couple of people in the room, and one of those appeared to be his girlfriend.

McCreadie gave the barfly up by the till a wide berth; he looked like the nosey sort who liked to listen to other people's conversations. The sour-faced girlfriend at the other end of the counter looked like she had personal issues except when she was talking to her man. Once he disappeared through the swing doors into what looked like the kitchens, she began acting demonstrably irritated which was evident to everyone else through her incessant tapping of her shoe into the wooden front of the bar counter.

It was another barman who re-entered the bar. McCreadie watched him carry a money float and place it in the cash register. He was obviously just starting his shift.

"Our fella; Can I speak with you?"

"Sure, how can I help you?"

"I am supposed to be meeting a Belfast man here this evening. I believe he may have booked in."

"I don't think we have any guests from Belfast staying here, Sir."

"There were two Belfast men here earlier," said a voice from further along the counter. "They left about 20 minutes ago."

"Why thank you," said McCreadie turning towards the barfly. "You didn't happen to overhear where they were going."

"I was just minding my own business but I did hear mention of the new oriental restaurant in Gratton Street. It think it's called the Happy Huong."

McCreadie was grateful for the lead and called a refill for the man's whiskey and a bottle of stout. He had found out all that he needed to know, and now it only remained to go and fetch Brady and head down to Gratton Street.

He left the bar with the intention of quietly slipping up the stairs but that familiar face of the friendly proprietor was waiting for him as soon as he reached the front reception. What's more, her frustrated Yorkshire terrier gave up dragging his hind quarters across the floor in search of sexual release to adopt guard duty where he was concerned. McCreadie felt like kicking him away but released that this would likely stoke up his zeal.

"There you are," said the dog's owner. "I wondered whether you had left, I am afraid the chef couldn't wait any longer as he had to get back to a busy kitchen. Maybe you can tell me what your dietary requirements are and I can ask him to get back to you later on."

"It's okay Missus. I will come back another time; there is somewhere I have to be…" McCreadie trailed off because he had just seen a ghost from his past coming out of the door beside to the small snug bar. He immediately turned his back to the man hoping that he had not been recognised. His standard calm and controlled demeanour was surrendering to an overwhelming urge for fight or flight. Strangely, his inner turmoil appeared to empathically reflect upon the face of the host. She too appeared to have seen something that both shocked and riled her. However unlike him, she wasn't prepared to stay calm or keep quiet.

"Can I help you, young man; may I ask you what was your business going upstairs to the guest's rooms?"

Brady looked shaken by her challenge as he quickened his pace down the stairway and tried to avoid eye contact.

"Yes, I am talking to you young man. What were you doing upstairs," she said as she walked to the bottom of the stairs to block his clear exit.

Brady had no choice but to speak up and front the woman. His problem was that he had no idea what excuse to come up with.

"I am sorry Ma'am; I was just looking for a bathroom to use."

Brady's harsh Derry accent didn't go unnoticed by the older man that had just come out of the snug bar. This customer stared intensely at him assessing him as a potential threat. Brady who still looked rattled glanced at the proprietor and then at the tiny but overtly aggressive Yorkie that was spinning around in circles psyching itself up for confrontation. His business eye noticed the stranger staring at him with suspicion, and as a natural reaction, his eyes sought out McCreadie seeking clues as to whether they were ready to leave. McCreadie met his stare but then looked away back at the other man.

It was obvious to Brady that something was wrong and that his colleague was worried. There was little he could do but push his way past the mature woman using as minimal force as he could manage, but the dog got the sharp end of his boot.

McCreadie followed his cue and with his eyes cast down he headed for the exit. He was still immensely troubled, and in half a mind to have pulled out his Beretta pistol and shot the man. He just couldn't. Instead, all he could manage to do was stare back at him through the glass panel. Just like Lot's wife, that tempting glance was to cost him dearly. The man had definitely recognised him. McCreadie turned to Brady, and very uncharacteristically shouted, "Run!"

He led the way, and Brady matched his stride and kept pace even though he ran with his head craned looking backwards. They had cleared the corner around into Castle Street and didn't slow down until they reached its junction with Market Street. There, a small public house provided a temporary safe haven where they could rest up a while and McCreadie could explain what the hell was going on.

This pub was called 'Shoot the Crows' and its patrons seemed to be a very shady sort. Brady called for two pints and the barman topped off two that had already been sitting idle next to the pump and handed them to him quoting his price. Paying him, he squared up to the sullen bartender who returned his aggressive look with practised indifference. Brady let it go; he was seeking explanations rather than aggression.

"Are you going to tell me what that was all about?"

"You don't want to know."

"Yes I do," said Brady wearing his best 'don't feck me off face'.

"We used to work together," said McCreadie simply as if it explained everything.

"What on the roads? Or gutting fish? Could you perhaps be a little more specific?"

"You know what I mean. We were in an active unit together," said McCreadie spelling it out.

"Okay, so why not just say hello."

"Because he's a Stickie, and I shot his brother."

"Why didn't you just kill him? Nobody knows us here," said Terry Brady stating the obvious.

"Well he did, and we used to be best friends. It's complicated. There are many unmarked graves as testimony to the past violence. OIRA tried to wipe us out no sooner than we had split away from them."

"Well, there is your justification."

"Séamus didn't try to wipe me out," said McCreadie. "In fact, he tipped off my girlfriend and saved me from an initial ambush."

"So why did you kill his brother?"

"Lord knows I didn't mean to. It just sort of happened. After that, the gloves were off and we have both killed many of each other's colleagues, whoever we came up against. Except we somehow gave each other a wide berth, or maybe we were just spared the reality of facing each other."

"I see," said Brady feigning understanding. However his pretence of compassion didn't fool anyone; McCreadie was well aware that Brady was a sociopath.

The Guinness had coated McCreadie's moustache which was a source of irritation for Brady. Beards and moustaches were worn as a badge of pride by many of the older members of the republican movement. These veterans of the early troubles from the late 60s, up to the mid-70s, had either been introduced to them during internment or when they were on the run. To many of them, a healthy outcrop on your top lip or chin signified gravitas or at least experience.

To the clean shaved Brady, it signified losers who had either got caught or else had soft faces that needed to look harder. Facial hair wasn't the only badge of a twat; this bar was full of them, yet there were no beards in sight. Just a bunch of Guinness patriots at least who tried to talk and look hard but crumbled as soon as you shook them up a little.

McCreadie surveyed the roughshod interior of Shoot the Crows and thought the place had character. He liked the look of the patrons too. He had a certain amount of respect for a man who was comfortable drinking in a spit and sawdust environment with just a good pint in his hand and a good friend by his side. His own pint was lovely and he duly finished it off, although he was disappointed that he could not feel the same about his present company.

"Come on, we need to get going. We can take a recce of the restaurant and its clientele. Gratton Street starts across the road. We can take a measure of this Aden Clancy and see who he is hanging out with before we approach him. I want to know what two Belfast Provo's are doing down here — something nefarious for certain."

Brady liked McCreadie's 'business first' attitude and didn't even bother to finish his own pint. McCreadie collected both glasses and returned them to the bar counter. The landlord gave him a nod, and he replied in kind.

10 Séamus Tooley

When Shane saw his mother being roughly pushed aside by a stranger at the bottom of the stairs, he rushed to defend her. However, by the time he reached the reception hall, the man had already departed through the front door. Shane's instinct was to run after him and jump him from behind, but he felt the restraining hand of Séamus Tooley holding him back.

"He's not worth the trouble Shane," said Séamus and turning to the proprietor he asked, "You are okay, aren't you Margaret?"

Shane's mother was over it. For her, it wasn't his aggression or rudeness, but it was the contempt of the man walking freely about upstairs. Nor was this the first instance. There had been other unwelcome prowlers who had either robbed customer's rooms or fallen asleep in beds that weren't theirs. Shane had ejected many such bums on her behalf. He was a good lad in that respect, and would always try to do the right thing. She just wished he would settle down and stop taking those damned drugs.

Later on, she was pleased to see him head out with one of the McGowan daughters. They were publicans too and Margaret reckoned this daughter was called Maureen. In fact, she opened the front door slightly ajar and both she and Guinness, her faithful hound, watched their son walking over the bridge, hand in hand with the McGowan lass. She wasn't too sure about Shane's present girlfriend; Enya seemed a bit highly strung, and more than a little controlling over her son.

Séamus Tooley looked perplexed and troubled as he stood opposite the reception desk dialling a number on the payphone. He had just been talking with the proprietor and now she remained standing behind the small counter by the main entrance.

"Could I have a little privacy please Mrs.G," asked Séamus respectfully.

Margaret was happy to oblige Séamus who was one of her most respected and loyal customers, so without further ado, she took the opportunity to go and check on the restaurant. Having known Séamus since she took over running the hotel, she had made sure to retain his regular fortnightly booking. She appreciated that the club represented the aims of the official IRA, but that wasn't a problem for her. In her youth, she had done her fair share of supportive visits to republican prisoners incarcerated on the mainland. Séamus respected this and even felt protective of this strong matriarchal figure.

With privacy ensured, he started speaking to the person who was holding on the other end of the line.

"We have a problem. There are a couple of snakes arrived in town. They were here in the Bective; I identified them myself and I think they may have gone to check out the Chinaman's restaurant in Gratton Street. So thinks one of the barmen here who says they were enquiring about two Belfast men that had gone there. Can you get anyone over to that place fast, to eyeball them, and follow them. Make sure to tell them not to engage; I want to do the meet and greet part myself."

Séamus paused to listen briefly to the recipient of his call and seemed to be considering a question they had asked. "What no, it's the two Derry men we need to follow. Sure the Belfast men are of interest, but our priority here is to catch those snakes."

Once again Séamus listened to the other person with applied concentration. "Listen Feargal, you can follow the Belfast men if you want, but get Mickey on the snakes, and tell him not to let them out of his sights. You can't miss them, both wearing leather coats, and one is my age with a thick moustache, the other is in his early twenties; a mean looking fella and both of them have strong Derry accents."

Séamus was about to end the call, but had one last epiphany, "And don't take Maxie with you."

He looked surprised that this request was even questioned.

"Why! Because he's like a fecking mountain and he will blow your cover."

Séamus Tooley hung up shaking his head in frustration.

Regardless of Séamus' instructions, three men departed their private room above the Ship Inn on Quay Street but only two set off on foot in the general direction of O'Connell Street. Maxie Jinx was going to drive to and park outside the Fours Lantern's takeaway. This allowed him to be on hand as backup muscle and transport support. It also allowed him to get double cheeseburger and fries.

Feargal Keohane and Mickey Donelon travelled light and walked at a fast pace reaching the Happy Huong restaurant in good time. Standing near the junction of O'Connell and Gratton Street, they both watched and waited for their respective targets.

11 The Happy Huong   (Friday)

Aden had studied to be a structural engineer when he was in college. A lack of concentration and a leaning towards 'the republican cause', ten years into the troubles, had helped curtail that ambition. Except now and again, the muse would come over him. Right now, he was studying the curves in Enya's tight blouse and wondering what degree of force was being applied on the two small buttons straining in vain to keep those blouse plackets firmly knit together. He was still marvelling at the odd shape of her breasts which seemed to point in perpendicular directions.

Kav had taken a seat on a table beside the door, which allowed him to keep one eye on the entrance and the other on the swing door to the kitchen. He was busy explaining his dietary requirements to Enya who was the only waitress on duty.

"Could you make me something with no nuts, dairy, fried food, or cured meat?"

"Do you have a medical condition?" she asked with interest.

"Yes Enya, he has I.B.S; Irritable Bastard Syndrome," said Aden winking at the waitress. "It means he takes forever to order from a menu."

Enya tried hard to suppress laughter. She found the younger man amusing as well as quite handsome, and she was impressed that he remembered her name.

"Actually, it is Crohn's disease; an inflammation in my colon," explained Kav unaware of the fleeting eye contact between the other two.

"Thanks for putting me off my dinner," said Aden addressing his friend directly.

Kav smiled back at him, unperturbed as usual at Aden's digs concerning his diet. Then he supplied a broader smile for Enya who was leaning over the table to help him find something that matched his dietary requirements. Aden took full advantage of the opportunity to continue his ogling at Enya.

"The beef in oyster sauce with steamed vegetables will suit me fine darling," said Kav appreciatively whilst he surreptitiously kicked Aden's shin under the table.

With their order taken, Enya turned around to face the kitchen whilst she wrote it down.

Aden took the opportunity to openly study the shape of her pert little derriere, which just like her breasts, seemed to have a life of its own, and presently seemed intent on moulding a permanent dent in her tight black waitress skirt.

Then, waiting until she had left the vicinity, he said to Kav, "Stop kicking me."

"Then stop staring lecherously at her breasts."

"I can't help it, she is like Medusa luring me onto the rocks."

"It wasn't Medusa, she had snakes coming out of her head; it was Pandora with her box of tricks."

"No it wasn't," said Aden who didn't like to be challenged on mythology or history.

"Was!"

"So what was the box for? Did she throw it at the shipwrecked sailors?"

"No, I think she made them look into it so that they could find their peril and doom."

"I look in a box every morning. I only ever find cornflakes in it," said Aden dismissively.

"They were sirens," said Enya, surprising both men by her stealthy return to their table. "They were irresistible, and they always got their man," she added winking at Aden, before walking away to clear another table after the previous diners had left.

"Did you see that?" Aden asked his friend with excitement.

"No," curtly replied Kav.

"Yes, you did."

"Forget about it, we have other business to attend to."

But Aden couldn't forget. In fact, he took another peek over at her jiggling backside as she busied herself cleaning.

"Can you imagine that thing bouncing up and down on your face," asked Aden rhetorically, in truth only seeking to inspire his own thoughts.

"You have a girlfriend," pointed out Kav in a reprimanding fashion.

"I know, but Enya is gorgeous, and I don't know for the life of me what she sees in that barman."

"I think she probably sees him as handsome in a rock-star kind of way."

"Maybe a person should be a rock star before they try to look like one."

"He is alright, he is just young," said Kav on reflection. "But he has a serious problem appreciating the difference between Vietnamese and Chinamen."

Aden didn't agree but chose not to comment any further on the subject.

ANGUS CACTUS

There were more things in life to ponder about, and two of those things were currently anchoring his attention as he watched Enya vigorously scrubbing a stain off one of the tables.

"You really should stop staring so much; you are going to spook the girl."

"I reckon she is wearing one of those conical bras like Madonna does."

"No, I think they're just naturally perky."

"Perky," said Aden repeating the word as if it were some mantra to chant that provided him with silent pleasure.

Huong Han had experienced many joys as well as much suffering in her life, but cooking was her eternal love. She liked the alchemy of turning base ingredients into something quite sublime. Nobody ever questioned her judgement and she loved the look of joy which good food brought to her guests.

"Table 5 wants duck pancake rolls for starters and a beef in oyster sauce with steamed vegetables and spicy chicken balls for mains."

Enya waited for her order to be relayed to Huong in Vietnamese first, before relaying a second message to her son Li Han.

The old lady spoke Chinese and French fluently, but English spoken particularly in the Irish dialect was a bridge too far. The necessity of learning this strange and colourful language had come much too late in her life. Chinese was the language of her husband who had survived the prison camps of the Japanese to die in another internment camp run by the French. She had never bothered to learn the language of the Americans soldiers who replaced the French. This was down to the lack of respect they showed. The Irish seemed different, but she was too long in the tooth to learn their ways and besides her son could manage for both of them.

Li Han walked with the lithe grace of someone who was very comfortable in his body. He was approaching forty but was healthier and fitter than most twenty-year-olds. With his dark hair, oriental complexion, and slanted eyes, he did have the appearance of a Chinaman. He was only 5'8" and more wiry than strong in appearance.

He commanded much respect in Sligo town on account of him providing inexpensive lessons and an introduction to the martial art of Kung fu. Until he arrived from Dublin, the best and only instructor in town was a black belt in Judo, and he chose never to demonstrate his prowess against this man who was allegedly a 2nd Dan master.

Li Han believed very much in the power of tenacity, and that strength came through conviction. He had a strong work ethic and admired this in other people too. What he couldn't abide were complainers who looked to find fault in everything. He walked over to the two new customers with different accents, who sat at the table by the door. Enya had relayed to him that they were unhappy that they were unable to purchase a beer or any alcoholic drink to go with their meal. Li provided them with two complimentary soft drinks, and also with an explanation that he was unable as yet to get a license to serve alcohol.

When one of the men asked him whether this was because he had failed to satisfy the licensing authority's background checks, he declined to answer. That man was far too inquisitive, and nor did he like the surliness of the other. He had already made amends with his offer of free beverages and now he had made his judgement concerning their character and it was not good.

"He doesn't look all that," said Aden assessing the potential threat of their target.

"Are you saying that you don't fancy him," asked Kav mischievously.

"Go away and stop annoying me shite with that talk. I meant that he doesn't look that dangerous."

"You saw what David Carradine could do; I am sure that he can put you on your back with one of his Kung fu kicks."

"I am sure he can't dodge a bullet."

Well, that is what I am banking on too. If he can bleed, then he can pay a ransom."

"A ransom?"

"Yeah, a gold ransom."

"But who are we ransoming?" asked Aden genuinely confused.

"Her," said Kavanagh gesturing towards Huong who was fleetingly visible as Enya passed through the door to the kitchen galley.

"What sweet tits. Are we kidnapping the girl?" asked Aden relishing the thought of spending more time with his latest fancy.

"No you's idiot; the man's mother cooking our food in the kitchen."

"Ah I get it," said Aden catching a glimpse of the correct target as she became visible when Enya returned through the door carrying plates of food.

Aden watched her every move as she approached with the duck pancake starters. He cleared a space on the table for the plates and was salivating at the prospect. In his mind, though, he was practising tying rope knots across her chest, tiny waist and bottom.

Enya smiled at him acknowledging his assistance, and Aden's heart melted with a desire born out of lust. No more lecherous stares were directed at her; only smiles and the odd wink.

As professional as ever, both men curtailed their conversation until Enya had left.

"Can't we consider kidnapping her instead," said Aden gesturing towards Enya who was heading back into the kitchen.

"No Aden. We need to seize his mother in order to break the man's resolve."

Then taking a bite out of his pancake, Kav's facial features were instantly gripped by gastronomic ecstasy.

"Look on the bright side Aden. We won't need to live on any more crappy takeaways whilst we have a master chef as our prisoner."

Aden who had also taken his first mouthful was inclined to agree.

"But where will we keep her until the ransom is paid?"

"I was thinking of bringing Maeve down here to take care of finding and renting a property. After all, she has experience in these things."

"Why would you bring that stone-hearted killer down here?"

"Yeah, she is a right bitch I know."

"That is why I never understood why you married her."

"We are divorced and separated now."

"You are not going to be very separated living out in a remote shack in Cliffony."

"Cliffony?"

"It's a wild and remote area where those crazy lesbians are moving to."

"Well, I don't want to live there."

"It was just an example. There are plenty of remote hideaways less than a few miles from this town. I was only making the point that Maeve might be difficult to live with."

"Yes that thought did occur to me, and she seems to scare you too."

Aden felt slightly stung by that observation and decided that Kav had drawn first blood.

"She will probably clip the old woman by mistake," he said with a wry smile.

"That is not fair, it was an accident before. That gun had a hair trigger."

"So she says," replied Aden sardonically.

"The man was only a grass anyway; no loss to the world."

"Maybe he was; we will never know now."

"Well, I won't let that happen again," said Kav, gazing pensively at the walls. "Hey, Aden; look at that photograph over there."

"It is some picture of Vietnam. It doesn't prove anything."

"Beside it," said Kav. "That's Li Han in a picture from another restaurant."

"So, what?"

"Well, he is wearing a waiter's uniform, and that restaurant is the Bain Marie in Glasnevin, Dublin."

"So it is; I will phone my cousin later and ask him to check it out."

*

McCreadie stood by the white marble statue of Lady Erin. The plaque said that she was positioned in the epicentre of Sligo Town. She was also a short but discreet distance away from the front of the Happy Huong's restaurant on Gratton Street.

He was waiting on Brady who was going in for a closer look. In the meantime, he gazed up at the statue marking the junction of the three busy roads and wondered who the heck the woman in the statue was. He had never heard of her and he had gone to Gaelic summer camp when he was a kid. This lady Erin had one hand held aloft as if she had just thrown something. Bizarrely, one of the windows belonging to the Shoot the Crows public house which they had just vacated was cracked and broken. He couldn't help think that the statue had thrown a stone at it.

Brady had just strolled up to the restaurant and then stopped outside pretending to study the menu in the window. McCreadie had to admire the subtlety of his younger counterpart. He doubted the target had even noticed him.

"That's him alright," said Brady upon rejoining his colleague. "He still looks just like his picture. Are we going in?"

"What does the other fella look like?"

"Kind of handy and dangerous; probably Provisional IRA too. They are maybe an active unit."

"If they are, we might need to seek permission before hitting them. We could find ourselves in deep water if we scupper a republican mission that has already been sanctioned."

"I very much doubt they are on that kind of mission. They may be taking out one of their own, or more likely robbing or kidnapping someone."

The older gunman was impressed by Brady's reasoning and had to agree.

"That is why we need to abduct Clancy when he is on his own and question him first. If their business is above board, we will just warn him off Walsh the solicitor."

"And if these guys are rogue?" asked Brady seeking confirmation on a rhetorical question.

"We kneecap'em, or worse," McCreadie replied matter-of-factly.

"Or worse?" asked Brady seeking clarification by also making the gesture of slitting his own throat with his finger.

"God, No! We are on the same side after all."

12 The Other Gun Club (Friday)

Mickey Donelon stood on the corner of Harmony Hill and Gratton Street watching the Happy Huong restaurant on the other side of the road. The pay phone he was using had become free once the previous user had clapped eyes on Maxie Jinx who was standing beside him. The phone at the other end of the line only rang once before Séamus picked it up.

"Are you there now?"

"Yes, Séamus, and them Belfast boys inside look like they are about to leave."

"Forget them. What about the Snakes?" asked Séamus applying his own colloquial slang for the Irish National Liberation Army.

"They are around, Feargal's got eyes on them but it looks like they are staking out these other two in the restaurant."

"Do you know where Maxie is?" asked Séamus. "I can't get hold of him at the Ship Inn."

"Not sure boss," said Mickey putting his finger to his mouth to elicit silence from the big fella.

"Listen up Feargal," said Séamus. "Wait till you know for sure which way those Derry snakes are heading in, and then call me. I will run along the Rockwood riverside path and capture them in a pincer movement, with you and Feargal fencing them in."

The line went dead, and Mickey pulled out his gun and gave it one last check before replacing it, and edging slightly around the corner for a better view.

The two Belfast targets came out of the front door and turned to their left heading in the direction of the Lady Erin statue and Castle Street. However, before they got there, they made an abrupt left turn and entered the dark unlit pathway between the old derelict warehouses heading in the direction of the Garavogue river walkway. Their surprise change of direction flushed out the two INLA gunmen from the shadows. Mickey briefly watched them rush towards the same walkway with Feargal in pursuit before he ran back to the phone.

Séamus answered immediately and told Mickey to follow them too, but to maintain a rearguard position. However, before he ran after them, Mickey told Maxie to stay by the phone and that he would call him soon.

"We shall see if we can book into the Bective first, then maybe I will come out for a drink with you," said Kav.

"When do you plan calling Maeve?"

"I will do it straight away when we get our room."

"Ah Jaysus, if you two are going to start on one another on the phone, I am going to need batteries for my Walkman," said Aden with serious intent. He had turned about face and was now walking back in the direction he had come from.

"Ah really Aden, can we please just go back to the hotel?" said Kav as he sped past two dodgy looking blokes as he quickly followed his friend.

"Nope, I am serious about this Kav. I am going to need loud music in my ears to drown out you two going hammer and tongs at each other. Come on, there is a late shop open in Castle Street. They sell batteries."

Feargal Keohane had to pretend he was urinating against the wall to hide his face from the Belfast pair and the two Derry snakes that pursued after them. Then as soon as it was safe for him to follow after them, he was joined by Mickey Donelon.

"Séamus is heading down the Rockwood riverside walk looking to capture them at the other end of this passage," said Mickey who seemed unsure what to do next.

"Well you run and intercept Séamus," said Feargal, "and then the two of you can head quickly up the riverside to reach the other end of Castle Street. I will follow them from this end."

"Great stuff," said Mickey appreciating the pure logic from his slightly smarter brother-in-arms.

The two men separated heading in different directions.

Mickey Keohane was fit as a fiddle and the youngest amongst them. The thin pencil moustache and the low fringe style that his black hair was cut in, did little to make him look any older. Being of small stature, it made his close friendship with the enormous 'Maxie' Jinx appear all the more bizarre. He was as committed to the republican cause as he was to his friend and saw Séamus more like a father figure. Nonetheless, he still ran past him because he was going so fast that he took Séamus by surprise. The man had been waiting in the darkest shadow and had his old Locke's revolver drawn and ready.

"Hold up," Séamus futilely shouted after him, and then the retired gunman started loosening up some of his old joints as he started running after him.

TO HELL OR SLIGO

Late opening shops were a rare breed in Sligo town. It wasn't because of any local civic laws; it was more to do with a 'can't be arsed' kind of attitude. It was probably because the small shop at the Market Street end of Castle Street was run by the town's only other Asian man that it existed at all. He wasn't allowed to sell any 'off-licence' products, but the Sikh shopkeeper happily supplied the batteries that Aden bought along with some bars of Tiffin chocolate. It was a small shop, and so the couple of people outside had to wait for Kav to exit before they could come in. Strangely they didn't, and this made Kav stare the older one in the face as he walked past him. That big moustache and sideburns seemed mighty familiar, but Kav couldn't place him at all.

Aden was already testing the new batteries in his Walkman cassette player when he copped his first look at these two. It was the younger meaner looking one that caught his interest. He looked like he wanted a fight, but Aden wasn't scared of the likes of him and the sounds of Simple Minds dampened out everything else from his mind. That was, of course, everything except Kav's nagging, and the headphones had to come off and go back into his pocket.

"What was their problem?" asked Kav as they walked away from them.

"He's probably feeling menstrual, or judging by the older one's whiskers, possibly the full moon."

Even though they kept their distance, Aden was aware that they were being followed, and he kept glancing back over his shoulder to watch whether these two were still behind. After turning left at the end of the road into Thomas Street, the two Provos could see the Bective Hotel up ahead on the other side of Bridge Street.

The two mean looking men were now forgotten relics as they now met another odd pairing waiting at the entrance to the riverside walk. They had seen the older one earlier walk into the snug bar. Both Aden and Kav looked at him as they walked past trying to evaluate the credibility of their earlier theory that he was one of 'them'; the Stickie IRA. However, he didn't return their stare, and whether he was or not, they had no beef with him and didn't really care. Instead, they entered the front entrance of the hotel and went straight to the bookings reception.

The proprietor and Kav were soon on first name terms as she showed them upstairs to an available twin room. The two single beds were too close together for Aden's liking because the big fella was likely to snore. At least they weren't sharing a double bed again, and he could always use one of his own socks to stuff in his friend's mouth. Kav looked pleased that there was a bedside phone but Aden was hoping it didn't work.

ANGUS CACTUS

"So shall I book you in for one or two nights, Michael?" asked Margaret.

"I would say probably two, but I will let you know for definite tomorrow."

"We have a band playing tonight in the long bar. Do you like Country & Western?"

Aden's face appeared ashen and drained of blood at the fearful concept.

"It is not my younger friend's cup of tea, Margaret," said Kav, halting Aden in his tracks before he started using any profanity. "I think we will be heading out locally for a few 'bevies' later and back for an early night."

"Your dog seems a bit highly strung," said Aden referring to her tiny Yorkshire terrier that refused to leave her side. Even now, he was emitting a low guttural growl from the other side of the closed door. On the way upstairs, he had always walked between Aden and his mistress, presenting him with exposed teeth the whole time.

"Oh, he is an excitable little man, totally harmless of course. I think he just needs a new girlfriend."

"Don't we all," replied Aden.

*

McCreadie and Brady had stood close to the ruins of the Abbey whilst watching the two Provos from afar.

"They did say they were booking in there when they walked past us earlier," said Brady, "and they haven't come out yet and it's been a little while."

"You are right, Terry. I don't reckon they are leaving the Bective tonight, let's head out to the safe house and come back early in the morning."

"Why can't we just go in now? We can easily sort them," said Brady who really didn't see either of the Belfast duo as a credible threat.

"Because, like I told you earlier; That place…" he said pointing at the Bective, "… is off limits to us. We cannot get involved with the Stickies while we are down here, or this will get very messy indeed."

"I say bring it on."

"Well I am saying, we stay well out of the way of the Officials, and I am calling the shots here."

"Okay Kapitaine," said Brady saluting him in mockery. "Let's head back to the Land-rover and get out of here."

13 Hazelwood   (Friday)

Séamus had seen the two Belfast men before they spotted the INLA gunmen standing by the Abbey. He didn't even care if those two were Provisional IRA. They likely were, because they were eliciting so much interest from the two Derry snakes. As far as Séamus was concerned, the two Belfast men were not his targets. However, Chuck McCreadie definitely was, and his young snake companion was also for the chop, and tonight if at all possible.

He couldn't even see Feargal, but he knew he must be watching from some vantage point. He had three people tailing these two, and a fourth somewhere in reserve. The lack of communication between them was very frustrating for Séamus, and he made a resolve to use at least two cars with CB radios and radio walkie talkies if this stretched over to another day. In the meantime, he followed behind the two snakes in the company of young Mickey Keohane. The two of them kept a close watch on their targets as well as keeping an eye out for Feargal.

Feargal thought that he would find Maxie still waiting by the payphone on Harmony hill. When he didn't, he knew where he could expect to find him. True to form, he found Maxie in a queue waiting to be served fast food in the Four Lanterns takeaway which was nearby on John Street.

"Come on Maxie, no time for that," he said to the younger man.

At six foot four, and weighing in at nearly 25 stone, the loss of the 2nd youngest member of the locally notorious Jinx family made quite an impact on the waiting queue, and a big loss of custom for the management.

The man who 'Maxie' had sacrificed his next cheeseburger for was impatient to get going. The 'cause' was strong with Feargal and he would have been a credit to any paramilitary force he cared to join. Currently in Sligo, there was only Sinn Féin as a political option, and realistically the Officials were the only effective local paramilitaries. Feargal was late twenties and looked more like a sportsman than a nationalist. His hair was cut short, shaved at the back and sides which was unusual for contemporaries of his age. To be fair to him, he did play a lot of hurling whenever he could, and probably saw more aggravation wrapping that stick around other player's heads than he ever did with the Officials. Today was a notable exception to that. These two snakes that they were following around town looked highly dangerous and were most likely packing weapons.

"We need to use your car," he said walking towards Maxie's vehicle which was parked across the road.

It was not a quick getaway; it never really was where Maxie was concerned. There was always a lot of repositioning involved to sit comfortably behind the wheel. Maxie always drove for three reasons. Firstly, because he couldn't fit in the back, and Séamus liked to always sit up front, but never drive. Secondly, he didn't drink alcohol, and that was a godsend which helped separate him culturally from his other six brothers. Third and finally, he was an excellent driver, and his extra weight helped provide some ballast which helped him corner at extremely fast speeds.

Turning left into O'Connell Street, Sligo Towns main thoroughfare, he cruised slowly along the one-way system, in the left filter lane.

"There they are," shouted Feargal with excitement. "See Séamus and Mickey over beside the 'Wood & Iron' store. They look like they are heading into Wine Street."

They were, and Maxie followed with maximum stealth; partly not to spook the INLA gunmen they pursued, and partly to keep outside of Séamus's vision. The boss man was always on his case and was probably annoyed that he had slipped away from his post at the Ship Inn.

The trail didn't last much longer. The two snakes walked no further than the Wine Street car park. Once there, they got into a grey Land Rover Defender which looked like it had seen more than its fair share of being driven off road. Maxie sat with his headlights off and waited for them to exit before starting his pursuit. Seeing Séamus and Mickey waiting by the toll booth, he stopped briefly allowing them both to jump in the back. Maxie then floored it across the changing lights, and by the time they reached Stephen Street, he had fallen in two cars behind the target. The Land Rover left the one-way system before Bridge Street and headed up along the Mall in the direction of Sligo's General Hospital. Maxie pursued them at a distance, and took the same right turn into the Ballinode road and eventually on to the Dromahair road.

They were well outside the town by now, and travelling along the scenic road which circled Lough Gill. The snakes' destination was not clear at this point until they took the small unmade road turn off towards Hazelwood. Maxie continued on straight so as not to alert them to suspicion, but once he saw the Land Rover disappear from his view in his rear mirror, he swung his car around quickly and sped back down the same unmade road with his headlights turned off.

Despite the full moon, the intermittent cloud coverage made it difficult to avoid the potholes and the car and its occupants were getting severely thrown about. Séamus was cussing under his breath, but he had been in a bad mood since he got in. Maxie made sure not to avoid the one big pothole he could see, and made sure to clip it with the rear tyre on Séamus's side. The bump made him hit his head on both the ceiling and side window and the under breath cussing renewed with fervour much to Maxie's personal glee.

Choosing not to drive as far as the Hazelwood nature trail's car park, Maxie pulled off the road and parked up behind some trees. This allowed them to watch the now stationary Land Rover. One of the two snakes had got out and was seemingly hacksawing through a padlock which prevented access to the nearby sawmill and factory.

He must have stopped when he saw the car lights appear from Hazelwood's main access road. They were not headlights shining from Maxie's car, but instead those belonging to a Garda patrol car which drove right past the four OIRA men without seeing them at all.

However, the Land Rover with its headlights trained on the gate barring access to the factory slip road did get the Guard's attention and he drove directly over and pulled up beside its driver. The Guard shined a torch light into McCreadie's face indicating that he wanted him to wind down his window. What the Guard failed to see was all too apparent to the four Official IRA members as they watched the other taller thinner INLA gunman sneak up on his driver side and pull a gun on the Guard as he opened the door.

Pulling the policeman to the ground, he gave him a few kicks before bending down and tying the man up with a length of rope. Then, using the Guard's own keys, they opened the boot and threw the trussed up policeman in his own trunk.

"What do we do now?" Feargal asked directly of Séamus.

"We could go down and free the Guard before they do any badness to him, but my inclination is not to get involved now that a Guard has been kidnapped. I fear that tonight's hit will have to be postponed unless we want to go to prison."

"We could call the guards and let them come rescue him," suggested Feargal "Hopefully; they might arrest the two snakes in the process, and save us the effort of hitting them."

"That makes good sense," agreed Mickey, and Maxie was nodding in agreement too.

"Okay, if that is what you lads want to do, I am happy to go along with it." Truthfully he wasn't though. Séamus's blood lust was in overdrive, and he wanted nothing less than to settle his personal vendetta with his old friend Charles 'Chuck' McCreadie. Regardless, he kept his thoughts of revenge private from the others but instead aimed to appear a man of reason.

"Come on, let's drive somewhere where there is a phone," said Séamus, although before departing, he made sure to swap seats with Feargal and get in the front, making sure that Maxie drove away slowly and quietly.

There was a payphone near the Fiat garage which was a few roads further back along the route that they had come. Maxie drove like one of the Dukes of hazard to reach it and using a handbrake turn, spun the car around to broadside the phone.

"Why do you have to be so extra?" asked Séamus as he got out, and then taking off his flat cap, he passed it around the occupants of the car like it was a church collection plate. "Come on, divvy up, I need all your change in case they leave me hanging on."

"Can you not just phone 999; that's free?" asked a voice from the back.

"No Mickey, there are ways and means of doing this," said Séamus in answer.

"He has to go through the official channels," added Feargal by way of explanation.

The coin slot appeared to be jammed, and the three members of the Official IRA sitting in the car watched as silent witnesses as their leader repeatedly smashed the telephone's receiver against the rest of the phone.

"Good old Department of Posts and Telegraphs; never one to let you down in an emergency," said Feargal wryly in an attempt to lighten the mood.

Séamus was in a foul temper when he got back into the car. He issued instructions, and this time, nobody dared question him.

"Drive back to town. I will use the pay phone in the Bective."

The journey was short enough, helped by Maxie's fast driving, but it looked like Séamus was thwarted once again. There was a police motorbike parked outside the Hotel.

"Ah feck it double time. That's TJ Bannerman's bike. We can't go in there."

"can't we tell him. He is a Guard after all," asked Mickey.

"Allegedly," said Séamus, "but I need to go through official channels and if he gets involved, it will surely go arse over face. Park up over there Maxie, we will go to into Furey's bar instead."

TO HELL OR SLIGO

The four men made an impression as they walked into the small bar. This place was a serious drinking den, and Feargal went up to the counter to buy a round. The barman wasn't quick to take his order because he was busy trying to strike a match without leaving any trace on the matchbox. Feargal thought that this must be some trial of dexterity until it occurred to him that the barman was just being tight-fisted.

Séamus and Mickey had found the pay phone over at the other side of the long bar, and Maxie stayed to keep Feargal company. This time, the phone worked and a few coins dropped as he connected to the local Gardai station.

"Am I talking to a guard?" asked Séamus.

"Yes, this is Garda O'Donnell."

"Codlaíonn an fear glas riamh," said Séamus in perfectly pronounced Gaelic.

"I don't speak Irish," said the Guard.

"Well then get me someone who does."

"That attitude will get you nowhere," said Garda O'Donnell taking some offence. "And besides, our only fluent Gaelic speaker transferred to Mayo. Can ye not speak English?"

"THE GREEN MAN NEVER SLEEPS," said Séamus carefully enunciating each word slowly.

"Is this a complaint about your neighbour, Sir?" asked O'Donnell.

"What NO! It is a code-phrase."

"For what?"

"It is the OFFICIAL code-phrase that a representative of the OFFICIAL IRA is meant to use when OFFICIALLY contacting the Garda Síochána."

"Well, you learn something new every day. So what am I meant to do now?" enquired the Guard.

"You are meant to get me Philips or Wilson, your official liaison officers."

"That might be a problem, hmm," replied the Guard exhaling nasally as if this might emphasise the point.

"Not mine," said Séamus in complete exasperation.

"Well, it might be. Sergeant Philips has retired, and Garda Wilson is on his holidays."

"Ah Jayzuz, YOU guards couldn't find your way out of a paper bag."

"There is no need to be facetious," said O'Donnell which was followed by a long pause for reflection before he continued. "I will get you Detective Sgt. Mahoney instead."

There followed an even longer pause until a familiar voice came on the

ANGUS CACTUS

line.

"Hello, who am I speaking to?" said Mahoney.

"GREEN EAGLE ONE," said Séamus enunciating his words again.

"Is that you Séamus Tooley?"

"No; it's fecking green eagle one."

"Green eagle whatever, Séamus, what can I do for you?"

"It is about one of your guards."

"Who?"

"I think it might be Liam Walsh. He has a habit of parking on the grass. So I think it might be him."

"What about him?"

"I just witnessed him being kidnapped by the INLA. They put him in the trunk of his own patrol car."

"Where?"

"Down in Hazelwood, near the entrance to the straight service road belonging to the saw mill. You need to get some of your boys down there before they drive him away or do something worse."

"How do you know they are INLA?"

"We have been tracking them since they came to town, but we don't want to engage them now that they have involved the Garda Síochána. We have no beef with the guards."

"We are dispatching backup. Thank you Séamus, I mean thank you Green Eagle."

Séamus hung up. He had a welter of emotions churning within. There was disappointment from having lost the opportunity to settle an old score, but a certain satisfaction from having done the right thing. He needed some time and space to get his thinking right. Seeing his ex-friend and enemy McCreadie had mixed him up in the head.

One thing was for sure; he had no time for being hassled by one of the towns famous bar flies. Owen Mulligan was a scraggly looking fellow whom he had gone to school with. He had seen Séamus on the phone and couldn't resist coming over to *yank his chain*.

"I Ran Away," said Owen as his way of introduction. He knew Séamus was Official IRA and this was the oldest jibe in the book against them. This was a reflection upon their earlier reluctance to get militarily involved in the troubles up North.

"How about you go away and stop bothering me, Owen Mulligan," said Séamus in the manner of a polite warning.

"You boys are a long way from the fight," said Mulligan slurring his words.

"The fight is here, Mulligan, and Ireland's heart is the prize," said Séamus taking the bait.

"But where were you, when the civil rights marchers needed your help?"

"Shut up, you're drunk, and I have no time now for your nonsense."

"Brrk..brrk .. Brrk"

"What in bejeezus are you trying to say man?"

"That's the sound that a chicken makes, Séamus."

"It sounded more like he has reflux to me," said Mickey Keohane.

"What would you know? Ya young gob shite."

"Feck off Mulligan before I knee cap you; you old drunk," said Keohane.

"I might be drunk, but YOU SIR are a coward, and I will be sober in the morning."

"I seriously doubt it," said Séamus before calling out for some assistance from across the room. "Maxie, come over here, and escort Mulligan outside."

The man-mountain moved in front of the drunken lost prophet. He said nothing, but he didn't need to. A few centuries of selective breeding and a mountain of cheeseburgers were doing the talking for him.

"Ah now, Young Jinxie," said Mulligan in trepidation, and with a mind to retract his previous words. "No need to get upset with me. I was just joshing your friend Séamus. We go way back you know..." Mulligan's flow was being interrupted by the distraction of being dragged across the floor. However he recovered his train of thought by the time he reached the door, and now it was coming out thick and fast. "It's Maxie, isn't it? Aren't you the second youngest; and HOW is your mother? She is a fine woman indeed."

Mulligan had managed to jam both of his feet against the door frame and was applying his entire strength in a vain attempt to remain inside. Maxie replied to the situation by dropping the man's upper torso in favour of grabbing hold of his legs. Then he simply dragged him out, letting the door close on Mulligan by accident. The blow winded him a little, and just enough to shut him up for a while.

A minute or two passed before Maxie walked back into the bar. For some inexplicable reason, he was holding Mulligan's shoe in his hand. A sight that was a little unsettling for the other drinkers.

"Er Maxie," called out Mickey across the bar.

"What?" said the big man.

"The shoe!"

Maxie Jinx looked down at his hand, shocked and completely unaware that he had been holding it. His expression suggested that he had just picked up something revolting and he turned and re-opened the door, throwing it outside.

"Ow!" came the distant muffled cry from a man who had just been hit by something.

14 Colleen's 21st (Friday)

It was a ten to fifteen-minute walk, uphill all the way, and Shane was regretting every step of it. As he got closer to Jury's hotel, this girl Maureen was trying to get even closer attached to him. There had already been two failed attempts at a kiss; both of which had been surreptitiously scuppered by Shane himself.

He noted that she couldn't even walk in step with him, and the long uphill walk seemed all the more uncomfortable as they bobbed up and down to a different rhythm. The fact that she was so considerably taller than him, made him feel as if he was going out on a date with a Nephilim. Nothing personal, but he really didn't like the girl and while his head told him to cut and run, his better instincts told him to do the right thing. And so, in a spirit of self pity, Shane found himself pondering how exactly he had ended up in this predicament.

Maureen McGowan was unknown to Shane, but she had secretly held a flame for him for quite a while. Therefore, when she received a plus one invitation to attend her friend's 21st, she steeled her nerve and came across to the Bective Hotel to ask the good looking barman who worked there out on a date. If he had known this, then he would never have accepted to be her date, but by saying yes, he unknowingly had agreed to become her boyfriend.

She didn't know much about him and therefore didn't realise that he, in turn, had received his own plus one invitation from Colleen. She didn't even know that they were mutual friends and somehow Shane wasn't able to convey this simple fact to her. Shane was famous for getting the wrong end of the stick, and when she started asking him about Colleen's invitation and plus ones, he assumed that she was asking him whether he might allow her to come along as his.

His own girlfriend had declined to be his plus one, which was testimony to her suspicion of his Belfast friends and what he might be getting up to when he was up there. Therefore, he said yes to Maureen's request, but it was only in the spirit of inclusiveness for a fellow publican's daughter.

That was a month before this evening, and during the intervening period, she had convinced herself that Shane really was her boyfriend. Recently she had been getting off work early so that she could come down every day and spend the last couple of hours sitting at the Bective's bar counter as he finished up his day shift. He tried telling her that he had a girlfriend and was spoken for. He even tried telling her that she wasn't his type, but Maureen only ever heard what she wanted to hear. What's more, she frightened him in a psychotic kind of way.

One particular morning after having ignored her for most of the previous evening, he received a hand-delivered Valentine's card from her. She didn't sign her name and didn't even bother to use a pen. Instead, it looked like it was written in crayon, and it said thank you for making my time with you special. What scared Shane even more, was the fact that it wasn't even Valentine's day. The girl had some serious issues, and Shane wanted to come out of this whole fiasco intact and without being stabbed or castrated.

As usual, he didn't have much of a plan, he just hoped to ignore her some more until she eventually went away. He had already prescribed himself a couple of pints and a big fat splif, and hoped that his distended perception might soon help him forget her presence.

His friend Sean was a mutual friend of Colleens, he was a manager and she was his deputy working in a large local retail store. He usually resided in Sligo during the week but he had taken a few days off and had returned to Belfast. Despite this, he had promised to come down especially for the occasion, and was supposedly driving down with Shane's other best friend Min, and they were both bringing their girlfriends.

Shane had waited on their arrival before setting off, but there was no word or sign of them. Now it was looking to all intent and purpose, that Shane was going to spending the evening in Maureen's company, and no matter how much he wanted to attend Coleen's 21st party, this prospect now filled him with growing dread.

They were about half a mile from the Jury's venue when a familiar car screeched to a halt on the main road beside them. It was Sean and Min, and their girlfriends, Caitlin and Mary. Shane peered into the smoke-filled interior, which despite being a tight squeeze to fit in, it represented a haven of comfort for him. In contrast, Maureen fought her best instincts not to get in and was convinced that the driver was one of the four horsemen of the apocalypse.

A bottle without a label filled with a liquid without a colour was being passed around. She took a swig so that she might feel more accepted, only to realise that it was industrial strength poteen. Even Sean had to wipe the tears which it brought to his eyes, and he was driving.

This invasion of new faces brought new resolve for Maureen to demonstrate that Shane was her man. To her credit, his friends were convinced initially that she was his girlfriend. They did their level best to accommodate someone who was outside of their circle of trust. Perhaps as friendly as twenty-year-olds could allow themselves to be. They even bought her drinks; mostly neat vodka, which was a growing concern to Shane who knew she never usually drank alcohol.

It was Colleen who first cottoned on to some malfunction in the dating game when she came to the table and greeted them as her own friends. She asked both of them whether they had received her posted invitations in good time, and the penny now dropped fully for Shane. As for Maureen, she was a dark horse wrapped up in a puzzle which he had no intention of solving.

As the party progressed and everybody let their hair down or spiked it up as was the fashion, he forgot almost completely about Maureen. When he did try to placate her or ask her to dance, it was all too little, too late. The girl was knocking them back at this point like some hardened drinker trying to forget the past or blot out the future.

By now his friends, and in particular Caitlin, were continually asking him whether she was alright. Even Colleen expressed her concern about Maureen to him, and Shane supplied the same answer to all; that he was not her keeper, and that he wasn't her boyfriend. He wasn't coping too well with this burden of responsibility laid on his shoulders, and he turned to the only medicine he knew helped him best at shutting out the outside world.

In fact, he didn't even need to rely on his friends stash as there was enough of it being smoked by many others at the party. Both speed and cocaine gave him a nice buzz, and a little amyl nitrate on the dance floor took him off to the land of the fairies.

Much of the rest of the evening remained a blur to him. He remembered Colleen introducing her new boyfriend who had been someone else's plus one. Tom was from Tipperary and surprised her Belfast friends by his cosmopolitan values. Ostensibly, he was a 'head' from a rural county famous for birthing culchies, Ireland's version of the hillbilly. The Wacky-backy was a cultural leveller, and for the rest of the evening, he remained inseparable from Shane and Colleen and their cosmopolitan city friends.

He matched them drink for drink, and smoke for smoke. The trouble was, so did Colleen and Maureen. Neither of them was used to intoxication but tonight the gloves were off. Colleen who was the bell of the ball was probably enjoying herself a little too much. Maureen on the other hand, was just being strange.

ANGUS CACTUS

They were amongst the last to leave, and Shane and his friends likewise were still raring to party. They declined the venue's offer of taxis to take the hostess and her friends home. Most likely, this generosity had been prepaid by Colleen's parents who just wanted to see their daughter safely home that night. They trusted Colleen and were not overly worried, except her father was a plain clothes detective sergeant in the local Garda, and as such he preferred that she not take any risks.

Another problem presented itself on the way home. It happened once the group had stopped to allow the men to urinate against a stone wall. Maureen sat down, but comfort was her primary aim, and she was opting out of this evening's party. There was nothing anyone could say or do to persuade her to get up from the cold pavement where she sat. Min said he would carry her, but Maureen struggled violently preventing any assistance of any kind. Colleen, although worried about her friend, knew her best and said that she would be alright as she didn't have far to go.

The intoxicated party which now included Shane, Min, and Mary, Sean, and Caitlin, Collette and Tom, set off without her and by the time they reached the Bective, they had pretty much forgotten about Maureen. The Belfast foursome had already been allocated rooms, but Shane offered to host the after party for everyone present which was to take place in his converted attic room.

15 After-Party (Friday)

Enya had long since finished her shift and was waiting for Shane up in his converted attic bedroom. These days, she would more than occasionally stay over which was a bone of contention for her parents as well as for his. Shane had forgotten about the message she had relayed earlier through the two northerners, and this made it a nice surprise to find her there. Thankfully she was dressed and up for having some fun because Shane was still buzzing and wanted to start the 'after-party'. This was fortunate because whether she liked it or not, three couples had just followed Sean through the attic door.

Shane wasn't the kind of host that made his guests initially feel relaxed and welcome. It was more a matter of fending for yourself and finding a comfortable spot to stand or sit. He was more likely to disappear or else busy himself with unknown tasks.

Without any explanation, he had fully opened the sash window and climbed outside onto the expansive flat roof of the building. It was a dry cloudless summer night and the first thing that was carried outside were the 150-watt speakers which were Shane's pride and joy. The amp stayed in his bedroom in the glass cabinet which housed the tower stack system and vinyl collection into which he had invested so much of his wages.

The record deck was suspended in the air by four strings, which was the second image that most people processed upon entering the attic, the first being the general untidiness of the room and the lack of furniture. There were mix-tape cassettes strewn about everywhere which displayed just pictures and numbers. The playlists of each were indexed only inside Shane's head; a simple feature that guaranteed his position as resident DJ.

Most of that which Shane needed was already positioned outside. The flat roof housed chairs, a small table, a hammock, some bean bags, and lighting. He only required beverages, snacks and food and Min kindly volunteered to help him forage downstairs for most of that.

The restaurant was locked, but he could get through to the kitchen via the bar. There was no need for him to unlock that door because his sister Bernadette and brother-in-law Jimmy were conducting an early hours lock in. The two lads attracted some attention as they entered and walked through the bar. Shane made sure to greet everyone he knew so as not to disturb the craic that appeared to be going down. Min kept a low profile at first until Bernadette spotted him and beckoned him over to say hello.

Shane knew that his sister had a soft spot for his fireman friend. He was hoping that his friend was sufficient eye candy to distract her whilst he went behind the counter and began pulling pints and enough shots to fill a set of trays with complimentary drinks for his friends upstairs. There was an unspoken truce between him and his sister. Each, in turn, could generously 'comp' their friends, just so long as they kept this fact secret from their mother.

Shane could see that Bernadette and Jimmy's usual entourage were all here, and they looked set for another all-nighter. What confirmed this notion was the presence of 'TJ' Bannerman wearing his full police motorcycle uniform propping up the other end of the bar as usual. This was his preferred spot as it allowed him to quickly reach the toilets so that he could answer his police radio in privacy without any pub noises in the background.

His presence always gave some legitimacy to the late night bar extension. It was also a good yardstick for the usual late night entourage to measure their own potential alcoholism. If you could drink as much as their resident Garda and then ride a motorcycle home at the end of your shift, then you were probably a lost cause like him.

The other benefit of a late night lock-in was the extended banter and a generous supply of drinks on the house. 'Billa' who was one of the regulars, was presently sitting alongside TJ and Bernadette. And her husband Jimmy was standing the other side of the counter and laughing at the ribbing TJ was getting from Billa.

This concerned his failure to bring to justice one of the bar's other regular denizens. That would be Owen Mulligan, a painter and decorator, who looked uncannily like Stan Laurel. Owen had decorated much of the Hotel's interior and had taught Shane how to paint and skim over plasterboard. As such he had earned his seat at the all night bar but had been conspicuously absent recently since stealing that police car. Everyone assumed that he was wary of TJ's wrath seeing as he had directed much vitriol at the absent man.

Billa had a bizarre lazy eye that seemed incapable of ever synchronising with its fully functioning partner. He also had a bit of a stutter which would get progressively worse as he got angry or frustrated. This could sometimes make him seem a cheap target for abuse. However, despite his quirky appearance and his bizarre vocabulary of colloquial slang words which seemed to be characteristic only to him, nobody ever made fun of Billa. They took the piss out of him mercilessly regarding everything he said, especially challenging his unexplained obsession with homophobia, but they never picked on his disabilities.

"How did a drunken man manage to steal a feckin police car?" asked Billa for the umpteenth time.

"That arse Callaghan left the keys in the ignition when he stopped at Feehily's corner shop," explained TJ. "That fecker Mulligan came out of O'Dwyers across the road, and drove it off for a laugh."

"How many police cars were in the chase after him?" said Jimmy asking a rhetorical question that everyone already knew the answer to.

"I heard there were three police cars chasing him for most of the 26 miles around Lough Gill," confirmed Bernadette.

"I think you will find that there was motorcycle chasing him too, Bernadette," said Billa mischievously.

"Was that the fella using all that bad language over the police radio?" asked Jimmy.

"Yep, no doubt he was employing a whole heap of language that was outside official Garda vocabulary," said Billa struggling to say the final word before landing the coup de grace. "But what I don't understand is, how you could arrest Owen, but then drop all the charges?"

The memory seemed too painful for TJ who looked around seeking an understanding face. He chose Min's and directed his defence at him. "That fecker Mulligan recorded us. He recorded me, god dammit! Unprofessional conduct and language, he called it. So we had to let him go, but I tell you, he is going to have to answer to me some day. He can run, but he can't hide from me forever. I will have my reckoning."

Min nodded in full agreement although, for him, the gist of the story had got lost somewhere in translation. But not for everyone else present who were all falling about laughing thinking about the antics of their absent compatriot Owen Mulligan. Mirth was something that Min particularly appreciated. Thus he began to laugh heartily as well, and this was more fuel on the fire for the others re-treading this often repeated anecdote. Laughter is contagious and right now they had a pandemic on their hands.

Shane took the opportunity to slip into the kitchen and with practised and with consummate skill, he quickly made up a few rounds of his speciality sandwiches which he carried in a closed wicker basket back out to the bar. He wasn't hiding them; he just didn't want to share.

Nobody noticed anyway. They were still preoccupied with tears in their eyes and uncontrollable laughter. Shane was confused because this was not normal behaviour, but then he realised that his friend was as high as a kite, and he was the furthest gone in the party. He had fallen off his chair and hadn't managed yet to stand up as he was bent double on the

ANGUS CACTUS

floor and crying with laughter.

Shane collected his friend and used the collective responsibilities of carrying trays full of plunder back upstairs as a sobering influence.

"What was so funny?" asked Shane as they headed up the stairs.

"I don't know. I didn't even know who they were talking about. I was just laughing at them laughing."

Shane smiled at his friend thinking that the demon weed had struck him again.

When they reached the attic room, they found that everyone had already moved outside. They passed all the trays out through the open window and Min distributed all the goodies. Meanwhile, Shane cranked up the amp and put on mix-tape No.7; that usually hit the spot. He adjusted the volume up to level 5.5 which was pretty loud for 2pm in the morning. The only saving grace was the river Garavogue which was fast flowing below. It always delivered a subliminal roar in the background, and the breaking water had the effect of dragging the sound of his music at least 200 yards downstream.

Sean had gone back inside the room and was sitting on the side of Shane's bed. His purpose was cutting up some more lines of speed, and he was doing this on a small mirror. This, in turn, rested upon the laminate wooden casing of a large cathode ray tube television which he had slid over and was using as bedside table.

"Nice enough gogglebox. What size is the screen?" asked Sean.

"36 inches and about another 36 inches in depth," replied Shane.

"Yes, I noticed that it is a bit cumbersome."

"Why is it sitting on the carpet anyway?"

"It's broken."

"But you just bought it," said Sean familiar with Shane's purchase.

"I know but the vertical resolution won't hold still. That shop in Enniskillen must have sold me bomb damaged stock."

"Can't you just take it back? It must have some warranty," said Min who had climbed in through the window.

"I went back there already, but the guy pretended he didn't recognise me or the television."

"You've got a receipt. Get the police on him," said Min who was unfamiliar with the cross-border trade.

"If he does that the RUC will do him for smuggling the set across the border," explained Sean. "The bastard knows that he has Shane by the short n'curlies. He probably sells bomb damaged shit to ever Teague that crosses the border."

"You should have hit him," said Min.

"He wasn't alone; he had back up."

"Can you fix it then?" asked Sean.

"Not economical."

"So why are you keeping it?"

"I was waiting for my brother in law to help me throw it over the side of the building."

"Not into the river?" implored Min.

"No, the other side; into the car park."

"Why can't you just take it down the dump?" asked Sean.

"I just wanted to see it explode and get some satisfaction for my hard spent money."

"We can help you do that," said Min.

"Sure we can," agreed Sean.

It seemed like a plan, and the three of them helped pass the TV out through the window and then carry it down to the western perimeter of the roof. Sean relinquished his hold and allowed Min the privilege of helping Shane cast it down to oblivion. Holding a firm grip with both hands, the two of them stood close to the edge and above the external fire stairwell. It was dark below, but there were no cars parked there, just empty tarmac waiting to accept the incoming projectile.

The TV seemed extra heavy after carrying it the distance, and the two of them started to sway it back and forth getting ready to throw it. It was Shane that started the count. One; and the swing developed a much wider arc, then Two, and Shane immediately let go of his end. Min hadn't let go of his, and the momentum of the downward plunging TV nearly dragged him with it. It was only Shane's quick reaction, to grab hold of him and anchor him to the roof, which stopped him from keeling over.

All three young men stood and watched the large television hit the tarmac and explode into smithereens. This was accompanied by a loud bang as the cathode ray tube imploded.

Once that excitement was over, Min turned angrily to rebuke Shane.

"Why did you let go on the count of two? You could have killed me."

"I caught you, and why didn't you let go on two."

"Nobody lets go on two; you are meant to let go on three."

"Not in Sligo; we let go on two."

There was going to be no compromise to this debate, so they put it down to a cultural difference, and went back to join the others and party some more.

ANGUS CACTUS

16 The Troubles (Friday)

When Colleen didn't arrive home by 1am, her father Detective Sergeant Matthew Mahoney of the Sligo Garda decided to get in his car and drive up to Jury's hotel in search of his daughter. It was her 21st and he wanted her to have fun, but enough was enough.

He was not happy that the hotel staff had failed to order her a taxi home. After all, he had paid for two taxis to be on standby and neither had been employed. He was annoyed with the members of staff who were working this graveyard shift and when they could supply no clue as to his daughter's whereabouts, he promised to take his complaint to the day manager.

Meanwhile, he intended to drive around the usual haunts that were frequented by most twenty-year-olds in Sligo. At this time of night, there weren't many. Only two clubs were still open. One was Maxines at the Great Southern Hotel, but that was too far away for them to have walked. The other was a disco at the Claremont Hotel on Wine Street, and he knew the doorman there. So before he set off from Jury's, he used their phone to call to the Claremont and talk to Terry on the door.

Terry the doorman knew his daughter well and confirmed that she wasn't inside the venue tonight. This left only the late night takeaways and Sergeant Mahoney got in his car and headed first to the Four Lanterns on John Street. That was a negative, so he backed into O'Connell Street and pulled up in front of the other late night takeaway.

When he failed to find his daughter there, he went and parked up beside the bridge near the Silver Swan hotel and walked along the river walk investigating the final youth haunt that he knew. The walkway was dimly lit and offered excellent privacy for a lot of young courting couples. In some respect, he was hoping that he wouldn't find her here, as he had not yet come to terms with her dating any man.

His search was interrupted by the distinctive sound of distant music. It was difficult to pinpoint where it was coming from, although the silhouettes of at least five people were visible, standing on the flat roof of the Bective Hotel which was about a hundred meters further along on the other side of the river. Then he noticed three more silhouettes standing at the top of that hotel's external fire stairway and they were carrying something large in their arms. He stood and watched what looked like a large television being heaved over the edge, and heard the loud bang as it crashed to the ground.

Reprobates, he thought. Then he remembered that Colleen had a friend who lived there who spent a lot of his time on the roof. He had met him just once and didn't like the look of him at all. He looked like a druggie and had his hair bleached white at the time.

Matthew Mahoney put two and two together and wondered whether this was where his daughter had ended up and whether she was one of those silhouettes partying up there now. He worried that she was perhaps on drugs too, or worse, maybe sleeping with that reprobate.

He decided to walk back to his car and drive around to Bridge Street and investigate. Then changing his plans, he decided instead to park up on the Kennedy Parade facing the Bective Hotel and watch the goings on up on the roof for a little longer. After all, he was a detective, and he wondered whether a full investigation into that friend of hers was warranted. Sligo was awash with drugs and someone had to be bringing it in. Maybe it was this friend of hers with his druggie demeanour and his connections in London and Belfast.

His train of thought was interrupted by his police radio bursting into life and the message was an eye-opener for sure.

It was Garda Liam Walsh that stumbled across Maureen. To be more exact, he nearly ran her over as he attempted to reverse park into a reserved Garda parking space in front of the local police station on the Pearse Road.

The girl was lying there comatose or sleeping in the road, and when he jumped out of his car to rescue her, he could smell the stench of alcohol off her.

Once he had got her sitting up, he recognised her. She was Maureen McGowan from McGowan's public house literally across the road and beside the court. The girl didn't drink as far as he was aware and was a shy type. This behaviour wasn't her at all and was most disturbing.

He helped Maureen to her feet and brought her inside the police station and sat her down with a big mug of black coffee which she only took small sips from.

She was talking to him, but her explanation was a little incoherent. She was saying something about her boyfriend who was called Shane and that he didn't love her like she loved him. Frankly Garda Walsh couldn't give a damn about that until he found out that this same fella Shane had walked off and left her lying on the ground alone. What's more, the girl had given some disturbing answers to his direct questions. She had taken a range of drugs tonight, and these it seemed had been supplied by this boyfriend of hers.

Sergeant Mahoney could not believe the serendipity of the officer assist message he had just heard over the radio. The call was for a drugs search on a group of people known to be staying at the Bective Hotel. This assist request came following a police incident in which another girl had been nearly run over by a Garda patrol car. She had been left lying comatose in the road outside the police station and had been given a cocktail of alcohol and drugs by the Bective Hotel's barman.

Even though he was off duty and a plain clothes detective to boot, Matthew Mahoney was about to take the call until the unmistakable slur of TJ Bannerman, one of Sligo's pair of motorcycle cops, came on the radio. As far as Sergeant Mahoney was concerned, TJ was an embarrassment to the force, a heavy drinker and an old school cop who was seen to get by using his own methods. Mahoney picked up his radio and call signed in; circumstances had made up his mind and he was going to get involved now whether that was a good or a bad thing for his daughter.

It was definitely the chill part of this evening's session. The music had been turned down a bit, and the collective of couples had paired off and separated. Min and Mary had disappeared to their room, and Sean and Caitlin were lying in Shane's bed and either chopping up lines, sleeping, or perhaps being romantically inclined.

Shane was laying down on the beanbag outside and Enya was cuddling up with him. Colleen was entwined in the hammock with her new boyfriend Tom and they had started kissing each other. She seemed very content and happy after a truly great evening.

Shane didn't pay any heed to the music being turned off, but he nearly jumped out of his skin when a man in a Garda uniform started climbing awkwardly through the window. He recovered somewhat when he saw it was only TJ, but this was still a shock because he didn't really know him that well and he couldn't understand what his business was up here.

Sean was up on his feet by the time the TJ had climbed through and noticed his brother in law Jimmy following after him.

"What's up Jimmy, TJ," asked Shane nervously.

"Don't what's up me young fella," said TJ slurring his words a little. "Which one of you is Colleen?"

"I am," she replied from the hammock.

"You need to make yourself decent," said TJ speaking directly to her, "and get downstairs and pacify your father before he brings half of the North-West's guards up here."

"And you Sunshine," said TJ now leaning forward and attempting to have a private word with Shane. "You have a couple of minutes to gather up all that crazy stuff you boys be smoking or snorting, and throw it into the Garavogue."

Shane didn't know if he should take him seriously or whether this was some prank that Jimmy had put him up to.

"What are you waiting for Shane; get it done, or you are going to get arrested tonight," said TJ, this time without slurring and with a serious look on his face. Shane turned to look at Jimmy, and he wasn't grinning, so this probably was for real.

Shane felt way too charged and too tired to carry out any of those instructions or even to motivate himself to any form of response. It didn't really matter because Sean had climbed out of the bedroom window in his underpants and shoes and had hurled a small mirror and a small package down into the river below. Tom could be seen searching his pockets, and more contraband found its way into the river. Shane sheepishly followed suit, and Enya took hold of his personal stash and disposed of it.

"Someone needs to inform that fireman friend of yours as well," said Jimmy now beginning to show that trademark smirk of his. "And Bernadette asked me to ask you, to ask him and his girlfriend to put their clothes back on and stop pillow fighting in the corridors."

"I'm on that," said Caitlin as she rushed away in the direction of the brace of hotel rooms she and Min had been allocated.

17 Saturday Morning

The legacies of last night were the repercussions that disturbed the tranquillity of his own special world. After the mayhem created by their late night after-party, his father had shouted at him particularly pissed off by the debris of a shattered television which littered the yard. He had also relayed his wife's main point of contention: Margaret was really upset because the guards were involved. She had already lost three points off her publican license through an earlier mistake of Shane's in serving underage drinkers.

Now his mother wasn't talking to him, and conversation would have to stand in line behind the ice cold looks of disappointment which were all she was prepared to offer him. His friends were off the hook as far as she was concerned. She expected Shane to take on the burden of their sins because he was meant to be the responsible host.

The Garda weren't finished with him either. They hadn't found any drugs in their late night search of his rooms, or those of his friends. However, just like his mother, they were seething with him, and he was very much still on their radar. And so he was with Colleen's father too; he just didn't realise how badly. The man had taken a professional interest in someone who he now saw as a reprobate and a potentially dangerous influence on his daughter. Out of vindictiveness, he had taken the opportunity to investigate Shane's two means of transport.

If it wasn't for his desire to see his friends before they set off back to Belfast, he probably would have stayed in bed. Enya, who was already sharing it, was down for that; a sleep-in was a perfect way to spend her Saturday morning. She had no work today, and no agenda other than persuading Shane to drop her back to Grange. She also had no repercussions to face, and it was only his stoic resolve to go and face these, that had driven him from the safety of his duvet.

By the time he found his friends in the restaurant, they had practically finished their breakfast, and were rinsing out the last dregs of tea from their second refill. However, Shane was not the only late arrival to the breakfast club. The two northerners from Belfast had just managed to walk in before the waitress changed the sign on the door to read 'closed'. He hadn't realised that they were guests here and nodded out of respect.

ANGUS CACTUS

They recognised him too and saluted him back from their table across the room.

There was so much that he had to tell his friends, but just like Min, Sean, Caitlin, and Mary, he too was wasted, and not in the correct frame of mind to talk. Silly pranks were more the order of the day, and pouring the last of the milk down his friend's trousers seemed a fitting revenge for the used teabag that Min had just flicked with a teaspoon in his face. Slapstick and fooling around had always been their favourite form of camaraderie. It was so much more poetic than the use of mere words. It was also contagious, and the small border war between him and his tall fireman friend, soon spilled over into open warfare between all five of them, as any leftover food and beverage became eligible ammunition.

Regardless of the way things had played out, it had been a great evening and they had all had much fun together. Now it was time to collect their things and hit the road, and if there had been enough room in the car for him, Shane would have happily gone as well.

They walked out of the restaurant as a group, but the protection of the herd didn't save Shane from the beckoning finger of his mother. Now she was ready to talk. A reckoning was due, and it was much worse than expected and was to be delivered piecemeal to him over the next few days.

The two Provos were in no rush to head anywhere this fine Saturday morning. In fact, they just made the restaurant before the cut off time for breakfast at 11am. A hearty cooked breakfast, followed by a walk around the town was the order of the day, and Aden looked forward to stretching his legs. Sharing a room with Kav, always gave him feelings of cabin fever. It wasn't just the smell of his socks, but there was a whole multitude of reasons for him to find irritation, and his long phone calls throughout the evening to Maeve were definitely high on his list. Thank God for headphones and a liberal policy allowing alcohol in the rooms.

The crazy barman was sitting across from them at a table with his Belfast friends, and northern accents dominated the room. Both members of the provisional IRA scoped out the others who were engaged in some childish food fight.

"His friends look a right motley crew," said Aden.

"Belfast people are always troublemakers away from home; present company excepted," replied Kav philosophically.

"Do you still think that we should trust his story about the Vietnamese ex-monk," asked Aden more than a little concerned that their venture was based on the barman's hearsay.

TO HELL OR SLIGO

"God No! He is a head banger and so are his friends. Today we shall ask around, and substantiate the truth," replied Kav reassuringly.

Later, Aden was finishing his cigarette at the table, when Kav departed, on route to the reception, intending to pay their bill. Seemingly another account was also being settled between the barman and the proprietor who appeared to be his mother.

"It wasn't a pillow fight," said Shane protesting in all innocence. "And they weren't running around in their underpants. Min and Mary were temporarily locked out of their room."

"But they woke up the other guests, and the guards said you were playing loud music on the roof till past two in the morning."

"Well, he didn't wake me, Margaret. I had a lovely sleep." said Kav acting the mediator and trying to lessen the crime.

"I was awake all night long," said Aden interjecting into the conversation as he walked out of the restaurant.

Margaret looked at him with empathy, and back at her son with some anger.

"Oh it wasn't his antics, Mrs.G; it was this big heifer's," he said pointing a finger at Kav. "He was snoring so loud I couldn't hear myself think, let alone sleep."

"I am sorry to hear that Mr. Clancy, and I hope your remaining stay here will be quieter."

"Actually Margaret," said Kav. "We need to book out today. My ex-wife is coming down, and I think she has found us a place to stay."

Aden looked at his friend with a surprised look on his face.

"I will miss you, Michael. Come back here whenever you are passing through."

She gave Kav the warmest of smiles, before turning again to her son with a scowl on her face. "You have embarrassed me, Shane. The guards have been asking me some sensitive questions about you. You might even be facing charges, and Sergeant Mahoney has issued you this," she said holding up a folded document, "He wanted to speak with you personally, but in your absence this morning, I took it off him."

"What is it, mum?"

"He said it is a 'producer' ordering you to supply your tax, insurance, and ownership papers for your old Fiat parked across the way, and for your motorcycle too."

Shane, who was looking very worried, asked his mother, "When do they want them by?"

"Tuesday at the latest."

ANGUS CACTUS

It should have been private, but nevertheless, Aden found himself drawn into the conversation. "Will that be a problem for you?" he asked directly of Shane.

"Very much so, seeing as I don't have any."

Aden wanted to offer some form of help or advice to the young barman, but he had nothing to offer except a cocked head and an embarrassed smile. Kav was shaking his head as well, assuming the worst outcome for him, but neither one of the two Belfast men was aware of the way in which official paperwork and such things were dealt with in the south. Shane knew, and his intention was to lay low or bugger off somewhere until the whole episode had blown over.

His mother, taking in their combined looks of reservation, looked very disappointed with her son, and she turned and walked back into her private office. Guinness, her faithful Yorkshire terrier gave all three of them one last scowl before he did the same and followed her.

"It's Shane isn't it," asked Aden.

The barman nodded disconsolately.

"Shane, I am sure it will all work out fine, but can I ask you a question on another subject we were talking about."

"Sure thing."

"Well, I wanted to ask you where you originally heard all that gossip about the Vietnamese guy."

"Which guy is that?"

"The Chinaman, perhaps?" offered Aden in suggestion.

"Oh yes, that would be Corky's bar on Markievicz Road. Let me tell you, there are some tales told in there."

"Cheers friend, maybe see you around," said Aden not really wanting to hear about them, but still offering his hand for a friendly handshake.

"That goes for me too," added Kav taking a grip on Shane's hand once Aden had released it.

Kav got out his wallet, and asked to settle his bill, whilst Aden went back to their room to check that they had not left anything. Very soon, the two men had walked out the door and were heading back into town along the same route they had walked back to the hotel last night.

This didn't go unnoticed by another two men who watched them from the vantage of their grey Land Rover parked across the road in the small riverside car park. Brady turned the ignition, and they got ready to follow the two Provos, to keep an eye on their movements, and seek the ideal opportunity to abduct Clancy.

The occupants of two other cars parked on the other side of the river in

TO HELL OR SLIGO

Kennedy Parade took notice of the Land Rover's manoeuvre. They had been watching them all morning.

"Green Eagle One to Green Hawk, do you read me? OVER!"

"What is it Séamus?" shouted Maxie in reply through the open windows of his precious MK1 Volkswagen Golf and the Vauxhall Astra beside him.

"Use the friggin walkie talkie ya big idiot?" was Séamus' reply heard with a slight delay over the radio receiver.

"Someone's in a bad mood," replied Maxie this time into his handset.

"Use my call handle and say over, will ya," said Séamus getting more irate.

"You didn't use it either."

"My mistake, sorry, Green Hawk; OVER!"

"Mickey says can we be Green Hornet instead; OVER!"

"What; no you can't. Listen, drive yourselves back to the Ship Inn, and both of you stay put in the office until these guys are ready to leave town. They seem to be following the two Belfast Provos who are on foot. Feargal can follow on foot too, and I will tail the Land-Rover. Keep your walkie talkie charged and turned on. I will call you later; OVER!"

"Sure thing boss, see you later," said Maxie talking directly to Seamus through the open windows before reversing onto the road and driving away. Seamus waited until the Land Rover was three cars in front, before setting off on its tail. He was still grimacing; sometimes Maxie had that effect on him.

It appeared to be a beautiful warm sunny day as Aden and Kav left the Bective hotel and set off across the bridge. But, by the time they had reached the other side, it was raining again. With no umbrellas or even hats for protection, they were forced to pull up their coat collars and walk quicker with their heads down looking for a suitable place to hole up inside.

"It sure rains a lot here," said Aden. It was more a statement of complaint than a conversational opening.

"I spotted an interesting looking bar yesterday."

"Where?"

"By that statue of the woman, that looks like she is throwing a rock. We can try in there first."

A couple of pints in Shoot the Crows public house was to mark the start of a pub crawl that continued with Beezies Bar in O'Connell Street, Hannigans in Knox Street, and it was going to end up in Corky's Bar on the Markievicz Road.

They had both agreed earlier that they weren't going there, but necessity was the mother of invention, and this was where the story of the monk may have been invented. Frankly the previous three pubs had provided no answers at all. Shoot the Crows was empty, and Beezies was full of kids and adolescents putting Guinness heads on glasses of coke, and they had failed to find anyone familiar with Li Han's story in Hannigans pub.

"That Hannigans was a strange place, absolutely no women at all."

"They must be hardened drinkers," said Kav.

"Hmm, I had a few men looking at me strangely in there; made me feel uncomfortable."

"Aggressively staring?"

"No, not really, but I didn't like the way one of them was fondling his pool cue."

"Well, you did touch one of his balls."

"That was a mistake. He had snookered me behind the black with it."

"Anyhow," said Kav changing the subject. "Did you call your cousin in Dublin last night?"

"Yes, he said he was going to check out that restaurant today."

The roar of a loud exhaust pipe distracted Kav from what he was about to say. He squinted his eyes and stared fixedly at the trials bike that was making the noise. He thought he recognised the barman, with a girl in figure hugging trousers and tight cashmere jumper riding pillion. They had just crossed Sligo's main bridge and were heading out of town on the Markievicz Road.

"Is that our fella on that motorcycle?" he asked.

"Yes, and with Enya."

"Noisy old bike."

"I know, but she is beautiful," said Aden in agreement.

Corky's Bar was definitely not open for passing public trade. It was the haunt of its regulars, and there was a distinct clandestine atmosphere when they walked through the front entrance.

They had a couple of pints sitting up at the bar counter, where they found it easier to engage some of the regulars in conversation. Of course, the subject of the Vietnamese restaurant owner of the Happy Huong was brought up, and as expected, the story of the fighting monk escaping the clutches of the North Vietnamese and battling through the jungles of Cambodia was retold with embellishments each time they asked someone new.

TO HELL OR SLIGO

Aden was bored of hearing it, so he opted to use the pub's pay phone to call his cousin and rely on some real information rather than hearsay. It was Aden's absence which prompted Kav to look at his watch and realise he was already late for his rendezvous with Maeve.

The realisation hit him like a shot of adrenalin, and without explanation, he left his pint and the barstool to head outside onto Holborn Hill through the pubs back exit.

He really couldn't be bothered looking for a car, and half of the ones parked outside looked like they had already been stolen. Regardless, an older red Datsun took his fancy, and necessity being the mother of a quick getaway, he smashed in the driver-side window with a loose brick.

His actions didn't go unseen. The occupants of a Land Rover were watching from their vantage point further down the hill, and across the road from them, a brown Vauxhall Astra was watching the watchers.

18 Maeve (Saturday)

Maeve Kavanagh was at home and was studying a desk map of the County Sligo area. It was spread open on her desk which was situated in her improvised office in her two bedroomed terraced house in the Short Strand, a small catholic enclave in East Belfast. As a bedroom, it was surplus to her needs because she lived alone and had no children.

For someone else, it would have made a fine boudoir which could have housed a walk in wardrobe, and the desk could have served as a vanity station for her makeup. Maeve didn't wear much makeup, and vanity was definitely not an inspirational muse for her. She was still slim for a woman in her early forties, and these days, she tended to dress in a very androgynous way. However, this had not always been the case. She used to wear heavy makeup and short skirts in her salad days. In fact, she paid a great deal of attention to her appearance and used her youthful good looks as a honey-trap to catch off-duty soldiers and lead them to their doom. She was still blessed with piercing blue eyes and lustrous dark hair, but that was now cut in a severe bob hairstyle, and her lips had grown small and mean, to match her nature.

She had pinpointed the remote village of Ballyconnell, just north of Sligo Town on the map. It was not far from Mullaghmore where they had taken out Mountbatten five years earlier. She had a limited knowledge of the locality but knew that it was both remote and wild. Aden Clancy had suggested looking in this area, and she had already cross referenced a few cottages advertised for rent in the vicinity. It needed to be private and well off the beaten track, but a small place located in the Raghly peninsula seemed to tick all the boxes. She had already spoken to the owner, a quietly spoken local man; and as far as he was concerned, he was renting the place to two couples coming down for a summer break from Belfast.

The place was immediately available and so she would drive down and take possession of the keys later this afternoon. Raghly Point was over 200 miles away and the drive would take at least three hours; so she would set off shortly.

Maeve was the epitome of organised efficiency. If she could have channelled her passions into a more conventional career, she might have become a successful PA to some corporate CEO. Instead, she channelled most of it into the republican cause. What she set her mind to was usually accomplished with the uber-efficiency of a German industrialist. She assessed criminal enterprises through risk assessment analysis, and as a result, the Belfast Command were very much enamoured with her. She was also a very good fundraiser, which meant that the war council was prepared to sanction nearly any operation that she participated in. She knew this was the real reason why her ex-husband had approached her and asked her to join his kidnapping venture down south. His credentials were not so appreciated and his maverick attitude was seen as self-seeking and not appreciated by Belfast Command. He wasn't even on the payroll, and so he technically wasn't even a commissioned volunteer. In truth, he was just a useless heifer of a man and she often questioned why she had married him, but never what she had first seen in him. Michael was also a lovely man, warm and affectionate, and clever in a bespoke way. The shame was that his unregulated laissez-faire attitude towards the republican cause had been the downfall of his paramilitary career and their marriage.

She reached Raghly Point by early afternoon. The cottage was everything she hoped it might be; in fact, it couldn't have been more secluded. It was difficult even for her to find it, but this she did after backtracking a good distance around the Ballyconnell area.

The owner was there to meet her and enquired about the others in her party. She told him that her husband was coming down separately and bringing along her brother and his mother. Although she paid fully with cash, there was no reason to disbelieve her unremarkable story, nor distrust the pleasant middle-aged blond woman who went by the surname of McGovern.

As soon had he gone, Maeve removed her headscarf and pulled off the blond wig. In her experience, witnesses had difficulty in giving detailed descriptions of blond women in terms outside of the spectrum of their hair. In a small rural area such as this, an outsider was going to stand out, but it was better to stand out in disguise.

She investigated the interior of the cottage and then took a brief walk around its grounds. She marvelled that it was such a beautiful place with fine panoramic views of Sligo Bay and its various strands of yellow sands. Queen Maeve's cairn on top of Knocknarea Mountain was clearly visible in the distance, whilst the stunning backdrop of the Dartry Mountains and Benbulben, in particular, were close by to the east. This mountain was unique with its uniform angled sides and flat top which resembled a raised plateau. Of course, what really endeared this mountain to Maeve was the clearly visible slogan H-BLOCK which had been marked in 25ft tall letters on its side. This was great tribute to the brave hunger strikers of Long Kesh prison, but personally, she had preferred the original sign which simply said BRITS OUT. She had seen that once before when she had come down on a pilgrimage to the site of the Provisional IRA's victory and Mountbatten's sacrifice at Mullaghmore.

Maeve looked at her watch and realised that it was time to get going. She had the address of a meeting point supplied by Aden which was not too far from here. It was a remote stop where she could wait for the others without fear of CCTV cameras or too many witnesses.

Putting her disguise back on, Maeve got back into her car and headed for the nearby town of Grange. Once there, she took a country lane off from the main road and headed towards Ballintrillick. This place wasn't difficult to find, being the only shop or petrol station on the entire route. It was situated at the junction of the only crossroads she had encountered. An ancient road sign offered opposing destinations of Mullaghmore and some place called the Gleniff Horseshoe Pass which had three signs pointing in different directions. This epitomised the peculiarity of the South for her. This thatched roof shop, that sign, and the whole damn area were lost in some time-warp.

She pulled up beside one of the 1950's style glass Shell logo petrol pumps in the shop's courtyard. Then before she had a chance to get out and fill up, an old man came out of the shop with a bucket and promptly splashed soapy water that didn't look that clean on her windscreen and gave it a quick wipe with a dry chamois leather cloth. Then without asking, he proceeded to open her petrol cap and insert the old style nozzle from the pump.

She rushed to wind down her driver's side window as she felt the jolt of the pump kick in. "Just a fiver's worth," she quickly prompted, and the man just nodded. When he had finished pumping and replaced the cap, she asked him whether it was okay to park up and visit the stop. "Just leave it there if you want; we have two pumps and they aren't too busy."

"I'd rather park somewhere else if you don't mind," she said, and the man nonchalantly indicated to a parking spot around the other side of the building.

Entering the shop through its front entrance, it wasn't clear to her where she should pay for the petrol. In fact, it wasn't even clear at all what kind of shop this was. This part was definitely a grocery and provisions shop. There was a counter for bread, cakes and pastries. And there were central deep bins of potatoes and mixed vegetables. All of them looked like they were probably grown out back, or else in some dirt beside the road. There was a section of counter that looked like somewhere she might pay, but it turned out to be the local post office and here, a closed sign sat in place beside what looked like a cashier's till. To the other side of the post office, the last yard of shop counter showcased some pictures of coffins under a glass panel, and the wall behind held a few wreaths and flower decorations.

Then there was an open doorway which seemed to lead on to a small licensed bar on the other side. The old man had crossed between these two rooms via a small opening behind the counter. He went and stood attentively behind the main grocery section of the counter which solved the riddle of where she should pay. Thus, she handed him a five Punt note, but now wondered where she could wait for the others. "Is the public bar open?" she asked gesturing at the other room. "It surely is," said the old man removing his grocery apron and replacing it with his bar keeper's one as he walked away through the connecting hatch.

Maeve hastened after him through the main doorway and looked around in awe at the bazaar of antiquity which passed for a pub. There was no carpet, just wooden floorboards and a sprinkling of sawdust. The seating was mostly benches fitted along the walls with a few comfy chairs parked beside some small tables. The place was empty, and if it wasn't for a sign above another doorway which said 'toilet and exit', she would have thought that she was inside the owner's living room. Although, it didn't look like any living room she had ever sat in before. There was all manner of flotsam and jetsam either hanging from the ceiling or pinned to the walls.

It was only the small bar counter which made any sense to her. With its three mandatory beer pumps of Guinness, Smithwick's, and Harp lager, it remained a breath of normality, and she promptly approached it and ordered a pint of lager.

The old man reached for a half pint bottle of Harp lager which he opened and served to her with a wine glass.

"I asked you for a pint of draught Harp," said Maeve annoyed with the man, correctly guessing that he was old school in his belief that women shouldn't drink pints.

In answer, he opened a second bottle of harp and placed it beside her glass, and said- "The pump isn't working." He then reached to take another five Punt note which she proffered ready in her hand. Maeve held it back.

"I want a Bushmills and ice too," she said eyeing up the whiskey which was on an optic behind the bar.

ANGUS CACTUS

The old man produced another wine glass and pushed it up against the optic, allowing the amber Northern Irish mixed malt to flow in. Then proceeding towards a small decrepit fridge, he opened up the frozen compartment to pull out an empty tray which he then filled up with tap water.

"I am afraid that you will have to wait for the ice," he said reaching out, successful in his second attempt to take her five Punt note which she had put down on the counter. Then fiddling with a cash box stored in a hidden recess, he produced some coins and deposited them back in place of the note.

Maeve in frustrated annoyance grabbed her change and promptly walked back through the internal doorway and into the shop section of the thatched premises. Earlier, she had seen a small freezer in the grocery section, and rummaging through it; she took out a bag of frozen sliced carrots and brought it back into the pub section of the building. Before she sat down in one of the comfier chairs, Maeve placed a 50 pence coin on the counter and told him that should cover the carrots. She was in no mood to be messed around anymore; she had shot a man for less insult. Then placing her drinks beside her on a table, she sat with her back to the old man and facing the door instead. Tearing open the bag of vegetables, she dropped four slices of frozen carrot into her glass of whiskey and waited for the others.

19 Two Car Tail (Saturday)

Once beyond the town limits, Maxie floored the accelerator just long enough for the fuel injection on his VW Golf to kick in, allowing him to cruise past Séamus' brown Astra effortlessly. The leader's new car was nice enough, but couldn't compete performance-wise with the car which was Maxie's pride and joy. Both he and his co-pilot Mickey were bopping their heads in time to the sound of Bob Marley's Buffalo Soldiers playing loudly on the car cassette deck. So loud in fact that neither of them could hear the words of Feargal coming over the walkie talkie.

"…Stolen from Africa, brought to America," Maxie loved singing Bob Marley nearly as much as he loved driving. It was in his honour, that he allowed Mickey to light up a small splif in what was usually a smoke-free environment. Sligo was presently awash with the stuff, and although he had taken 'the pledge' and remained a teetotaller, Maxie was partial to the odd cannabis joint. Filling his big set of lungs by taking a long draw on the joint, he then exhaled slowly releasing several puffs in rhythm with the music. Meanwhile, he kept the grey Land Rover firmly in his sights while maintaining a safe distance.

Despite making him a little lightheaded, he found that this stuff helped him concentrate and aided intuition. It also made him like to sing, and so he joined in with Mickey on the chorus. Sure, this song was almost a republican rebel song.

"Said he was fighting on arrival, fighting for survival,
said he was a Buffalo Soldier, win the war for I.R.A."

The impromptu duet hit a crescendo as they added their own lyric, and kept the fervour going throughout the next bit which thankfully had easier lyrics to remember.

"Dreadie, woy yoy yoy, woy yoy-yoy yoy."

Meanwhile, there was a different vibe going on in the car following closely behind. Séamus' irritable mood had not subsided and its contagion had started spreading like a plague across his body. He kept twitching and twisting in his seat as if in discomfort, and his infliction seemed all the worse every time he heard Feargal's repeated call sign being ignored over the radio waves by that pair of head nodding imbeciles driving up ahead.

"I thought that we were meant to be on point, and they were to stay behind us," said Feargal complaining; but he was just preaching to the choir.

"Feargal, I swear that boy is driving me to the end of my tether; hand me that walkie talkie."

Séamus snatched it from his preferred deputy and then gripped the transmit button tightly and bellowed down the receiver.

"Green Hawk Two, come in Green Hawk Two; OVER!"

"GREEN HAWK TWO," Seamus repeated even louder while flashing his head lights once.

"Hello Green Hawk, this is Green Hornet replying, OVER!"

"This is Green Eagle. I'm not friggin Green Hawk; you are, and who the hell is green hornet anyway. For the love of mercy, can you two idiots learn the call protocols? That way you won't interrupt me again before I have said the word 'OVER'. That is the corr…" Séamus trailed off as he was interrupted by an incoming transmission.

"Sorry Séamus," said Mickey.

"Jaysus, you interrupted me again. I hadn't finished speaking," he said in an increasingly irate tone.

"You did say, OVER, boss; Maxie says he heard you say it too."

"I was friggin talking about the word, and not saying it. Ah, forget it! I will get no sense from talking to the two of you; and what the fecking arse are you boys up to with all that head banging going on. Just turn off that bloody music so I can hear you, and turn your CB radio onto channel 44, because we may need to split up later." Seamus let go of the transmit button, and listened for their call signal over channel 44.

He allowed ample time for them to switch it on and tune in the radio, but their reply remained suspiciously absent. He decided to go first instead.

"Breaker breaker, green hawk two, this is green eagle one. I have been waiting for your call signal. Are you receiving me loud and clear; OVER!"

"Yes green eagle, we didn't think we should reply, because you hadn't said 'over'; OVER!"

Séamus didn't even want to grace that with a reply, but the business of the day demanded it. Both he and Feargal were also casting a cold eye on the old red Datsun far ahead which contained the two Belfast Provos. Their interest only lay with them, due to the fervent interest shown in them by the INLA snakes they were presently tailing.

20 The Road To Ballintrillick (Saturday)

Kav was driving north on the Bundoran road in the direction of Grange. Aden was sitting beside him with an annoyed expression because of the cold breeze circulating uncontrollably around the interior of the car. The undesirable wind kept turning the pages of the road atlas which he was studying, and he had just picked out another fragment of broken glass from under his trouser seat.

"I'm stealing the next car," he said moodily.

"Right so; whatever," replied Kav.

"What I mean to say is that you would think a man of your age might have learnt by now how to steal a car without always breaking a window."

"You made your point Aden."

"I know, but I am just saying."

Kav had heard this same speech many times before and was in no mood for its repetition. Nevertheless, Aden wasn't going to drop it. As Kav drove faster, in an attempt to shorten the travelling time and curtail his friend's nagging, the wind was wreaking extra havoc as it blew the road atlas off Aden's lap and posted it all across the inside of the windscreen in front of him.

"Jayzuz, son of a frigging camel herder, would you ever let me show you how to pop a lock without just busting the glass."

"Look; Aden," said Kav trying his best not to sound condescending. "You have your way of doing things, and I have mine."

They drove on in strained silence in the stolen red Datsun until Kav broke that silence.

"Shall I take this next turn-off to Ballintrillick, because there is another one further up as well?"

"Yes; take the one before Grange. You will pass the pub that way."

"You said it was a petrol station."

"It's kind of both; you will see for yourself."

The last stretch of country road was straight and narrow, but when they saw the signs at the crossroads up ahead, the thatch roof of the country shop became visible and they pulled up in the front courtyard making sure not to block access to the petrol pumps.

ANGUS CACTUS

A mud splattered grey Land Rover which had been following the red Toyota also stopped, but at a healthy distance from the country store. It had tailed them all the way from Sligo, and now McCreadie and Brady didn't want to make their presence obvious. Therefore, they stayed back and watched the two Belfast Provos walk into the thatched shop ahead. They watched and waited some more, but the delay in those two returning to their car was getting longer.

"What do you think they are doing?" asked Brady.

"How am I meant to know," replied McCreadie. "Drive the car to the pump and fill up whilst I have a gander inside and see what they are up to."

As Brady pulled up in front, McCreadie who had already got out, gently opened the shop door and quietly slipped inside. Brady who was waiting for the petrol pump to be switched on, stood facing the entrance with his left hand holding the nozzle, and his right touching the butt of his colt pistol which was tucked into the back of his jeans.

He held the advantage whilst he controlled the exit, but the long wait made him anxious to get inside because he was experiencing that disassociated feeling which usually meant that bloodshed was following. The next person who came out of the store, if it wasn't McCreadie, would get it between the eyes.

Fortunately, it was McCreadie who walked out of the store next.

"Leave that," he said referring to the petrol pump nozzle in his hand, "We have to get going. They left by the other exit and are heading on the road to Mullaghmore."

"On foot?" asked Brady as he climbed back behind the wheel.

"No," replied McCreadie as he buckled up in the front seat of the Land Rover. "The shop keeper said that they left with a blond woman who drank pints and put carrots in her drinks."

"How did he know that?"

"Because he served them to her," replied McCreadie bemused by the question. "You do know it is a pub as well?" he added as an afterthought.

Brady nodded and turned left at the crossroads beside the shop and floored the accelerator in the direction of Mullaghmore. Both men remained quiet letting the adrenalin of the driving and the ongoing situation do the talking. However, before they reached Mullaghmore, they met the main road to Bundoran, and now had a choice of three directions. They chose to carry on in the direction of the infamous harbour. It was a wrong decision, but then even if they had turned left in the direction of Sligo, they wouldn't have caught up with Maeve's car which had taken the next right exit after Grange in the direction of the rented cottage at Raghly Point.

Brady parked up on the approach to the grey stone harbour walls and looked out to sea. It was obvious to them now that they had lost the two Provos and the trail had gone cold.

"Do you think they watched it from here," said Brady envisaging the hit back in 1979.

"No, probably from the headland over there, or maybe from another boat out at sea. Those remote controllers have a decent range of about half a mile without electrical interference."

"So what now?" asked Brady seeking a wise reply from the older hitman.

"Right now, we go back to Sligo, but I think we should stake out that country shop in the coming days. The shopkeeper said that he had never seen the blond or the older fella before, but he said that the younger man has had a pint there a few times."

"Clancy?"

"The same man," confirmed McCreadie.

"I will head back there tomorrow. If he comes back, I will be waiting for him, said Brady, removing the gun from the hollow of his back, and returning it to the glove box."

"We need him alive to talk," reminded McCreadie staring at his colleague with suspicion.

21 Cheeseburger Express (Saturday)

The fast driven red Datsun was leading the chase, and so seeing it indicate a right turn before Grange, he knew in advance that the snakes in the Land Rover in front would follow suit. Seamus knew this area well, and he realised that he could set a trap.

"Breaker breaker, Green hawk two. Continue on the Bundoran road and take the turn off for Ballintrillick at Cliffony. We are taking this next right turn and will follow behind the snakes. Then whatever their intended route, we will have them in a sandwich; OVER!"

"Sure thing, green boss eagle; OVER!" said Maxie transmitting the reply, with sandwiches very much on his mind. Then turning to his best friend, he said with amazing powers of misdirection and a complete lack of intuition, "He seems pissed off with you."

Mickey initially questioned his friend's judgement, but having smoked most of the joint, paranoia got the better of him.

Neither of them considered their decision to stop at Grange village to buy snacks as a poor judgement. After all, Séamus's road to Ballintrillick was long, and Cliffony was only a mile or so up the road. There was plenty of time to kill, and seeing as the cafe was open, probably enough time for a cheeseburger and fries.

With due consideration that he was on active service, Maxie instructed that he wanted the order to take away. The pace of life in the village of Grange, however, was not very blistering, and the cook took far too much time heating up the chip pans and flipping the meat patties.

Mickey wasn't in the mood for fast or slow food. He just needed to satisfy his craving for sugar, and after visiting the sweet section of the nearby grocery shop, he sat back in the car and started tearing wrappers and getting his fix.

His private moment was broken by the sound of the CB radio crackling into life. "Breaker breaker, Green Hawk Two, are you receiving me? OVER!"

"Green Hawk receiving," spluttered Mickey in reply showering the dashboard with toffee crisp shrapnel.

"The snakes have stopped outside the post office in Ballintrillick. Have you reached the other exit at Cliffony yet?"

Mickey's paranoia was off the chart. Suddenly he felt very stoned and needed a quick reply to get Séamus off his case.

"Yes, we are there, green eagle."

"Well; be ready to block the road, and I will let you know if and when we flush them down your way."

Mickey agreed verbally, but mentally he had reservations that Maxie would allow his prized Volkswagen to be used as a road block. Regardless, he had already agreed to do this, but that was for the sake of covering up for Maxie who was presently moonlighting in a cafe in Grange.

As the wait for his friend grew longer, Mickey's paranoia grew greater. Then at its peak, as if by some force of synchronicity, the CB radio burst into life once again. "Breaker breaker, green hawk two, are you receiving; OVER!"

Mickey had a bad feeling as he gripped the radio handset. He pressed the transmit button and his lips pursed to speak, but no words would come out. All Séamus could hear on the other end was distorted static, and in his impatience, he broke protocol and interrupted.

"I cannot hear your transmission, there must be something wrong with your receiver, but if you can hear me, get ready to seal the road. The snakes are on route to you. Hold them until we block them from behind, and if they shoot at you; shoot back; OVER!"

Not only could he not speak, his heart was going like the clappers. He pushed down long and hard on the steering wheel until the long burst of the car horn drove Maxie out of the cafe. The big man ran over to his car and jumped in, but he did have a burger wrapped in tissues.

"What the hell, Mickey. I had to leave without my chips, and didn't even get my change,"

"Quick drive fast, Maxie. I told Séamus that we were forming a road block on the Ballintrillick road. The INLA are on their way. There is going to be a shootout."

"Not if we are not there, and why would you think I would use my car as a barricade. They might ram it."

"You were taking forever, Maxie. I was just trying to save your bacon, and besides, I was feeling a bit paranoid and couldn't speak to the man."

Maxie pulled out into the road and floored the accelerator. He knew this road and they were five to ten minutes away.

"How long ago did he call?"

"Maybe five minutes ago at least, but he called earlier to let me know what was going down."

Maxie looked quizzically at his friend, "Then we won't make it in time."

ANGUS CACTUS

Probably won't get there before Séamus does either. Why didn't you shout out to me when he first called?"

"I dunno; I thought you were nearly done in there."

"Feckin idiot forgot to turn on the chip pan; sorry about that. I guess we better get there and face the music, the snakes are probably long gone."

Mickey jumped up alert in his co-pilot seat. His head swivelled around unexpectedly like he was the possessed girl in the exorcist, and from an inhumanly looking contorted position, he yelled, "Turn around, Maxie. That's them, or at least it's the Provos that those snakes are chasing. If we follow them, the snakes will follow us."

"Can't be," said Maxie. "They were driving a red Datsun with a broken window."

"Well, it looks like some blond is driving them now in that silver Ford Escort."

"Are you sure?"

"I'm certain, Maxie. I spent yesterday following them around town. I would know them anywhere."

Maxie whooped, "You're the man, Mickey," as he cranked up the handbrake and spun the car in a full circle skid. Then without pause, he kicked it into first, and followed the silver Ford Escort for the next half mile and continued following it after it took a right turn onto a small country lane whose signpost said Ballyconnell, 5 miles.

In fact, they followed them all the way to the small peninsula at Raghly Point. They couldn't follow them down the single access lane, but drove on and parked up within sight. Here, they waited for quite a while, expecting the grey Land Rover to turn up, and Maxie used the opportunity to eat his cold burger.

"At least, we know where these guys are staying," said Mickey making a consolatory remark.

"Do you reckon, Feargal and Séamus might have sorted the others? Maybe we should contact him over the CB radio and find out."

"Good lord, don't do that Maxie. Our only saving grace is pretending that our radio is broken and that we never heard any of his instructions."

"I get it," said the big man cottoning on. "If we didn't know any better, then us following a car with the Provos in it was the logical choice to make."

"Exactly," said Mickey smiling back at his friend.

Then with intuitive understanding that was born out of friendship rather than weed, they both started stamping and kicking the CB radio unit until it made a fizzling noise and its lights went out.

22 Eileen's Pub (Saturday)

The weather had turned by the time she parked up at Raghly Point. It was only a localised squall coming in from the bay, and the late afternoon sunshine would probably return soon enough. Even so, the cottage looked cosy and inviting as seen through the fast moving wiper blades of her Ford Escort.

It was warm inside which was the product of the wood burning stove which had been lit earlier by the owner. Maeve filled up the kettle and placed it on the burner's hob. She looked around and almost sighed with contentment. She had her boys with her, and the mission was on. Their initial reaction had been one of surprise. They were probably expecting some run-down shack, and she imagined their reactions as she heard their footsteps investigating the other rooms. Maeve smiled again, this time like a Cheshire cat. She wanted them to appreciate how well these things could go, when and if they were planned right.

"What are you thinking?" Aden asked Kav as he joined him in one of the rooms.

"I am freaked out, Aden. There are only two bedrooms," Kav said looking worriedly at the double bed.

"She is a fine looking woman," pointed out Aden.

"That is what I am scared about. I am sure that those are the last words heard from the male tarantula before the lady tarantula bites off his head."

"You are divorced," reminded Aden.

"And that is for good reason. That woman scares me these days."

Aden smiled at his friend in acknowledgement, but in truth, he knew that his friend still loved his ex-partner. He liked Maeve too, but kept that to himself; more than that, he respected her. Nonetheless, he did appreciate that she could be utterly ruthless and a scary opponent. With that in mind, he decided to go join the dragon in her lair and have a cup of tea with her.

Other than the carrots, Maeve had also picked up some other groceries in that weird shop in Ballintrillick, enough to make a passable hot meal, and something to sustain them for the night. As they sat together at the table in the kitchen, they were treated to a wonderful panoramic view of the sun setting over Sligo Bay. It almost seemed romantic, except that there were three of them.

ANGUS CACTUS

Dessert was two pint-bottles of Guinness for the boys and another bottle of Harp for herself. That had come from that store too, but the bottle of Bushmills had been brought down from Belfast. This time, she had all the ice she needed, and the company of those she cared for and was willing to lay down her life to protect.

Even Kav had to admit that there was a warm atmosphere in the cottage, for which the wood burning stove was not wholly responsible. There were, however, two things on his mind. One being that double bed he was expected to share, and the other being that they had run out of Guinness. Whiskey wasn't really his thing, and he craved and needed at least another pint if he was to get through this evening intact.

"Do you know if there are any pubs around here?" he asked timidly.

"Always seeking the comfort of a pint and the company of strangers," said Maeve in a rebuking tone.

"I think there must be one somewhere near," said Aden trying to keep the peace. "Maybe a couple of pints will be a nice way to cap the evening off."

Maeve looked at Aden fully aware that he was trying to fix things. This was what she liked best about him, so she volunteered her agreement and went into the bathroom to put her blond wig back on.

They didn't have to drive too far, because, setting off in the direction of the local village of Ballyconnell, they soon came across Eileen's Bar. It was a single storey thatch cottage similar to the shop in Ballintrillick, but this time, the welcome signs and beer adverts outside advertised a proper pub. There were even a few cars parked out front in the courtyard.

Inside, it didn't look so promising. There were old wooden barrels which had been cut out and furnished as chairs which made the bench seating which skirted the walls look more inviting. The bar looked well stocked, though the mature barman behind it didn't at all explain away the woman's name on the pub's sign.

There was a decent crowd in the bar, and the atmosphere was fairly inviting, even though many of the locals gaped at the newcomers and in particular at the blond woman in their company. Maeve drew quite a bit of attention as if she was the latest model of tractor unveiled by Massey-Fergusson. She was the only woman there, and perhaps the only one many had ever seen. With her pleated skirt and fake blond wig, she might as well have been an alien descended amongst them. More than likely Eileen didn't exist, and if she did, she was likely a man who was a cross-dresser.

"Let's try and fit in and not try to stand out," said Kav.

Maeve wasn't sure whether he was taking the piss. Her husband's humour was something that she had never really understood.

Aden who probably had the biggest thirst in the room made his way forcefully to the bar and ordered two Guinness and a pint of lager. He was elated to see that they had pork scratching and Tayto crisps and took three sets of each as well. He was looking back and smiling at Maeve over his shoulder when he purposely decided not to order her a whiskey. She had had a few already, and he didn't trust her when she drank spirits. After all, she was a finely tuned republican killing machine and it was always best to keep these sedated with lower strength alcohol and happy company.

One of the locals who judging by his appearance was probably a local sheep farmer got brave and walked straight up to Maeve seeking a closer inspection. He was particularly short and no threat at all, and so Kav humoured his inappropriate behaviour as the man stood staring at Maeve's breasts. They weren't even large, nor particularly her best feature. However this poor fellow looked like sheep's udders were about as close as he had ever come to witnessing a pair.

Kav stepped forward; not menacingly, but just enough to gain the man's attention.

"Do you like her?" he said with suppressed mirth.

The man looked her up and down as if taking the proposition seriously.

"She's a bit skinny," he said, staring and mostly addressing her breasts in reply. "She could do with some fattening up," he added as if referring to his prize ewe.

"Don't mind him at all," said another man who began to push him out of Maeve's vicinity. This man in his forties was almost as small and unkempt, but the collection of glasses he held in his hands suggested that he worked for the bar.

"And who are you?" asked Maeve.

"I am Michael. I work for the management here," he stated proudly, turning around in surprise to answer Maeve's question.

"She's up there fella," said Kav pointing at her face, and redirecting the second local from staring at his ex-partner's breasts.

"Very Sorry, I was distracted," said Michael apologetically before he hurriedly scuttled away.

"You scared him off Michael and he was your namesake too," said Maeve laughing.

"Haven't you guys found a table yet?" said Aden rejoining them and carrying their drinks on a bar tray.

"Maeve has been busy feeding the wild animals," replied Kav to his friend. He then pointed out a nearby spot and led the way to a vacant table which the other Michael had just cleared. He let Aden sit down next to Maeve on the bench seating whilst he pulled over an improvised barrel for his own use.

A few of the other patrons who they had assumed to be regulars had produced some instruments and started to play. A bodhran drum, a button accordion, and a fiddle put down a lively rhythm and tune, and the evening turned even better. The musicians played at the other end of the room which allowed Aden and Kav to talk comfortably and without being overheard.

"So this is not just some imaginative fantasy of that Bective Hotel barman?" asked Maeve.

"No this appears to be a general rumour shared by many people in the town," said Kav.

"Yes, we spent today asking around and heard the same fighting monks and gold story repeated a few times," added Aden with enthusiasm.

"And were those stories repeated to you in pubs?" asked Maeve suspiciously eyeing up the empty glass in front of him. She added caustically, "Shall I get you a refill, Aden, and then perhaps you can tell me a story about a fighting monk."

"Yes please," replied Aden not even realising that she was making fun of him.

"No let me get the next one," said Kav, seeking to spare his ex-wife from having to fend off the randy shepherds.

Maeve understood and appreciated his motive. She had known for a while that Kav still held feelings for her. "Same again, but I want a whiskey as well this time," she said, causing Kav and Aden to exchange knowing looks with each other.

"What?" demanded Maeve.

"Nothing dear, a Bushmills is on its way," said Kav sheepishly.

Maeve looked satisfied at his reply but was still perplexed as to why both he and Aden had a problem with her drinking whiskey. She let it go though because she had more important fish to fry.

"So Aden, you are a clever and smart man, even if you do spend too much time in pubs."

"And your point is?"

"I need to know whether you are really on board here. What I mean is…" she reached out to grip both of his arms as if she wanted to badger the truth out of him. "Do you believe that this Vietnamese restaurant owner actually does possess a hidden stash of Gold and jewels."

Aden thought long and hard mulling over his reply. "Yes Maeve, I think I do, and I will tell you why." He paused either for effect or perhaps waiting for Maeve's permission to continue.

"Go on, please tell me," she said.

"It's like this. He was a refugee for sure, and by all accounts was as poor as a church mouse when he worked as a waiter in Dublin. All of a sudden, he has this new Mercedes and has bought a restaurant. Now, I can't ascertain the truth about him being a fighting monk unless I ask him, but he does teach Kung fu lessons at the sports centre which makes that part of the story sort of ring true."

"But have you actually researched any of this?" she asked suspiciously. "Did he really work as a waiter in Dublin, and has he actually bought that restaurant in Sligo?"

"Okay, no he hasn't. But he is leasing it from the owner and that requires a good financial standing. The Dublin part has all been corroborated. I phoned my cousin in Dublin and he even visited Li Han's former employer. They said that he was quite hard up when he worked for them."

"I am impressed Aden. You are not just a pretty face," said Maeve as she clasped his facial cheeks with both hands.

Aden grew uncomfortably nervous and wondered whether she might soon let her inner beast out. However instead of the beast, he was visited by a full-scale charm offensive.

"Does Kav ever talk about me?" asked Maeve in a quiet inquisitive tone.

"Sometimes."

"What does he say?"

"That's private between him and me," said Aden assertively preparing himself to repel her aggressive rebukes.

"I respect that, but he may tell you things that he hasn't told me."

Aden remained silent, crossing his arms as if he was a defiant child.

"Look, Aden, I just want to know why he hates being with me so much," said Maeve with apparent sadness, "And why he left me?"

"Because of all the killing, Maeve. He left because you kept killing; he couldn't stand it."

Maeve looked shocked and hurt, although not necessarily by Aden's words. She seemed more upset by the epiphany that they had released inside. With this realisation, came understanding; which she now digested in contemplative silence.

"I think I will go and take a piss," stated Aden, hoping that his voice or body language didn't betray his concern. Although he did need to use the bathroom, it was more his discomfort from being alone in her company which motivated him.

Meanwhile, Kav was getting his large order filled by the barman. He had doubled up on everything to make it fair on Aden, but he made sure to only buy the one short for Maeve.
"I'm sorry if Michael was bothering you and your... friend, earlier," said the barman fishing for information.
"That's okay, he was no bother at all; he said that he works for you. Is he the potman?"
"Not at all, I give him a few free drinks if he collects some glasses for me," replied the proprietor smiling, "Now, there you go; enjoy!" he said as he placed the last of the Guinness on the tray.
Kav thanked him and returned to where Maeve was sitting. Aden had gone away somewhere, and the Ceili band were taking a break. Kav looked across at Maeve as he crossed the room, fearing the worst; that she was going to want to hold a conversation with him. The prospect filled him with dread; communication had never been their thing.
It was Maeve who broke the uncomfortable silence that followed after he sat down beside her.
"I have talked to Aden and I am feeling much more convinced by the merits of your plan," she said referring to the prospective kidnapping.
"Nice to know that his opinion holds more value than mine."
"Look at it more as if he has seconded your proposal and endorsed your plan. And besides that, he also told me something about you."
"What?"
"He told me why you left, and why you do not want to live with me now."
"He did, did he?" said Kav with visible anger encroaching on his face.
"Aden says it's the killing," she quickly blurted out before he had become too distracted by his perception of his friend's betrayal.
Kav's habitual response would have been to stay silent on the matter. Regardless, the cat was out of the bag now, and from her tone, she seemed more than willing to listen. He decided to confess the truth.
"He is right Maeve; I could smell death on you when you used to come home after a hit."
"Well; you have killed people too." It wasn't really a challenge, more like an observation.
"A couple; well maybe a few, but that was different. I had to, but you ... You revel in it. You enjoy killing and that makes me feel..."
"Go on," she said seeking a fuller explanation.
"Well not like the man in the relationship."

"So this is about the fragility of your male ego?"
"No, it's about being scared of my own wife."
Strained silence pervaded. They briefly looked each other in the eye, like two stags with horns locked upon each other, but a weakness was showing in the window to Maeve's soul.
"I can stop killing," she said meekly and almost apologetically.
"It's not in your nature."
"It might be; it could be. I could do that for someone if they cared for me."
"Do you care for me, Maeve?"
"Yes, and I know that you care for me too."
More silence ensued, but this time, it was contemplative rather than strained.
"I don't have to kill, I can wound them instead. Would that bother you?"
"No Maeve."
It would be a start, like a small bridge cast across the deep chasm that had developed between them; but the ghosts of their marriage would require a more thorough exorcism. Nonetheless, it was food for thought and was served up with equal portions of contemplative silence.

The toilets were in an outhouse out back. Aden could only see the Irish sign for the men's toilet, and wondered what facility the eponymous Eileen had to use.
The inside of the latrine was a sight for sore eyes. How it had been passed as acceptable by the licensing commission was a complete mystery. There were no wall standing urinals at all; instead just a small gully in the concrete floor which ran the length of the shed. The one basin to wash your hands in had fallen away from the wall and had bent the pipes under its own weight until it leaned forward at an angle exceeding 45 degrees. There was no light to see where to pee, apart from the bright one outside which illuminated the Irish word 'Fir'.
He had to acclimatize his eyes to the dark in order to accurately target the gully. There was another man already finishing up his business and zipping up, and Aden acknowledged him, realising that it was the potman Michael.
Michael seemed taken aback by Aden's greeting, and made of show of washing his hands in order to impress the visiting Belfast man. This action required him to have to kneel down in the urine soaked gully in order to reach the taps, and the running water just flowed out of the fallen sink and ran down his trousers. They looked soiled and soaked by the time he had

ANGUS CACTUS

finished washing his hands, and Aden watched the pot-man walk away with a self-satisfied look on his face. Aden, in turn, had a look of concern on his. He was worried for the man's sanity.

He took a look at his own hands and decided that they didn't require cleaning. He just zipped up and returned to join Kav and Maeve inside.

He saw them sitting in silence and grew concerned that Kav might have said something stupid. He probably had, but the mood lightened as soon as he joined them at the table.

"Kav thinks that we should proceed with the kidnapping tomorrow," announced Maeve.

"I didn't say that," he protested. "I said that maybe we should pay the Hans another visit tomorrow so as to develop a plan about when and how we kidnap the mother."

"That sounds fine by me," said Aden in his usual peacemaking role.

"I can't come with you tomorrow, I need to stay by the phone at the cottage; Belfast command is going to phone me," said Maeve disappointed to be left out of the planning. "So yous two better not feck this up."

"We will be the model of professionalism," said Kav reassuringly.

"That is what worries me," said Maeve with a wry smile and looking less than reassured.

23 Sligo Sunday

By mid-day, Sligo Town was being buffeted by strong winds and intermittent rain showers, and even though the people of Sligo were used to this kind of weather in May, it still had the effect of chasing people off the streets.

The Sunday opening hours were also limited and restrictive for pubs and restaurants, and most of the shops remained shut for the Lord's Day. All the same, the town felt liberated as far as Aden and Kav were concerned. In Belfast, the ruling Presbyterians had made sure that you couldn't even buy a bottle of air to breathe on a Sunday.

So Aden, in particular, was looking forward to an afternoon pint later on. Before that, lunch was on the menu and it was to be served up in the Happy Huong restaurant. That meant more Asian food accompanied by a soft drink, even though he had his heart set on the roast beef dinner and a pint of Guinness which was on offer in the Bective.

"We are on a mission, for god's sake. You don't find our enemy in the SAS feasting out on roast beef and Guinness. Those boys sit in wet ditches and eat worms together."

"I am not feckin' eating a worm with you."

"I am just saying, let's case the friggin' joint first before we eat it."

"I get that; a joint of beef, very clever Kav, but you said we were eating in here," said Aden casting a cold eye over the Happy Huong's menu in the window.

"I was talking figuratively,"

"So are we, or are we not, eating in here?"

"For the love of mercy! of course, we are. I was talking figuratively about the SAS, and our duty coming before pleasure."

"But we could just have starters here, and then head back to the Bective for the full slap up meal," said Aden offering a compromise which he felt ticked all the boxes.

Kav decided that Aden's question didn't warrant an answer, but instead opened the door wide and said, "Come on, they are closing soon."

Taking up his preferred seat at the table closest to the door, his friend Aden sheepishly followed him in, picked up the table menu and sat down to study it.

A tall thin waitress with ginger hair and a ginger complexion walked straight over to see if they were ready to order. Aden looked disappointed that his favourite girl wasn't on duty to serve them. Nonetheless, he had a question for her replacement, who introduced herself as Geraldine.

"Does the crispy chilli beef come with roast potatoes, peas and gravy?"

"No Sir, it comes with stir-fried asparagus, sliced carrot, and mange tout in an oyster sauce."

"Is that like gravy?"

"Not really sir. Would you like to try it?"

"Okay, and give me a club orange to drink as well, please."

"And you sir?" said the waitress directly to Kav.

"I hadn't decided yet, but that sounds quite nice. Can you double up on that order," said Kav trying to be accommodating. "Oh and excuse me miss, is it Mrs Han doing the cooking."

"Yes Sir, Huong Han always does the cooking. She is really exceptionally good."

"Oh I know, we have eaten here before."

"Yes," said Aden interrupting. "We were served by a girl called sweet ti… actually, I forgot her name." Aden had blushed with embarrassment at his near slip-up. The waitress had worked out what he intended to say and was smiling with amusement.

"That was Enya, but your name fits her well. She doesn't work here on Sundays. She is probably at home."

Geraldine was still smiling as she left them to go and place the order. As far as she was concerned, Enya had been christened with a new nickname.

Every time the fire door to the kitchen opened, Kav seized the opportunity to study the room. There were glimpses of Huong cooking in the kitchen, but he was hoping to see whether there was a back door exit, and he wanted to check who else worked with her in the kitchen. One thing he knew for sure was that Li Han was not working today, and this was the kind of circumstance he would require for an easier kidnapping.

As he engaged his meal with enthusiasm, he wondered what other days Li might be absent. The answer to this was supplied by the waitress who in answer to his query about Li Han's absence, pointed to a small poster about Kung fu on the wall.

"Mr. Han doesn't work on Sundays," she said, "Or on Wednesday evenings, because that is when he trains his martial arts students at the sports complex."

Geraldine looked pleased at Kav's look of satisfaction, but she also appeared keen to clear away and close up for the day, Aden and Kav being the only remaining customers.

"If there isn't anything else, I can get your bill for you," she offered.

Kav nodded back at her but then noticed Aden was nodding his head exaggeratedly gesturing towards Huong who had just walked into the dining area. She was wearing a coat and a hat and she spoke quietly to Geraldine who then proceeded to make a call on the wall mounted phone for a taxicab to take her to some shop.

Both men studied her intently and then looked to each other.

"Are you thinking what I am thinking?" asked Kav.

"Yes, I thought the shops were closed."

"No, not that! I was thinking we should do it now. You could go and nick a car quickly and pretend to be the taxi," said Kav who wanted to seize the opportunity.

"There is no time to steal one, but Maeve's car is parked just around the corner."

"We can't use that to abduct the woman. Maeve would kill us," but Kav really meant 'himself'.

"Why not, it's a perfect opportunity. Maeve doesn't have to know, and I can steal another car later," said Aden. "But one of us should stay in town and contact Li Han and issue our ransom demand before he has a chance to get the police involved."

"I can do that," volunteered Kav.

"I can leave Maeve's car somewhere for you to collect. I still have the phone number of the Bective hotel. You should go there and wait for my call, and I'll tell you where I have left it."

Kav was nodding in muted acceptance as Aden quickly exited the restaurant leaving Kav to settle the bill. He remained behind until Aden pulled up outside, but before exiting, his light fingers snatched Mrs. Han's hat from the counter where she had placed it. It would come in useful as proof of kidnapping, and to help initiate this, he casually remarked, as he departed, that there was a taxi waiting outside.

Upon recognising the word taxi, Huong stood up and grabbing hold of her umbrella walked out the door and climbed in the open door of the ford escort which had mounted the pavement outside her shop.

Kav crossed the road and surreptitiously watched while standing beside the statue of Lady Erin, who appeared to be waving them goodbye. All he could think of right now was lots of buried gold.

The rain had stopped and the Sun had come out for Michael Kavanagh as he made his slow triumphant walk around town. He took it as a metaphor that signified a new chapter in his paramilitary career. Of course, he would take a percentage of the ransom and use it as seed money. This kidnapping would be the first of many successful enterprises that his unit would execute, and which he would mastermind. His prowess would become known and recognised by all the leaders in Belfast Command. He would be respected as an 'earner' with all the kudos that comes with that. He would be known by some cool alias or code name, and he would hand pick his team which would operate in Dublin or London. There he would become a living republican legend.

It was a sound plan even though it had begun with a few hiccoughs. Using Maeve's own car was one of them, and abducting Huong Han on the spur of the moment was the other. Regardless of that, he had taken the initiative and seized the opportunity that presented itself. No doubt a celebratory pint of Guinness was in order, and as he turned the corner at Castle Street, he could see the Bective straight ahead. If he hurried he would make it in time to order a couple before the licensing hours would close the bars until the evening.

The lingering aroma from the busy Sunday lunchtime trade filled his nostrils as he walked in the entrance. Maybe Aden was right; perhaps they should have eaten a roast beef dinner here. Anyhow, the restaurant was on the verge of closing now, and so was the main bar too.

The small snug bar was open, and so this was where Kav pointed his compass. He stopped only briefly to talk with the Lady proprietor who sat at her front desk adding up long columns of figures.

"Bookkeeping?" he enquired.

"Double entry. I was trained before the war, and I still like to do my own accounts."

"You'll never get ripped off that way," agreed Kav. "Excuse me Margaret; I am waiting for an important call on this pay phone of yours. Can I wait for it in your snug bar?"

"Of course, Mr. Kavanagh; I will listen out for it. You will meet my husband Paddy serving in the small bar. Don't mind him, he's in a bad mood. We are a barman short today, and he drew the short straw."

Kav heeded Margaret's warning and made sure to be disarmingly friendly to her husband who sat behind the counter in a nearly empty bar, doing the Times crossword. He was an imposing figure, though this seemed more to do with his air of grumpiness and irritation than with his size. Dark hair combed across with greasy wax, a roman nose, and a full grey beard made him resemble the singer from the 'Dubliners'.

Paddy was a man of gravitas, and yet he also resembled a caricature of a bushy-bearded republican prisoner of war. He had the Buddha belly which so often signified satisfaction, yet this man was obviously far from being content with his current predicament. He displayed a complete lack of enthusiasm in getting up off his stool to come over and serve Kav; and in his mind, he may well have been dragging the stone of Sisyphus up that hill.

"Hello Sir, Lovely day for it, the weather I mean," said Kav intending his comment as an icebreaker.

"So lovely, you felt the need to come inside," Paddy replied with irony.

"No, I was just walking around town and appreciating the blue skies," offered Kav in manner of explanation for his current good humour. "I mean it was raining earlier on, and the weather in Sligo seems so unpredictable. I am not from around these parts."

"Belfast man?" enquired Paddy.

"Born and bred."

"So do you want a drink?" the barman asked with an air of impatience.

"Yes, a Guinness, please. In fact, can I have two?" said Kav who was planning to sink a few while he still could.

"I am not closing," came a perceptive but gruff reply from a man who was so obviously out of his depth running a public bar.

"Just the one then," said Kav smiling like a Cheshire cat. "You don't sound like a Sligo man either, sir."

"I couldn't think of a worse fate."

"Why; do you not like living in Sligo?"

"I love Sligo; the only problem with it, is that it is full of Sligomen," said Paddy who paused before proudly stating, "I am from Kells, County Meath."

"So, did you name this hotel after the Bective abbey in Meath."

"That is perceptive of you. Have you been there?" asked Paddy.

"Yes I passed by it last summer, but it was raining that day; bucketing down, a bit like the other night. No, my preference is definitely for a bit of sunshine," stated Kav, still equating today's lovely sunshine with his potential bright future.

A few minutes later, another customer entered the bar, sidling up to the counter tentatively, looking for a drink outside of licensing hours. With a thick Sligo accent, he asked "Ah howayeh Mister Gee? Nice to see you behind the bar, and looking so well."

Seemingly Paddy wasn't in the mood for greetings or small talk, but he did look up from his crossword to see if the man had any intention of getting to the point.

ANGUS CACTUS

"Tis a mighty fine day outside," said the man still nervous about asking for an illicit pint. "I believe we are in for a fine spell. Do you think we might, Mister Gee?"

The bearded proprietor erupted; he had had enough.

"Look if you want to talk about the bloody weather, talk to him," he said pointing at Kav, "He's a fookin expert."

The couple sitting at the small round table began to snigger, and the man winked at Kav who smiled back in return. That was all the introduction needed, and the man got up from his table to come and sit next to Kav.

"I'm Jimmy," he said offering his hand in friendship. "That is my father in law, Paddy," said Jimmy gesturing at the barman who had returned to his crossword. Then, in an inclusive manner, seeing the man's look of disappointment, he shouted over at the other customer.

"Don't be poking the bear, Reggie. Just ask him like normal for a pint. Paddy doesn't do small talk."

Jimmy's wife had come over and joined them. She offered an outstretched hand as a welcome. "Bernadette; pleased to meet you," she said. "Kav," he replied taking her hand.

"So, you are from Belfast," said Bernadette. "My brother spends a lot of his time up there."

"Yes, I know. I met him."

"In Belfast?" she enquired surprised.

"No, not there," he lied, "I was talking to him here last Friday. He seems a nice kid. A bit crazy though."

"That's Shane alright," said Jimmy. "A complete head-the-ball," he said, parodying the symptoms of concussion.

Is he around?" enquired Kav.

"No, he is out of town. He pissed off a few people like the local Guards and he has skedaddled and run away until it all blows over."

"I'm sorry to hear that. I hope things work out for him."

"Ah don't mind him. He always comes up smelling of roses," said Bernadette.

"Or dope," added Jimmy sarcastically. "He smells more of dope than roses if you catch my drift."

The door into the snug opened slightly and Margaret the proprietor popped her head inside.

"Michael, your friend Aden is on the phone for you."

She then turned towards her husband, who was looking perplexed as if 6 across was incorrect, and announced, "Paddy; Look after these three officers whilst I find a room for them."

Everyone looked up at the mention of the word 'officers', and one of the three burly men who now walked into the snug bar could be seen grimacing at the job title which he would have preferred to have remained secret.

It wouldn't have remained secret from Kav. There was no mistaking the ill-fitting extra large suits which poorly disguised the underarm gun holsters. The standard issue black shoes with Dr. Martin soles were another clue, but it was really their smug and imperious attitude which labelled them as Dublin Special Branch detectives. This fact was confirmed by Bernadette who whispered conspiratorially to Kav.

"They are detectives that have come up from Dublin because of that Guard that was kidnapped the other day. They are doubling up in the rooms to save expenses. One set sleeps whilst the others are on duty."

Kav supplied Bernadette with a knowing nod though in truth he was very much in the dark. He didn't have the faintest idea what was going down here, but he knew that whatever it was, Maeve was going to blame him for it.

He emptied the remnants of his pint glass and said his goodbyes to his hosts. "Lovely to meet you but I better get to the phone."

One of the special branch officers stared intently at him as he passed, and the Provo looked back in muted challenge. Then against his better nature, Kav decided to speak to him.

"Paddy the barman has stopped serving, but you boys might get lucky if you mention the weather. He's an amateur meteorologist."

The cop nodded in reply, not sure what to make of his advice, and Kav could see a beaming smile breaking out on Bernadette's face, and her husband Jimmy, crippled and bent double with suppressed laughter.

24 Amelia   (Sunday)

Enya's phone call to Bernadette had confirmed that Shane had gone missing. Bernadette didn't seem worried because her brother was prone to disappear whenever he got into hot water, and right now, as Enya was well aware, the shit had well and truly hit the fan in his world. Shane's mother wasn't speaking to him and he had one Guard accusing him of peddling drugs and another asking for valid tax and insurance certificates for his motorbike as well as his old car.

Enya knew that he possessed none of the above, and even though Bernadette suggested that she might try contacting him in Belfast, she had a pretty good idea where he might have gone. Shane would always camp out in the same spots. They were his bolt holes, and also his place to sit and think. Although lord knows, he did far too much of that.

It was turning into another glorious day despite the rain showers earlier on, and it would make for a lovely Sunday walk around the Gleniff Horseshoe Pass. Enya took her Collie dog along for the walk and for company, in case she was mistaken about Shane's whereabouts.

The walk would take her through Ballintrillick, which wasn't really a village, but just a designation for a few local houses and a post office. It was her dog, Molly, who particularly wanted to shop there. She liked her mistress buying her ice lollies, and Enya wanted to pick up a few treats as well to share with Shane if she found him.

She knew the couple that ran the post office, who would often take turns to man their bespoke set of counters. Today it was Moira's turn. Enya was about to busy herself choosing items from their single refrigerated unit but let another young woman, who had just come in through an entrance in the adjoining bar, go before her.

She was tall, slim and very elegant, and wearing a long plain white dress which looked hand woven. She was definitely not a local, though there were no guest houses nearby. Across her arm she carried an old-fashioned wicker basket into which she placed a few choice items.

The young woman was quite pretty and this had invoked a reaction from one of the bar customers who had a mean face and a coarse Londonderry accent. When she had entered through the bar, he had called out 'hello', and asked her if she wanted a drink, and she had replied curtly by telling him to shut up.

The man took exception to this, and so as she walked past him on her way out, he called out, "Lesbian." However, this did not seem to bother her, and she simply replied, "Get lost creep."

Enya admired her assertiveness, and was more than intrigued to find out who she was; therefore, she quickly paid for her items and taking Molly with her, left through the same exit.

The girl wasn't far ahead and so she hurried after her calling out as she went.

"Hi, Excuse me, may I walk with you?"

The girl stopped in her tracks and seemed surprised to have found a friendly local.

"I am Enya, and this is Molly," she said as they joined the girl and fell into step beside her as they both proceeded onwards.

"My name is Amelia," she said supplying a warm smile for Enya. "You are the first friendly face I have met around here."

"I have not seen you around before. I think you have great style and you're very pretty," said Enya who was a firm believer in giving credit where it was due.

"Thank you for the compliment Enya. We have just moved in up the road, and I find myself missing certain items in the move. We normally produce our own food and make our own things."

The penny dropped following the second plural reference.

"Are you one of the Screamers?"

"That is not a name that we use, but I have heard people use it before in reference to us."

"What name do you use then?"

"We are the Sisterhood of Sardonis."

"I wonder why they call you Screamers."

"I think the local perverts listened to us screaming in our Donegal commune."

"What do you guys scream for?"

"We often scream during religious ceremonies; to invoke the earth goddess and also for other things."

"Such as?"

"Well, usually we scream during sex."

"I thought you guys were lesbians."

"Some of us are and many are bisexual."

"I've heard that you mistreat your men. Do you not like them?"

"I prefer women, but men make good pets if you know how to train them."

"Can you really train men?" asked Enya with some doubt in mind.

"They're easier than some dogs. It is natural for them to be obedient, but they just don't like rules."

"So how do you do it?"

"We make them learn our rules until they know them by heart. I simply enforce them, but they usually police themselves. I reward good behaviour and punish bad. So long as you remain both strict and assertive, you will never have a problem."

"I hope you don't take offence Amelia, but it sounds a little cruel and a bit strange."

"I appreciate that our ways are different and seem bizarre to others, but there are benefits involved."

"Such as?"

"We have servants who work hard to please us in any way that we desire."

"But how do they feel about it?"

"I can't say I really care. They get basic provisions and they seem content enough, and none have left us yet."

"Well, I am happy enough with my boyfriend. Sure he has got his faults, but hopefully, I can change that."

"Good luck with that."

"Are you saying that I can't change him?"

"Probably not, but with my help you could."

"Well thanks for the offer Amelia, but I think I can manage by myself. I do enjoy talking to you though."

They had reached a small forestry path which led off from the road that they were now walking along. The path was wide enough for single vehicle access, but a locked chain between posts prevented that option. It didn't appear to lead anywhere except deeper into the forest.

"Our commune is down here. Do you want to come and visit?" asked Amelia in a very welcoming way.

"Maybe, but not today, I am looking for Shane right now, but I hope to see you again sometime."

25 Doorly Park (Sunday)

Kennedy Parade was across from the Bective on the other side of the river. Jimmy had set Kav straight as to where to find Sligo's leisure centre. Apparently it was two miles further along this bank of the river and was the other side of Doorly Park. He had decided to walk there and take advantage of all the positive ions from the fast breaking waters of the river Garavogue.

It certainly was a nice walk in the sunshine, and he was enjoying watching two pairs of swans defending their territories which seemed to conflict or overlap. As they launched into shallow flight, they appeared to be running across the water when they attacked each other. It was amazing to watch such graceful creatures acting so aggressively when resorting to violence. It made him think of Maeve. These pairings mated for life; maybe the male swans were frightened of leaving their females.

The news from Aden was fairly positive. Although he hadn't yet found the opportunity to switch cars, he said that he was in Ballintrillick and had just stopped for some provisions before he boosted another car in Grange. He still had the old lady captive in the Maeve's Ford Escort and said that she was no bother at all. In fact, she still thought he was the taxi driver.

Kav was a little disappointed that Aden hadn't switched cars on the other side of town. Now he was going to have to steal one himself. He had been looking forward to walking through Doorly Park, after having been informed that it was a visual treat and the muse for the famous song 'Sally Gardens'. That was a song he had sung as a kid and yet had never realised that it was based on a poem by Yeats, or that those gardens were here in Sligo.

However, time was running away with itself. It was nearly three o'clock, and Li Han's class would be over soon. He was going to have to leave Doorly Park for another day, which was a pity because he had enjoyed watching the swans and this riverside walk. In fact, he had enjoyed today; the lunch, the drink in the Bective, and the kidnapping had all gone swimmingly well. Even the two swans he had been rooting for had won their territorial dispute, and they were now on the bank beside him grooming themselves and basking in the sun. That was Maeve and him, the eventual winners after completing all the hurdles in the human race.

ANGUS CACTUS

Pressing time constraints helped Kav concentrate on the job in hand and he looked around for a decent vehicle to pinch. The best prospect was a maroon Range Rover. Its main credentials, other than its pleasing colour, were the fact that it was parked on the kerb right in front of him and it also had some gardening tools in the back. Kav reckoned the spade would come in handy for digging up buried treasure.

Sure it had a few failings in that the owner appeared to be a messy man. There were magazines all over the floor, and it had a general untidy appearance. Regardless, he took out a new car-thief's pouch which Aden had given him only yesterday, more as a dig at his ineptitude in this department, than as a present. Kav opened it up and inspected its contents.

He took out the slender but sturdy jemmy and forced it between the door and the frame. There was a small inflatable pouch to push between them which had an attached hand operated pump, but Kav found it too fiddly and opted instead to use brute strength to bend the weakest part of the door open enough for him to reach in and pull the door lock with a length of strong but very flexible wire. It was like solder but stronger and formed a perfect hook to wrap around the lock lever. Wasn't technology wonderful he thought as he felt the grip and began to gently pull upwards.

"AVAARRVAARRKK!" screamed one of the swans behind him as it stood as tall as it could, spreading its wings to make it appear as large and threatening as possible. Kav caught sight of this in his peripheral vision and thought the loud shriek was a siren going off behind him. He was so shocked that he dropped the wire inside the car, and the jemmy fell to the road bounced once and dropped into a storm drain leading into the river. He was so pissed off that he threw the rubber inflatable at the offending swan and shouted at it.

"Ugly Goose; have that for your piles." His remarks were directed at the pen. The cob swan remained quiet but seemed to look at him with understanding.

"I know son," he told it. "And you've got a damn life sentence ahead of you."

As for the car, Kav selected the largest stone he could find and used it to bash in the driver's side window. He then got in, bypassed the ignition, started the engine and drove off.

The leisure centre was only a short distance away, so he was careful to hide the car behind a bigger truck just in case some friend or neighbour of its rightful owner should recognise it. Then he went into the building.

TO HELL OR SLIGO

There was no viewing chamber as such, so he just purchased a ticket for the sauna, but then went and stood at the other end of the main gymnasium instead. From there, he watched Li Han walking amongst the ranks and rows of his students, often correcting poor stances with a sweeping leg movement of his own that usually put the student on the floor.

Kav who had christened every knuckle of his hands in fist fights during his youth had to admire the fighting prowess of the man. His movements were fluid and graceful, but Kav was most wary of his speed. That twinge of fear made him reach inside his heavy jacket to feel the stock of his Walther pistol. The touch of the cold gun metal was reassuring for him. Aden was right. The man was good; in fact, he was very good, but he still couldn't dodge bullets. Besides, experience had taught him that it was all about feeling in control. He had the man's mother, and this put him very much in control.

It was obvious the class was ending because the students were bowing in respect and thanksgiving for their instruction. These martial arts instructors always seemed to have power complexes. All this bowing, standing in line, and answering in unison wouldn't go down well in the 'Ra'. Despite the punishment beatings and the kneecappings, the Provisionals were probably a little more footloose and carefree.

He waited and watched now, alert for any opportunity that presented itself to speak with the man in private. He wouldn't achieve that in a changing room full of his students, but he was presented with the perfect opportunity when Li Han visited the men's room.

Kav sidled up alongside him at the urinal. He didn't really need to go but this was always a good place to make introductions. Rule one, to put people at unease, was always to invade their personal space. However, in this case, it also provided him the opportunity to satisfy his curiosity about cultural anatomical diversity.

It must have worked because Li Han looked very disturbed and Kav capitalised on this by raising the subject of his mother.

"I met your mother today; nice lady. She is with my friend presently but—"

"Who is with my mother," said Li looking very alarmed. "Where is she and who are you?"

"Don't worry, he intends to look after her like the gentlemen he is. However, if he doesn't hear from me, or have his demands met by you, or if he should hear from the police he has the potential to turn really nasty. However, I am pretty certain a gentlemen like you will be quite willing to exchange a little information for the safe return of his beloved mother."

"This better not be some joke," said Li Han.
"It is no joke, Mr. Han.
"Prove it."
"Here, look, I took this from her earlier," said Kav producing her crushed hat from inside his jacket.
"You cock sucker, you better not upset or hurt her."
"Please don't use that language Mr. Han, at least until after you have zipped up your flies."
"Who are you anyway? Why are you doing this to me?"
"You don't need to know my name, but I am a soldier of the Provisional Irish Republican Army. It's nothing personal."
"You could have just stolen that hat and be trying to con me. How do I know she is not at the restaurant right now? I want to speak to her; I want to know she is okay."
"Well then phone the restaurant. Speak to Geraldine. I think that was the waitress's name. Ask her. There is a pay-phone at reception, but don't try any funny business, because..." He shows Li the gun concealed beneath his jacket that is draped over his right arm.

Geraldine confirmed Li Han's fears. She explained that under normal circumstances she would have already gone home; she had only stayed on because Huong Han was missing, and she wasn't able to lock up. She told Li that a booked taxi had arrived to take her to the cash and carry, but Mrs Han was now nowhere to be found.
Li looked worried when he came off the phone, and Kav led him out of the building to prevent anyone else from intervening.
"Come on let's walk to the car and drive somewhere more private."
Li Han walked alongside him like a zombie with no will of his own, yet this did not portray the intense consternation in his mind as he tried to figure out what he should do.
"Okay I believe you; what do you want; money?"
"Gold!"
"What do you mean, gold? I don't have any gold."
"Really? Are you going to play that game, Li? It is not going to work out well for you or your mother if you do."
"I am serious. What gold do you think I have? I am not a wealthy man."
"Don't take me for a fool, Li. I know all about the shed load of gold you buried when you arrived in Sligo. Now this is how we are going to do it. You are going to stay with me tonight, whilst your mother stays with that friend of mine. You can call her and speak with her later, but you

can't see her until you have shown me where you buried your gold. Once I have it loaded into my car, I will drive you to meet your mother and she will be unharmed, as will you if you don't play any shenanigans on me. But if you do, my friend will kill your mother."

Just when Kav was beginning to put all the pieces back in the correct order, Li went and upped the ante.

"Why don't I just take you to the gold now?" He said appearing genuinely compliant. "When you see it, you can release my mother first and then me. I will even help you load it into your car if that gets me my mother, back safe and unharmed.

"So you are saying that you do have it," said Kav seeking confirmation.

"Yes, we go now and I give you it, but I must get my mother back today. She doesn't speak English; she will probably be confused and afraid."

"Well I must say; I am a little surprised by your rapid change of heart, but then if that is how you feel, I am certainly game. Where is the gold?

"It's buried in Streedagh."

"Where's that?"

"Its about twenty miles north of Sligo, near Mullaghmore. Do you know Mullaghmore?"

"Oh yes, I know Mullaghmore; there is not a republican alive who doesn't. Come on, get in. Let's go."

26 Taxi for Huong (Sunday)

There are two types of characters in the world. Those that immerse themselves in a complexity of social veneers, and those that are more forthright and straightforward. Aden classed himself as the second kind, but he wasn't sure whether Huong was also or whether she belonged to a third type made up of people who only inhabited one of these groups through necessity. He wondered whether the ravages of a hard life and encroaching age had stripped away her previous social persona and left behind a simpler person.

He was watching her in the rearview mirror, but he couldn't quite figure her out; she was almost complex in her simplicity. For a start, he didn't even know whether she had yet realised that she had been kidnapped. As far as she was concerned, Maeve's car was her taxi, and he was her driver.

She could be just playing along with him; trying to lull him into a false sense of security. Then again, it was a possible that she really was oblivious to what was going on. After all, he didn't know her medical history; she could be half doolally for all he knew. The last thing that she had said to him was, "You take me to shops now," and that was over 20 minutes ago. Since then, Aden had driven her out the town on route for Raghly Point. She stared outside of her window watching the majestic Benbulben get closer, surrounded by a backdrop of lush green beauty. Aden wondered what kind of shop she was expecting to visit.

There was also another possibility; perhaps she already knew that she had been kidnapped, and was now applying some advanced Kung fu practice of mental withdrawal from a potentially threatening situation. He may have to keep a close eye on her because it was possible that she could flip at any moment and go all "hong-kong-fuey" on him. In fact, the more he watched her in his rear view mirror, the more he became convinced of her fighting prowess.

She was only about 5'5", petite and almost demure, but he reckoned that she might be able to snap bones with a single kick or punch. He wondered how Kav was fairing with her son. His friend hadn't even seen 'Enter the Dragon' yet, so he was going to be in the dark concerning the Kung fu aspect.

Aden felt an adrenalin rush and he realised that he was spooking himself and should probably stop and tie her up. However, perhaps it might be expedient to try and talk to her first, and maybe suss out if she was actually doolally, or a Kung fu master that was capable of fighting her way out of the Cambodian jungles. He realised that she could only speak English with some difficulty, but perhaps a few simple questions might serve the purpose.

"Hello, Huong."

She turned to him at the mention of her name. He had her attention at least. Aden spoke slowly making sure to enunciate his words.

"How long before your son gets back?"

"Maybe more than thirty years," she replied, convincing Aden that she probably was a few loaves short of a dozen.

"He started very young, now he is best."

An expression of confusion developed on Aden's face, but he soon realised that she was probably answering some other question. Li Han was only about 40, so maybe she was referring to cooking or maybe even Kung fu. He could have started learning either or both when he was ten. He may as well ask her the one question to which he really needed to know the answer.

"Do you know Kung fu?"

"Kung fu move rocks, yet flow between like water. It is Tai Chi."

This was some kind of oblique David Carradine answer akin to walking on rice paper without leaving a trace; a lesson in life to be sure, but definitely not an explanation. He was going to have to rephrase the question.

"So can you Tai Chi Kung fu?"

"I live Tai Chi, every day even I cook or shop. I Tai Chi Kung fu." She made a slow but sweeping gesture with flowing hand movements as if to emphasise her point.

Aden was none the wiser, but he thought it worth trying one more question.

"Where did you bury the gold?"

"By mountain and by sand. We go this way. I want shop now."

The confusion etched ever deeper lines on his brow. What he needed now was some clarity and a pint. He looked at the dashboard light indicating a nearly empty tank and thought about the one shop he knew where you could get all three.

"We are off to Ballintrillick, Missus Han. There is a shop there."

"Good, I need duck."

Definitely doolally, thought Aden.

It wasn't far to Ballintrillick, and Huong sat patiently and quiet for the rest of the trip. She seemed to like the mountains because she craned her head to study Benwiskin as they passed it.

When he reached the thatched post office, he pulled up beside the petrol pump.

"Is this shop?" asked Huong who was staring at the old advertisements and posters in the courtyard.

"No, this is MY shop. YOUR shop is next. STAY HERE, DO NOT GET OUT!" said Aden mimicking her stuttered style of speaking as if this made his English easier to understand.

Huong looked disappointed, but her demeanour indicated someone who was brought up to be obedient to rules and commands. For this reason, he decided not to bother tying her up. Besides, if she got out, she wouldn't get far, and he would soon find her.

Regardless, he kept his eye on her as he put a tenners worth of petrol in the car. Then before paying he made a couple of calls from the pay phone located outside in the courtyard.

The old call box must have been one of the originals. It was made in the British style of red phone box but painted green. Someone had positioned it incorrectly because the door, which was half off its hinge anyway, opened into the pillar post box beside it, allowing only the thinnest to get inside.

Aden called Kav at the Bective and used up half his change waiting for the big heifer to come to the phone. The next call was important and required some thought about what he was going to say. It was a difficult call, to say the least. Kav had chickened out of phoning her, so it was left up to him to explain how they had jumped ahead with the schedule for kidnapping Huong Han. Aden explained how the opportunity had arisen and pointed out how the simplicity and ease of taking it had made it the obvious thing to do.

Maeve was uncharacteristically easygoing about the change of plan. She only seemed interested in who had her car, and so Aden point blank lied and said that Kav was driving it and that they had split up. He told Maeve that he had stolen a car in Sligo but had not yet left town. This would buy him a little bit of time to steal another car somewhere else like Grange or Cliffony.

All in all, by the time he had used up the last of his change and ended the call, he felt that it had gone rather well. Now all he had to do was pop inside, buy a few groceries, polish off a quick pint, then set off for Cliffony and look for a car to steal.

Huong appeared happy enough sitting in the back of the car, and Aden reckoned she would be fine for a little while longer while he popped inside. There was an old lady behind the counter; she was probably the wife of the old man he was more familiar with. She was certainly friendlier and more helpful than her partner, and he asked her to start pulling him a pint of Guinness whilst he busied himself selecting a basket of groceries. Kidnaps usually entailed long waiting periods locked away inside so he would need some supplies. By the time, he was ready to pay for the goods and the petrol, the pint would be nicely settled and ready to down in a few thirst quenching slurps.

In fact, he was salivating at the thought as he walked through the house divide and into the public bar. The pint was ready for him and sitting on the counter enticing him towards it, no doubt trying to lure him on to the rocks, like Pandora and her box. He raised the glass to his lips and closed his eyes as he let the cold nectar slip down his throat. Although that was not the only cold thing touching his neck, the other thing felt more like gun metal and was being pushed hard into the nape from behind.

"You're coming with me Sunshine," said the voice with the brash Derry accent.

Aden had little choice but to comply.

"Don't turn around; just walk out the door, nice and quiet like."

The man was left handed and that is all he knew for now, but his mind raced to work out more. He tried to recall if he had any enemies in Londonderry, but no one came to mind, except a vague intuitive feeling that this was something to do with that solicitor from Letterkenny.

Once through the side exit, the man shoved him roughly in the direction of the rear car park, really, it was just a bit of gravel out the back. There was a grey Land Rover parked there, and also the red Datsun with the broken window which Kav had stolen the day before. The proprietor was possibly intending to keep it.

The Derry gunman made Aden kneel down while he opened the rear door of the off-road vehicle. He didn't feel fear, but only resignation, together with disappointment that his life-story didn't flash before his eyes. The last thing he felt was the hit to his head, and then there was nothing but darkness.

27 Streedagh (Sunday)

"Now for security reasons, I am going to have to tie your hands and blindfold you before we set off. Please turn to face the window and put your hands behind your back."

Li did as he was instructed, presenting his clasped hands to Kav who sat beside him in the front of the car. Securing Li's hands only took seconds and was accompanied by a dull ratchety sound. Kav then manoeuvred the much smaller man back into his seat so that his hands were pinioned behind him.

"Now there you go. You won't be slipping out of those in a hurry."

"What did you just tie my hands with?"

"They are cable ties," said Kav, holding one up in front of him and demonstrating in a salesman like way, how they operated. "See! Works like a charm, very tough, and a lot less messing about than using rope."

"I like them. I could find many uses for them," said Li sounding very impressed by this new innovation.

"Me too, I use them all around my home. No loose cables and wires, and I even use them when I am gardening. The British Army taught us to use these. I should thank the soldier that first imprisoned me."

Next Kav, took off his own tie and tried to fashion it into a makeshift blindfold over Li's eyes.

"How am I meant to direct you to Streedagh, if I am blindfolded?"

Kav took of Li's blindfold as quickly as he had put it on. "Sorry, force of habit. Of course, you are right."

Li was starting to question the professionalism of his captor. Meanwhile, Kav was fiddling awkwardly with the ignition wiring trying to find the end of the red cable which seemed to have got into some Gordian knot. Li couldn't see what the big man's hands were doing, but assumed he was a little ham-fisted.

As they drove off, Li watched his captor with a much deeper level of scrutiny. He was assessing him all the time, studying his strengths and weaknesses, and trying to figure him out.

Kav initially thought that the man was just quiet, and probably inscrutable. He welcomed the brief period of solace interrupted only by the sound of rushing wind inside the car. They had now left Sligo town and were travelling north towards Bundoran on the N15. As the road widened, he responded with increased speed, but this was causing the wind to whip up a furious maelstrom inside. It appeared to be annoying Kav rather than Li who was more concerned with finding answers to his questions.

"How did you break your window?" Li asked.

Any other question might have provided a better opening gambit. Kav was feeling overly sensitive about his car stealing skills following Aden's incessant nagging the day before.

"Oh I didn't do it, the ex-wife did," he said, deflecting the blame anywhere that wasn't on him.

"How did she manage that?"

"I don't really know. I think a bird might have hit it?"

"I have never heard of a bird flying into a side window."

"Maybe they are attracted to her. Can you please stop asking me questions about this car?"

"Does your wife live here in Sligo?"

"Or about my wife, in fact, enough with all the questions. Can we just journey to Streedagh in some peace and tranquillity?"

"Okay, no problem," said Li who then set about looking for other stimulation for his overactive mind. He was in fact very worried about his mother, but his concern only showed in an impulsive need to find answers to everything that remained inconclusive or unknown. It was his way of dealing with uncertainty.

There was a pile of magazines on the floor in the foot well in front of him. Li strained to read the top cover which was upside down. It appeared to be a farming journal and it included a special feature edition about animal husbandry. He looked to the big man beside him and wondered whether he was a part-time farmer as well as a paramilitary.

He used his foot to surreptitiously turn the magazine cover around so he could more easily read the smaller print. However, the glossy cover, slipped sideways off the top of the pile, revealing another glossy cover underneath and further fuelling his intrigue. It was different from the first one and appeared to be pornography, but not the usual kind. This magazine seemed to feature only animal sex. Li squinted at the gunman beside him, his judgemental eyes becoming mere slits.

"Are these your magazines?"

"No, they are the ex-wife's."

"Does she like animals?"

"Somewhat; she is very fond of the neighbour's dog," said Kav, thinking it a strange question.

"I see."

"Why do you ask?" said Kav more than a little intrigued by his new line of questioning.

"No reason," said Li who now possessed a fresh understanding of these inscrutable westerners.

Streedagh was not so much a town, more a location. To reach it, you generally took the turn off at Grange, about two to three miles from the ocean. It was a headland jutting out into the sea at the end of a peninsula. That headland acted as a natural shield, against all the ravages that the Atlantic could throw at it, and behind it, sheltered a long spit bar of sand which was almost sealing off a shallow lagoon. The spit bar was known as the 'back strand' and was over a mile in length.

It was the back strand that was their destination and in particular the long tall ridge of central dunes which separated the ocean from the inner lagoon.

"This seems like a strange place to bury your gold," said Kav as he followed Li's directions and drove along a single track access road that skirted the lagoon.

"It offers total privacy, free from onlookers. There were lots of dog walkers upon the headland, but very few come down this far," said Li.

"How much further shall I drive?"

"Keep going. I will tell you when," and Li kept craning his head from left to right, seemingly trying to orientate himself to some unknown landmarks. "Here, stop here," and as Kav parked the car closer to the dunes, Li said, "From here we walk."

Li kicked off his shoes and used his feet with some dexterity to peel off his socks before setting off up the dunes at a slow and steady pace. His hands were still secured behind his back, he compensated for this by leaning forward, enabling him to retain perfect balance.

Kav, preferring to keep his own shoes on, grabbed the shovel from the back of the range rover and scrambled up the dune after him. His clumsy climbing method paled in comparison to the lithe agile movements of Li Han, as did his state of health and fitness. At the top of the 20-foot dune, Kav dropped to his hands and knees to support himself as he tried to catch his breath. Li, on the other hand, looked completely unaffected by the exertion.

The trail continued for another fifty yards along the crest of the wind breaking dune. Those fifty undulating yards had taken a considerable toll on Kav by the time they reached the spot to dig.

Kav was still having difficulty catching his breath and his shoes and socks were sand soaked. He sat down briefly to rest awhile whilst the

Vietnamese man seemed to be studying some invisible line from two distant landmarks either side of him.

"What are you checking for?"

"The point of that mountain and the visible wreck of that ship in the sand, out by that reef."

Kav stood up and traced the same line of sight. It was clever and it made perfect sense to mark something that was buried.

"How did you find this place?"

"It found me. They told me all about the Spanish gold which was buried here when I moved to this town. I thought it was poetic that I buried mine here too." Li drew a large X mark on the sand with his big toe, and said, "And here it is."

Kav used the shovel as an aid to standing up. He then relied on it like a walking stick as he walked over to start digging. Enthusiasm and excitement showed visibly on his face, but his body looked like it wanted to rebel.

"Do you want me to dig?" asked Li.

"No; I want you to sit down over there, where I can keep an eye on you."

"I was only offering because you look exhausted."

"I am only a little tired because I had a big lunch. I am fit as a fiddle thank you very much, and I don't like the idea of you having your hands free. Nothing personal; it's only your martial arts that I don't trust."

Digging in sand takes a certain knack which Kav obviously didn't possess. He was finding it harder to go deeper than one foot before the surrounding sand would slide back in and level it again. Li sat maybe six feet away and was still studying the big man in silent judgement. This had not escaped Kav's attention and it was irritating him.

"I suppose you could do better." He said to Li Han, but it was really a rhetorical question because they both knew he could.

He wondered whether wetting the sand might aid the dig, but he felt too proud to ask the opinion of other man who seemed to demonstrate a subtle air of superiority. Besides, the only source of liquid that he could feasibly transfer into this damn hole was in his bladder. So, not wishing to cause the Asian man any cultural embarrassment, he turned his back on him whilst he peed into the hole.

This had very little effect and left Kav throwing his last reserves of energy into shovelling the sand away as quickly as possible before the surrounding stuff could replenish the supply. Bit by bit, with some grit and determination, Kav was getting somewhere, he was going deeper and the payoff was the sound of the shovel hitting something hard.

He drove down the spade harder like he was ice fishing with a spear, and the resounding resonance had a metallic sound. Kav looked up at Li Han with a beaming smile on his face and Li returned his look with an inquisitive stare.

Now Kav used the spade more like a shovel, and definitely like a madman digging. Sand was being thrown in every direction as he sought to fully reveal the buried treasure. He ended up dropping on all fours and using his hands to grasp and pull back more sand as the buried object revealed itself. It was an old style dustbin lid which some kid had probably employed as a makeshift sand dune sledge.

Now Kav's eyes narrowed to small slits as the notion that this man was making a fool out of him took hold. He stopped digging, looked up and stared at Li Han trying to work him out.

"Did you find it," asked Li.
"If by it, you mean a dustbin lid, then yes I did."
"That's a shame."
"You knew about this didn't you?"
"Maybe, maybe not."

Li Han was smirking, and Kav thought it time to teach him a lesson about who was in charge here. It was then that he noticed Li Han's hands were still bound by a cable tie but were sitting on his lap in front of him.

"Hey, I thought I tied your hands behind your back."
"You did, but they are more comfortable in front."
"Come on stand up. I need to re-secure them behind your back," instructed Kav as he walked over to his seated prisoner.

Before he reached him, his head was shaken and a flash of stars was replaced momentarily with darkness before his vision returned. When it did, Li Han was on his feet and standing with his legs apart, feet firmly planted in a martial arts pose.

"Did you just kick me?"
"I did."

"You wily son of a fox," said Kav as he adopted a boxing stance which came natural to him. "Now I am ready for you. See if you can get past my southpaw defence."

Kav had spent the better half of his miss spent youth in the amateur boxing rings of the Ardoyne. Despite the onset of middle-age and the extra girth he carried around his waist, he had not lost his sharp reactions. He raised his fists to defend his upper body readying himself to strike out in vengeance. He had already adopted the back-foot fighter's stance and was bobbing and weaving as he approached to take on Li.

In one fluid move, Li dropped into a headstand and the back of his head and shoulders pivoted on the ground as he spun around in a near 360 arc. As he moved, his legs which had fallen into full splits fluidly swung around at the tremendous speed of a whiplash.

A sweeping spinning leg just missed his face by less than an inch as Kav evaded it with his bobbing and weaving. Li noticed the faint smile of satisfaction which broke out on Kav's face literally a second before his other spinning foot connected fully with the side of his head. The big man looked surprised and then stunned as his knees gave way and he dropped to the ground.

Li stood back allowing Kav to clamber back on to his feet, but Kav had decided that today's boxing match was postponed, but a gun fight was about to begin. The Walther pistol came out of his jacket pocket, but before he managed to aim it directly at Li Han, the man was turning quickly away from him and as he turned about face again, his extended leg connected fully with the gun and knocked it clean out of Kav's hand.

Kav stepped backwards in retreat, but Li Han did not pursue him. The men watched each other intently waiting for whoever made the next move. It was a Mexican standoff in which Kav was convinced he could negotiate the upper hand.

"Your hands are tied Li, and all I have to do is go over there," he said gesturing at the gun which was closer to him than it was to Li. "Then it is all over for you. I suggest that you just sit back down."

Li said nothing but dropped instead into a crouch with his tied hands reaching out in front of his face, he appeared to be praying or perhaps conducting some religious ritual. Then his arms were retracted fast into his body as his elbows slammed into his hips. The cable ties snapped under the intense strain, and Li's hand flowed into a Tai Chi twist stance position, as he signalled to Kav that he was indeed ready for further combat.

Kav stared at the man in disbelief, and then stared at his gun on the ground estimating how many paces away it was. No more than five, and over twice that distance for the Vietnamese man.

Li stared back at him watching intently. He knew exactly what Kav had on his mind but was waiting for him to make the first move. Kav was willing to oblige him in this respect, and he exploded out of his starting block driven by his conviction, determined to make those five steps as fast as he possibly could.

He made at least three of them, but ended flat on his face in the sand, winded by Li Han who had used his body as a springboard to then reach the weapon first. He now stood pointing it at Kav determined that it was time to get his mother back.

All the fight had left the big man and he was now resigned to becoming Li's prisoner. He suspected that the terms of his captivity would involve a lecture.

"What exactly did you expect to find in the hole you were digging?"

"Gold, you know, your temple gold."

"And what temple is that?"

"The one in Vietnam where you were a monk. The one close to the border with Cambodia which was being overrun by the North Vietnamese army."

"I was a caterer. My father owned a chain of restaurants in Saigon."

"But you trained as a fighting monk, right?"

"I trained in Kung fu ever since I was a child, and yes, my first teachers were actually monks, but they lived in Saigon too, and their temple had no gold."

"But you knew about the buried gold when I first talked to you."

"Actually, you mentioned it first, but everyone in Sligo knows about buried Gold. When I came to Sligo, I was told that the German's had buried gold in County Sligo during the final days of the war. I thought those stories were true until I realised that the Spanish were meant to have done the same thing after their Armada sank out there." He gestured to the remains of the Spanish galleon or its keel which he had used earlier as one of his landmarks."

"So what was all that business with measuring out the steps and the landmarks?"

"I was playing with you. I couldn't believe that you were actually serious."

"And the metal dustbin lid. How come you knew that was there?"

"I didn't, but I nearly pissed myself when you found it."

"But you are a relatively wealthy man in Sligo with your restaurant and Mercedes car, but you weren't in Dublin; we made enquiries."

"It is mother's wealth from Vietnam. When she was granted Irish residency, there was a delay until she could regain access to her offshore accounts. Anyway, we are not that wealthy. Sure I own a Mercedes, but the restaurant is only leased."

"Hmm," said Kav upon reflection. "I've been a bit of a dick."

"Don't be too hard on yourself. It's these Sligo people, they have completely warped imaginations."

"Tell me about it," said Kav with disappointment and resignation.

It was Kav who now walked in front on their way back to the car, but his hands were not tied. They didn't need to be. He and Li were on the same page now, except Li still wanted his mother back, and this would involve convincing Aden and Maeve that this was the right thing to do.

Li allowed Kav to continue doing the driving, their destination a harbour hotel and pub, only a couple of miles away at Mullaghmore.

When they arrived there, either the bar had opened early, or it had stayed open flouting the licensing laws. Neither man bothered to enquire which one applied. As blow-ins, they were both fairly familiar with the west coast's cavalier attitude to breaking the law; not God's law, though, that was still sacrosanct, just the laws made by men.

They found a table in the comfortable saloon bar beside a wall pay phone, and Kav dialled the number at Raghly Point.

28 Prisoner of War   (Sunday)

He regained his consciousness piecemeal: a feeling of being restricted, the smell of petrol, and lastly his vision. Aden was in the back of a Land Rover which was being driven down some very rough and unmade roads. He kept still, said nothing, and hid his awareness from the driver, who often glanced back at him, and occasionally checked his bindings. He had no idea how long he had been out, but the journey was coming to an end for him, both geographically and metaphorically.

Still pretending to be out cold, Aden let the driver lift him out of the rear and drag him along the ground and prop him up against a breeze block wall, half in and half out of a partially constructed building. Through furtive glances, he could tell that it was an unfinished boathouse, a shell of a building with a roof and workable joists above him only requiring floorboards and steps to access them.

There were two sleeping bags inside the building set up beside a camping gas stove and light. Whoever these guys were, they were professional and didn't want to leave an unnecessary trail of witnesses and accommodation bookings.

Outside, a ramp to the water was also an unfinished construction, but even if it worked, any boat would have to wait a while, because the estuary outside was tidal. Right now the tide was out and the sea had left behind at least 500 yards of damp sand; an ideal location to hide a dead victim.

Aden could hear the voice of another man talking. It was deeper and he sounded older, and he had a thick Derry accent just like his kidnapper.

"Has he come around yet?"

"I think so, I heard him moaning a bit when I was driving off road."

"First things first, let's go and question him," said the older man.

"Hardman-softman routine?"

"Be my guest," he replied offering the young mean-faced man first dibs.

Aden found himself being roughly shaken by his coat lapels causing his head to bang repeatedly against the concrete breeze blocks of the wall supporting him.

"Wakey wakey sunshine, you are now a prisoner of the Irish National Liberation Army."

There was no longer any reason to maintain the pretence of sleep, so Aden opened his eyes and answered with his own question.

"So what are you Bogmen doing down here?" The name was not necessarily derogatory. Its connotation was linked to the Bogside & Creggan neighbourhoods of Londonderry which were the birthplace of the INLA.

"You better get your shit together and answer truthfully, or this bleak hole will become the end of the road for you."

"Bleak? I think it looks rather nice here. Sure, the boat house looks like it could do with a lick of paint, but otherwise, this looks like a lovely place to die."

Brady waded in with an array of punches, viciously assaulting him around the head, using the beating to emphasise his words. "Shut your wise-cracking mouth before I cut your bollocks off and stick them in it."

Aden rolled with the punches; he had taken much worse, but they were still wearing him down.

The older man with the bushy moustache asked his first question. Seemingly, he was playing the soft man. "So would you care to illuminate us as to why you are in Sligo?"

"No,"

Brady already tense, rushed forward, but McCreadie restrained him.

"And why not, pray tell?"

"Because your man there," gesturing to Brady, "told me not to talk."

Terry Brady saw red, and this time, the older gunman couldn't stop him. One punch knocked Aden sideways and to the ground, and he then waded in with a few kicks, punctuated by his own line of hard man questioning.

"So what are you up to, PIRA?" said Brady using the acronym for the Provisionals. Then when no answer was supplied, another kick was followed by another question. "Why all this interest in the Chinaman?"

"Vietnamese," corrected Aden.

Brady didn't like being corrected and his instinct was to hit the Belfast man again, but McCreadie urged tolerance.

"Easy, calm down our fella, Mister Clancy here was trying to be informative."

Aden looked up at the mention of his name.

"Yes we know who you are, and who you are connected to," said McCreadie. "The Provisionals are not our enemy, Mr. Clancy, but I have checked you out. This little venture of yours is not sanctioned. So you are running a rogue operation down here, which means that you do not have the protection of the Provisionals command right now."

ANGUS CACTUS

Brady was impatient for him to talk and decided a few kicks to the gut might loosen up his resolve. "Tell us all about the Vietnamese guy, *Chucky*", he said using the slang word for members of the Provisional IRA.

"I think you should start talking to us Mr. Clancy," said McCreadie sounding aggressively assertive, and slowly slipping out of his role. "Whatever you, your friend, and that blond bitch have planned, is ours now. This is our backyard, not yours."

"There are some others who probably might not agree," said Aden referring to the Stickies.

"What the Officials? They are a spent force. WE are taking over down here," said Brady rising to the bait.

"Look, Aden, if you don't mind me calling you by your first name," said McCreadie backpedalling into Mr. Soft man.

"I do,"

"Well tough, because listen up Aden. We have no use for you if you don't start giving us what we want. Are you really prepared to die over this?"

McCreadie paused for gravitas, but the interval didn't induce Aden to speak.

"Okay; Terry, take him around the back of the building and clip him."

"Kneecapping?"

"No, plan B instead, but you can knee-cap him first if you want."

It was only after being dragged away from the building's wall which had propped him up, that he got his first glance of the majestic mountain that loomed behind the boat house. He knew it from pictures, and from his youth. It was Knocknarea, the same mountain with the large cairn on top which was visible from their kitchen at Raghly Point, all the way across the bay.

Here he was at its base, a quite serene and majestic place to die, and yet he was not ready to go. He knew he was going to die as soon as he heard the first name of one of the gunmen being used. They were obviously not bluffing if they were prepared to reveal their names. Nonetheless, he had a change of heart now.

"Wait!" yelled Aden at Brady who then stopped dragging him along the ground. Dropping his legs, he looked back at McCreadie checking for a status update. There was none, so he grabbed hold of Aden's legs again and continued dragging him.

"We have kidnapped the Vietnamese man's mother. Kav is making him hand over his gold to get her back." The words spilled out of Aden's mouth quickly.

Brady instantly dropped the man's legs at the mention of gold.

"Gold?" enquired McCreadie seeking clarification.

"Yeah, he has a shed load of it buried somewhere. He took it from a temple in Vietnam."

"But why didn't you just torture him and make him tell you," asked Brady, no longer committed to the role of hard man, now that he saw a golden lining.

"We thought he probably wouldn't talk. Probably the inscrutable type."

Brady was nodding in full agreement, "Those chinks can be pretty inscrutable."

"So where did you hide the man's mother?"

"She's in the back of my car."

"Where's that?"

"Back at the place you friggin kidnapped me from."

Brady and McCreadie stared at each other in mute surprise, and then both looked at Aden Clancy with frustrated annoyance.

"What?" He said shrugging his shoulders, and then pointed out, "It's not my fault."

29 Buffalo Soldier   (Sunday)

Why was he pretending to be in Sligo? She could hear the vintage petrol pump humming and rattling in the background. It was an unmistakable sound made by an old diesel pump engine whose timer ran long after the customer had filled up. She had heard it droning on for hours yesterday afternoon whilst she waited for the boys to reach Ballintrillick. Where else would you find a 1950s petrol pump? He was so obviously in the very same place, and probably having a swift pint for Dutch courage.

Maeve didn't challenge him but she did wonder why he was lying. In fact, she said very little, instead letting Aden do all the talking, allowing him to slowly dig his own grave. She was restraining her anger, but inside she was furious with him.

He said that he had abducted Huong Han and had her in the back of his car and that Kav was on his way to intercepting the Chinaman and delivering the ransom terms in person. Typical to his form, this was an impromptu act, all planned on the hoof and based on decisions made on the spur of the moment. All her planning was to no avail, and now, this whole scheme was now probably doomed to failure. Her involvement in this whole debacle was a personal security risk and would not be seen in a good light by Belfast Command.

Maeve was convinced that they had used her car for the kidnapping, even though Aden was claiming that Kav was using it presently. That didn't make sense because he had already said that the kidnapping was a spur of the moment opportunity. For what reason would he have had a stolen car parked outside, if they had borrowed her car to drive to the restaurant.

For Pete's sake, they were only meant to have lunch there so they could case the joint for a future planned action. If she hadn't had to wait in for an important call from Belfast, then she would have gone into town with them. But she was seeking official sanction for this mission and they were going to get back to her tomorrow with their decision. Now, what was she going to say to them? 'We had a change of plan, and decided to go ahead without your permission'.

Lord, she was so angry with both of them, but a telephone was not the correct medium to express herself. She was using every last shred of her personal discipline to stay calm right now because she wanted to unleash her fury on both of them personally.

Maeve was resolved to be patient and wait here for Aden to arrive with their captive, Huong. He was probably on route from Ballintrillick right now and looking to switch cars somewhere down the road. Aden was just as predictable as her ex-husband — even their unpredictability was predictable.

The long wait did surprise her, but eventually she heard the sound of an approaching car crossing the gravel causeway to the cape of Raghly Point. Spying on it through a bedroom window, she realised that the approaching Volkswagen Golf wasn't being driven by Aden at all. Instead, a very large man stepped out of it and he was wearing a US army surplus jacket. She didn't know him, but as he walked towards the front entrance, a sense of foreboding alerted her to the possibility of danger.

Adrenaline made her mind work fast, and she quickly unlocked the front door, leaving it slightly ajar. The bungalow had a rectangular layout. The main entrance opened into a long living room and an identically sized kitchen-diner was positioned at the other end of the property, and in between were two smaller bedrooms, facing each other and separated by the interconnecting corridor.

Maeve was able to watch him standing at the front door using her bedroom window's peripheral view. She had correctly guessed his intentions because the man entered quietly through the unlocked door. In doing so, he signified his bad intentions.

The intruder would be extremely alert entering through the living room and would have no other option than to walk through the bungalow's central corridor. The trap was set in the other bedroom. It had a private bathroom comprising of a toilet and a shower, and this she had purposely left running.

The sound of the running water could be heard from the corridor. If the intruder was up to no good, then it would attract his attention and the sound of the other bedroom door being opened would confirm his enemy status.

She was literally facing him, but standing behind the closed door of her bedroom, directly opposite. Hearing the other door handle creak a little, she made sure that hers remained silent as she gently turned the knob and stepped into the corridor behind him. Then as the big man edged sideways through the other bedroom's partially open door, he got to feel the Walther PPK pistol and silencer being pushed gently into the back of his head.

ANGUS CACTUS

She led him into the kitchen and tied his bulk to a wooden chair. Kitchens were ideal places to interrogate people. A captive's mind usually raced through all potentials and possibilities, and a kitchen was ideal inspiration for a wider range of potential torture devices and tools. He was a big man, and she didn't expect him to talk - well not at first. However, unlike her first assumptions about his motives and actions, this one was proved incorrect.

He had already told her his name, and she hadn't even started working on him yet. In fact, he was chatting nineteen to the dozen, and although nerves played a part, he really seemed way too amenable for a paramilitary. She knew he was a Stickie because he had told her so. Not willingly, but she had managed to coerce the information and much more out of him using an unusual interrogation prop. This happened to be a bacon, cheese and broccoli quiche, served cold, and in small bite sized portions too, which she released piecemeal in exchange for each parcel of new facts.

She gleaned from his confession that he was part of a four-man unit of Official IRA. They were aware of this safe house and of the three-person unit of Belfast Provisional IRA using it. They were also aware that her unit was being watched and followed by two members of the Irish National Liberation Army from Derry. This was news to Maeve who was unaware that their kidnap mission had been compromised.

His name was Mathew, but he preferred to be called Maxie, and his role here today was only to visit the safe house and investigate. When he saw no cars parked here, he assumed that the cottage was empty. He swore to Maeve that his intentions when creeping around the house were only investigative.

Over the years, she had interrogated quite a few people, and not many of them got to live. Nevertheless, killing was off the menu; that was a given, seeing as she had promised Kav only the other evening, that she would try to abstain. Strangely, she felt no animosity towards the big man, and little desire to hurt him. However, maybe she should have provided a little more threat and aggression to ensure that he was telling the truth.

Nevertheless, she believed most of what he had told her, and therefore did not doubt his assertion that he had no backup outside waiting to come to his assistance. She mostly trusted him because he was amenable but, and as big as he was, he did appear to be scared of her. However, her next statement revealed that there was something he seemed to care about, more than his life.

"I am going to borrow your car, Maxie. I am just driving it locally, and

TO HELL OR SLIGO

I won't be long."

"Please don't. She doesn't like being driven by other people."

"I am afraid that I have to. I need to go and check something out, but I will make sure that I look after her."

"Please don't crunch the gears, and make sure you don't ride the clutch or yank the handbrake without releasing the cog teeth."

"Okay Maxie, but be a good boy and don't try to escape, and I promise to bring you back something nice."

"There is a cafe in Grange that does nice cheeseburgers," said the big man.

"I will see what I can do," she said as she closed and locked the door after her.

"And some fries too," yelled Maxie, loud enough to be heard outside.

30 Diarmuid & Grainne's Cave (Sunday)

The Gleniff horseshoe pass always delivered sublime views to anyone that made the six-mile circuit around it. The single track road was a horseshoe-shaped loop, and the two entrances or exits lay only two hundred yards apart. In America, it would be called a box canyon, because it certainly was not a pass.

It was the backyard of Benbulben Mountain and offered no through route to anywhere. Whereas goats may have found it handy enough, no vehicle or person on horseback could pass beyond the ring of mountains which contained it.

If she was wrong about Shane, it was going to be a long walk home for her and Molly, but she wasn't wrong. Enya always marvelled at how predictable Shane was in his habits. And a few miles further up the road, she came across his motorcycle. The trials bike was parked off road at the nearest accessible climbing point to Diarmuid and Grainne's cave.

The cave was a well-known local landmark which her boyfriend was convinced he had discovered all by himself; the supposed bolt hole for two lovers and mythical characters from Ireland's history. It was a deep cave with a cavernous opening, high above the pass towards the summit of Benbulben. It did not involve rock climbing as such, to reach it, but it was certainly a steep ascent.

There was a small canvas bag secured to the carrier of the bike which contained a small tent. It didn't look like it had been used, making Enya wonder where Shane had spent last night. His total disregard for the security of his possessions came as no surprise, except he had attempted to hide his helmets behind a small stone wall.

Molly had discovered these, and her reward had been the ice lolly wrapper which fell out of one of the helmets when Enya picked it up. Molly was quick to woof it down, swallowing the contents and the wrapper in one go. Her expression was one of surprise when she detected that there was no ice lolly inside it, however, the quarter ounce of dope that was inside it and which she had just swallowed would play havoc with her future expressions for the rest of the day.

Scrambling up a steep grassy path between rocky outcrops on the side of the mountain was easy exercise for Enya. For Molly too, except that her sense of direction was being challenged and the myriad of smells on the mountain were becoming strange to her.

It was the hunting dogs of Fionn mac Cumhaill who found the scent and chased Diarmuid up to the top of this mountain, and it was the keen smell of someone smoking a joint that helped Molly find Shane first. The aroma had a strange attraction for Molly too and, after finding him sitting at the entrance to the cave, she snuggled up beside him and rested her head in his lap. Shane immediately flicked the joint into the dark void behind him, knowing that the presence of Enya was sure to follow.

Enya was smiling as she climbed over the last obstacle. She was pleased to see him and enjoyed the look of surprise in his eyes. They usually lit up when he saw her, and for her, this was his most redeeming feature. His reward was a kiss and a cold drink from her bag.

Molly got her reward as well, the ice lolly that Enya had bought earlier. The collie climbed over Shane in a rush to get at it, and as she began to furiously lick the iced treat, she let out a silent fart that had the young couple running to seek protection in the back of the cave.

"I knew that I would find you here; you are so predictable," she said as they tentatively approached their original seating to see if it was safe to return.

"I've got too much going on at the moment. I needed to come here and think."

"Run away, more like it."

She was right and he knew it, so he chose not to challenge what she said, opting to change the subject instead.

"Don't you just love it here?" he said taking in the majestic panorama laid out before them. You could see all the way to the sea, and the view encompassed every idyllic spot that the west coast had to offer between Strandhill and the distant mountains of Donegal.

"It is a stunningly beautiful view from up here," she agreed.

"All things bright and beautiful," said Shane. "Do you remember singing that as a child?"

"The nuns that taught me loved that one. For years, I thought it was a hymn." Enya eyes gazed below in reminiscence.

"Do you know, the composer wrote that song, when he was a guest of Countess Markievicz at Lissadell House, right over there," he said, placing his arm around her shoulder and pointing towards Raghly Point.

"He must have been very happy when he wrote that song," said Enya.

"Yeah, she had probably given him some the night before."

Enya laughed, "You're funny Shane."

"So where did you go to school?" enquired Shane still wondering about her earlier comment.

"At the Mercy convent in Sligo."

"Isn't that the one run by those Sisters of Mercy nuns?"

"Yeah, but they were more like the Sisters of Misery as far as I was concerned."

Shane laughed and returned the compliment, "You're funny too", but not to be outdone, another anecdote sprung to mind. "You remember the Mother Superior with the exceptionally big bust."

"Reverend Mother Magdelena; how could I forget that old witch".

"Well, Owen Mulligan, the painter that decorated the Bective hotel—"

"That inebriated idiot."

"That's the man! Well, he told Jimmy that he was once asked by Reverend Mother Magdelena to give a quote for painting the exterior of the Mercy convent. So, him and the bloke who was helping him were in the company of a few nuns. They were all walking around the property inspecting what needed to be done. Anyway, Owen turns to the Mother Superior and tells her that it is difficult to give her an exact quote because she has the biggest front in town. I don't know how he managed to keep a straight face, but his assistant was bent double laughing and even some of the nuns were hiding their faces to prevent the mother superior seeing their smiles."

"Yet another example of your infantile humour Shane," but the words were lost on him as he had fallen under the spell of a fit of giggles, and had momentarily lost control laughing hysterically at his own joke.

Enya looked at him with an expression of dismay and bewilderment. "You've been smoking, haven't you?"

"Just a little."

"I wish you would lay off that stuff."

"It makes it all so much more beautiful."

"Such as?"

"You!"

"Shut up you charmer. Be serious tell me what you get from smoking that stuff when you could be running with me down there and getting fresh air in your lungs."

"I wish you would smoke a little and see for yourself. It's a matter of perspective so it's hard to describe."

"I get it, a kind of 'had to be there' sort of thing," said Enya trying her best to understand.

"Exactly."

"Well, you are there now, so tell me what you see and what you are feeling right now on that stuff." Enya preferred him to be open and less clandestine.

"I look out at this amazing view from up here and marvel at how beautiful County Sligo is. It makes me wonder if all those people who lived here in the past centuries really appreciated it. But then I think about how they butchered those Spaniards who washed up here, and how the town folk in Sligo built walls to keep everyone out. It makes me wonder how someone who wakes up to this view in the morning, could go outside with murder on their mind."

"It sounds to me like that fella who wrote All things bright and beautiful, must have been stoned like you Shane. You do realise that Sligo had walls because it was a fortress town built to subdue the rest of this area. The People who lived here were violent because they were hungry, and because what little they had, was often taken off them by force."

Shane sat more upright soaking in Enya's words before expounding his analysis of them.

"I think that what you are saying is that you can only experience the beauty of nature if you are separate from the affairs of the world, because once you are under the cosh of reality, life becomes difficult and hard."

"Seriously; you think this was the meaning of what I just said?" asked Enya perplexed by the complexity of Shane's thoughts.

"Yes I do," he said earnestly.

"That stuff must be stronger than I imagined."

Shane had the broadest smile across his face as he tightened his arm hold around her shoulder and pulled her towards him. "But you do love me though."

"For my sins," replied Enya.

"And I love you too Molly," said Shane grabbing hold of the dog with his free arm and squeezing her tightly. Molly looked up at him with initial suspicion and then licked his face from chin to nose.

"Molly and I need to get back for my mum's Sunday roast," said Enya hoping to inspire Shane to come home with her. "They'll be plenty of food, why don't you come with us?"

The idea of a roast dinner was very appealing to him right now," but the thought of it being served by her mother troubled him. They hadn't seen eye to eye for a couple of years now and he found it difficult to like her. And as for Enya's older sister; that girl he couldn't abide. However, he felt close to Enya right now and he could sense that it was important for him to come.

"Okay, Cave; it looks like I am leaving you for today. If Diarmuid comes back, tell him I left you the same way I found you."

"Come on Idiot," said Enya. "You are obsessed with them two, Diarmuid and Grainne."

"They remind me of us," he shouted back at her, as he took the lead taking giant steps as he clambered down the steep sides of Benbulben Mountain using gravity for momentum. The dog still beat him to the bottom, and they both waited for Enya to finish her descent.

"Not so fast at the hill running, are you?" he said

"Race you to your motorbike," she replied in challenge.

Of course, Shane with his cannabis soaked lungs didn't stand a chance. Enya was first, Molly was second and the both of them looked bored waiting for him to navigate the last 20 yards of heavy bog terrain.

One sharp kick on the Yamaha's starting lever was all that was needed to power up the XT250, and Enya jumped on the back and pulled up a slightly timid Molly who then sat in between them.

They were less than ten minutes from her house, but before they got there, Shane pulled over beside the petrol pumps of the post office in Ballintrillick. The decision to stop had been Enya's as she had seen her employer Huong Han sitting in the back seat of a silver Ford Escort. She jumped off the back, and much to Molly's consternation, went over to investigate.

"Hello," said Enya, opening the rear door and finding Huong Han waiting patiently.

"Hello dear," replied Huong, which represented about a fifth of her repertoire of English phrases.

"What ..are ..you ..doing ..here?" asked Enya clearly pronouncing her words.

"Taxi to shop," replied Huong, leaving Enya more bewildered by her answer.

"Where ..is ..the ..driver?"

Huong nodded her understanding and pointed her finger at the post office's entrance.

"Stay ..here ..while ..I ..check."

Shane watched his girlfriend disappear inside the shop and, after a while, return directly to talk to him and Molly, both still seated on the bike. Molly looked most disturbed that her mistress hadn't bought her another ice lolly.

"Shane, listen to me, whoever drove Huong Han out here left the shop nearly 30 minutes ago and hasn't returned. We can't leave her here by herself. She's not able to look after herself; she barely speaks English. We should bring her back to my house. Do you think you can fit us all on the back of your bike?"

Necessity is the mother of invention, and innovation is the product of many previous failures. Accordingly, it took many failed attempts before all four of them were balanced precariously on the back of the small trial bike.

Huong Han was surprisingly compliant when being given instructions, which Shane assumed was a product of much coercion in her earlier life. She had come along with them almost without due consideration, and regardless of her communication difficulties, she appeared comfortable and trusting that she was in safe hands.

He rode the final mile to Enya's house at a sedate speed. Mostly because he was unsettled by how tightly Huong Han was hugging his waist from behind. The thought of conversing with Enya's mother and sister was still foreboding, but the little china woman behind him would be the ace he would hold up his sleeve in order to escape that dire prospect.

Despite their communication problems, Huong Han turned out to be a real hit with Enya's mother who she joined company with in her kitchen. Cuisine seemed to be the international language they shared, and they spoke it fluently to each other.

This left Shane at the mercy of Enya's sister, Rosalyn, who looked set to beat her previous record for asking consecutive questions aimed at embarrassing him. It was some relief to him, that Enya wasn't getting any reply when she phoned the Happy Huong restaurant. Li Han wasn't home yet which was unusual for a man who was so used to following precise routines.

As soon as their meal was eaten, Shane volunteered to take Huong Han back to Sligo. Enya was obliged to agree, being that Shane's ulterior motive had not escaped her, or her sister. She waved to them as they set off and wondered when she was likely to see him next.

Huong Han's tight grip around Shane's waist disturbed him a little as she rode pillion back to Sligo, but once he hit town, his coolness meter dropped to a critical level as he realised that the old Vietnamese lady was seriously cramping his style.

For the first time, he actually wished that he had purchased that muffler to dampen his exhaust. The unwelcome noise which usually acted like a clarion call, identifying his presence was now attracting unwanted attention. Perceived looks of admiration for his wheelies were being replaced by embarrassing stares, and he was glad to drop her off at the Happy Huong. Shane was quite relieved to get back to the hotel where only yesterday, he had been so desperate to escape.

In his absence, The Bective had gotten really busy. A whole squad of the Dublin Special Detective Unit had just booked into tackle and solve the case of a local Guard's kidnapping. They were obviously taking the events of Friday evening at the lake very seriously.

These plain clothes officers were actually posing as a visiting Rugby team. However the fact that the bar remained open outside of Sunday licensed trading hours, and the swagger and alcoholic prowess they demonstrated in both of the hotel's bars unmistakably marked them out as Guards. That, and the chunky shoulder holsters that only partially hid their standard issue Beretta pistols under their ill-fitting dark grey suits. These were openly displayed every time one of them took a pool shot.

In fact, the bar was so busy that his mother hoped he could help out some, now that he was back. Although regardless of her need, she was glad to see him. His prodigal son routine had again worked a gem, and his unknown whereabouts yesterday evening and earlier today had rekindled a mother's love and brought forgiveness for his sins and past exploits.

They warmly embraced, as did the little dog too. Guinness, the toy Yorkshire terrier, was grappling the back of his ankle and was holding on tight. Shane accepted it as an emotional response empathetically passed to the dog from his mother until he felt the dog's pumping movements on his leg. Guinness was lost in some scent induced erotic fantasy about Molly the Collie. Regardless, Shane maintained the hug hold he had on his mother, whilst rejecting Guinness's amorous intentions with a deft back-flick of his foot.

The pay phone opposite the reception began to ring breaking up their private moment, and Shane, obligingly walked over to pick up. He was surprised to hear Enya on the other end of the line, but he listened intently because she seemed to be in some kind of trouble.

31   The Car Pool   (Sunday)

Her women's intuition was telling her that something was up. There was still no sign of Aden and no word from Kav. Maxie's admission about the INLA also worried her. Although they were not traditional enemies, the truce between the two organisations was fragile at its best. The INLA were a ruthless organisation that considered the 26 counties in the South to be their domain. Sure that was a ridiculous assertion for an organisation that only had a real power base in Derry, and that was weakened by their incessant internecine wars being raged within their own ranks. The INLA were their own worst enemy, but right now, she feared that they were hers too.

Ballintrillick was close enough to Raghly Point and her intuition had proved correct when she found her car sitting at one of the petrol pumps in the courtyard of the weird shop, post office, public house where she had collected her menfolk from yesterday. There was no one in the car and the doors were unlocked. Maeve prayed that the driver was still here and supping a pint inside. She walked around the building so that she could enter through the side exit.

She was expecting to find Aden, or even possibly Kav, but neither were there. In fact, the premises were empty but for an old lady whom Maeve assumed was the wife of the old proprietor who had served her yesterday. Her name was Moira and she was quick to relay everything that Maeve needed to know.

The pertinent facts were that she had seen the driver. He was a younger man with dark hair and he ordered a pint of Guinness which he had not drunk. There was another young customer, a man with dark brown hair brushed forward with a mean face, who had disappeared at the same time. Moira assumed that they had left together, but an old Chinese lady had remained behind but stayed in the car.

"Where is she now?"

"A local girl and her boyfriend were passing and they seemed to know her. I believe she went home with them."

"So where does this local girl live?"

"Well I don't know the exact house, but she is the ambulance driver's daughter, and he lives in the new estate in Yeats close"

"Where?"

ANGUS CACTUS

"Oh, just a mile further down this road and on your left before you come to the main road and Grange village."

"Thank you Moira. By the way, I will be taking that car, and leaving another in its place."

"Sound as a pound," said Moira, which Maeve took as her blessing.

As much as she wanted to return Maxie's car to him, it was not her intention to leave behind her own. The spare set of keys was still in place, taped just behind the car's radiator. She made sure to position the VW Golf's keys in a similar position after she parked it up. She would tell Maxie later where to find it.

However, the familiarity of her own car provided only a little reassurance for the situation she found herself in. Her feelings of anger and comeuppance which she had stored up for Kav and Aden, were now replaced by feelings of fear and concern for them.

One thing was obvious to her, these Derry INLA were after something. If their ambition had been a simple kneecapping or punishment beating, they would have dispensed that earlier. They were likely to interrogate Aden, and he was likely to give up whatever he had. He would tell them all about the Vietnamese monk and his mother, and more importantly about the gold.

If they had already known about the Vietnamese gold, then they wouldn't have left Huong Han behind. Her first move had to be to find the old lady and recapture her. Once she was her hostage, she could either ransom her for Aden or ransom her for the gold. Either way, she was a crucial asset to hold and hopefully, she would find her a mile or so down the road.

Moira's directions to Yeats Close were pretty accurate. Her description of this small community was not. The houses on this 'new' estate looked at least 25 years old. The estate comprised of eight cottage style semi detached houses in a crescent with a central green, complete with a rose garden. As estates went, this wasn't exactly the Ardoyne or Andersonstown. Maeve was more used to the term applying to run down corporation housing with vacant burnt out properties and car wrecks littering the streets.

The first house she knocked at supplied the address of the one she was seeking.

"I am looking for the home of the ambulance driver. I need to thank him for helping save my son," she lied.

She was directed to No.6, but rather than go and knock on the door, she got back in her car and slowly reversed into the houses small white picket fence as if engaged in a troubled parking manoeuvre, making sure to over-rev the car and attract the attention of those in the house.

The young woman who came out to confront her seemed to fit Moira's description; about twenty with piercing blue eyes, and shoulder length dark hair. Jumping out, Maeve quickly approached her and, with determined zeal pulled her by her arm and pushed her back against her car.

The young woman went ballistic, trying to wrestle out of her grasp but she poked her small Walther PKK, now divorced from its silencer, into the girl's ribs and told her to stay calm and inform her mother, who had just come to the front door, that they were friends. Enya complied afraid for her mother's safety, and relief showed on both their faces when she went back into the house.

However, it soon disappeared from Maeve's when she learnt that Huong Han had been ridden back to the Happy Huong by her boyfriend Shane. This was a complication for sure, but not an insurmountable one if she took this young woman hostage and ransomed her for Huong Han.

If he was so quick to take the old Vietnamese lady back to Sligo, then he would be quick enough to bring her back if his girlfriend asked him to do so.

She soon learnt her name, and Enya was reasonably docile once a passenger in her car. They even stopped in Grange to buy Maxie his takeaway meal though she made sure to keep Enya close and under her supervision at all times.

32   Missing Person   (Sunday)

The drive back to Ballintrillick was long and uneventful, but this time, Aden was allowed to sit in the back seat with just his hands tied together. He made sure to take note of road names and directions in case he ever needed to retrace this route. This area was called Strandhill and he noted that the boathouse was located nearby, just off the main road to Culleenamore Strand.

As the crow flies, they were a reasonably short distance from the post office where Huong Han had been left alone in Maeve's car. Regardless, their journey entailed going through Sligo Town and then heading north on the N15. The duration was frustratingly long, and the three men fully expected that the Vietnamese woman to be gone by the time they reached Ballintrillick.

Not only was she gone, but so was Maeve's silver Ford Escort. In its place was a sporty black VW Golf with non-standard alloy wheels. The shop keeper said that a woman with black hair took the original car. However, she didn't know her and didn't think that she was local.

"Whose car was it?" McCreadie asked Aden directly after exiting the shop.

"I dunno; I stole it," lied Aden.

"And this woman with black hair?"

Aden shook his head in mock cluelessness.

"Maybe the black haired woman was the owner reclaiming it," said Brady, a comment which betrayed naivety or even low intelligence. It just so happened that he was damn right.

What the old woman manning the post office, shop and bar had failed to impart was the fact that the woman with black hair, had only taken the car. She failed to mention that the old Vietnamese lady had left earlier on a motorcycle along with a girl from Grange and her boyfriend. She probably would have told them if they had bought something, or at least bothered to stop, chat, and pass the time of day. Northerners! Best left to fend with the British; they had no place down here. Bloody blow-ins!

Aden knew precisely who had taken the car. He pondered how smart Maeve actually was and assumed that she most likely held Huong Han now, and was busy transacting the ransom details with her son.

"So you have no idea where your hostage is now," confirmed

McCreadie. "Then what can you tell us about where the hostage and ransom handover are taking place."

"That was to be arranged once we'd contacted Li Han," said Aden easily passing off another lie to McCreadie.

"So, there is nothing he can do for us now," said Brady following McCreadie's train of thought.

"Plan A or plan B?" McCreadie was asked by his subordinate.

"Go with plan A," he confirmed. "Just take him up that rural road over there and knee cap him some place where it is quiet."

"Hey hold on a moment," said Aden, worried for his knees. "I did my part; what are you shooting me in the knee for?"

"Nothing personal," said McCreadie. "But we promised a solicitor up in Letterkenny that we would."

"Walsh! That lowlife piece of ass wipe."

"That sounds like him."

"Oh, I am so going to sort him out."

"I am afraid you can't do that, or we may have to revise this to plan B. He is under out protection now."

"Is there nothing I can do or say to make you change your mind?"

"Not really, unless it involves getting us back the Vietnamese woman," said McCreadie. "Besides, you will get over it, may even get to limp with some pride. Man up for heaven's sake."

Aden now faced with an imminent maiming, decided that he wasn't so brave. Actually, it was more a matter of vanity than courage. He didn't want to walk with a limp for the foreseeable future and his mind raced to find a way out of this predicament.

Then he had a sudden realisation, and that was that Maeve was a damn sight more cunning than him or these guys.

"Wait, stop!" he pleaded. "I know where the Vietnamese woman is and who has got her and you can phone her right now from that phone."

33   Switchboard Terrorist (Sunday)

Once back at Raghly Point, Maeve tied up Enya on another wooden chair in the kitchen. She then placed her two captives back to back and spun a second rope around them both securing their two chairs together. She allowed them one arm free and tied Maxie's right arm to Enya's left. It was a risk, but this limited mobility allowed Maxie to eat unaided, and Enya to hold a receiver and speak on the phone.

If he had realised that his car was not parked outside, it might have possibly put him off his food, but he had only asked Maeve if his car was okay and she hadn't really lied when in confirming that it was. In her opinion, the male mind was always too quick to jump to conclusions.

There was no reply from the Happy Huong restaurant when Maeve called on the phone. So she handed Enya the receiver and instructed her to call the Bective. She sat beside her and listened, and they were both a little surprised when Shane answered.

Enya had pledged that she could easily talk Shane into delivering Huong Han out to Raghly Point. However, Maeve detected a certain reticence in his speech, and so grabbing hold of the phone, she decided to introduce herself.

"Enya is a prisoner of the Provisional IRA. I will release her to only you if you come here immediately and deliver Huong Han to me. I promise that if you do this, no harm will come to either of you or to Mrs. Han, and after that, I will let you and Enya leave together. If however, you get any stupid ideas like involving the Guards, then you will never see her or speak to her again, and you will be endangering your own family too. Don't try to double cross me and this will all work out fine. You have the address, and the phone number here, so go and get Huong Han and bring her here immediately."

"That should do it," said Enya passing comment. "I usually have to nag him a bit more than that and bend his arm to get him to agree to something, but you did just fine. You are a very assertive Lady."

"Thank you," replied Maeve. "Maybe you should threaten him a bit more; let him know you are serious. When I give my fella too much leeway, he always fucks things up."

"Your boyfriend?"

"Ex-husband actually. This whole fecking business is another one of his screw-ups."

"I suppose I am not meant to know your name, but you seem like a nice lady. May I ask you a question?"

"You can ask, but I might not be able to answer and you can call me Alice."

"Well Alice, I guess I wanted to know woman to woman, whether that spiel you gave to my boyfriend was all true."

"I am not lying to you Enya, you guys can leave as soon as I have got Huong Han and returned her to her son."

"And where is he?"

"Truthfully, I am not totally sure, but I know my useless ex-husband is meant to be …" She trailed off because the phone was ringing.

"I bet that's my useless boyfriend ringing back to get the address again. He has got a memory like a sieve."

Maeve smiled at Enya's comment and picked up on the sixth ring. If Enya was right, then she needed to at least keep him stressed out and under manners. "Hello?"

"Ah Jaysus Maeve, it's good to hear your voice."

"Yes," she said curtly, not wishing to say his name aloud, or to come across too friendly to this oaf who had engineered another complete cock-up. "Where are you?"

"Can I say?" said Kav who appeared to be asking a third party, before speaking directly to Maeve again, "A place called Streedagh."

"Okay, it sounds like you have company."

"I do, I am with Li Han, and he wants his mother back."

"Well I am sure he does, but there is a little matter of a ransom involved."

"About that!"

"What, about that?" Maeve's word were clearly enunciated and served up cold and harsh.

"The thing is Maeve, is that there isn't actually any gold, there never was any. The whole thing is just a tall story cooked up in Sligo. Apparently they have been at it for years."

"Who has?"

"Sligonians; They have been making up lies and fables about any rich foreign sap that comes to town, no offence Li."

"And you believe him, just like that."

"Ah well, he makes a convincing argument."

"And the research about him from Aden's Dublin source?"

"Somewhat mistaken, Maeve. The wealth comes from his mother. She was minted back in Saigon; her husband had a chain of restaurants."

ANGUS CACTUS

"And you are taking him at his word?"

"Ah you see now, well I have to, and I promised him that you would deliver his mother to him here safe and sound."

"And why, pray tell?"

"Umm. It's a little embarrassing for me to say over the phone."

"Go on!"

"Well, I am sort of like his prisoner, and he wants to talk to you."

"Put him on," said Maeve looking like she was fit to explode. She had got to her feet and was pacing a little, to calm herself down. However, Maxie's outstretched legs were blocking her way, which was another example of how she was blocked in by men's stupidity in every move she made.

"Move! You big heifer," she shrieked at Maxie, causing him to recoil his outstretched legs in shock and response to her outburst.

"I am sorry to interrupt you in whatever you are doing, Mrs. Kavanagh, but I would like to speak to my mother now," said Li Han.

"Yeah you would, would you, well she isn't here presently. My colleague has her safely stashed away."

"Okay, well you have to get hold of her and phone me back at this number. We will stay here waiting for your call."

"It will take an hour at least, maybe two, but I will phone you then, and we can negotiate her handover."

"Nothing to negotiate, Mrs. Kavanagh. You get your husband back, and I get my mother, both unharmed."

"We will talk about this later," she said curtailing the call, hanging up abruptly, in order to maintain the upper hand in the negotiations, as well as in pure frustration.

The phone started ringing almost immediately upon her hanging up. Maeve let it ring for a good while because she wanted Li to get as angry and frustrated as she was. She picked up on the fifth ring, but it wasn't him calling again. It was Brady.

"Hello! Would this be a chucky bitch that goes by the name of Maeve?"

"Who the hell are you, and what the fuck do you want?" she replied in her most menacing tone.

"Language! Woman. You are talking to a representative of the Irish National Liberation Army; and I am also Aden's new best friend.

"Am I meant to be shocked Bogman? I already know you have got him, and I am warning you to release him before I am forced to come looking for you."

"Ooh; Am I meant to be scared Chucky tits?"

"You should be because I know where you are, and I know who you are with. I will get Belfast command to find out your name and any family you have outside of Derry will be taken."

"You are just a wee bitch who's bluffing."

"I know you are phoning from Ballintrillick right now."

The line went dead, which surprised Maeve, but gave her some measure of satisfaction too.

The phone started ringing again, and Maeve counted to five again, although she was hedging her bets as to who was calling her now.

"It's me you chucky bitch. I got cut off."

"Yeah, sure you did," said Maeve showing mirth in her voice.

"So you know where I am calling from, probably a lucky guess. What is more important is that I know all about your kidnapping plan and we want the Vietnamese man's mother from you."

"And why exactly am I supposed to give her to you?"

"To get your man back, of course."

"Nah, I think I will pass on that."

"You are bluffing, and you don't fool me."

"Whatever, but you will regret crossing me, I promise you," threatened Maeve, in probably the most genuine statement she had made today.

"Look we are not enemies of each other. Perhaps we got off on the wrong foot. What I am trying to say here, is that your mission in Sligo is not sanctioned. We know because we checked, but ours is. Therefore, if you drive on out here, seeing as you know where I am, I will give you Aden back, and you can hand over the old woman to a fully sanctioned republican active service unit. No need for us to fall out, and if this comes up trumps, I will personally sort you guys out a small cut of the proceeds."

"I am not heading over your way Bogman. I am far too busy. If you want the old lady, you best come over here and collect her. Aden knows where I am. Tell him I said so."

"You tell him."

"Hello Maeve, I am really sorry about all this. Do you really want me to tell them where you are?"

"Yes, Aden, I want you to tell them. When they return you here, I will negotiate with them about the exchange."

This time, it was Maeve who was the one to be cut off.

ANGUS CACTUS

The room had gone very quiet, and Maeve remained pensive, playing out a scenario in her head, but Enya soon disturbed her train of thought.

"You're going to give them Huong Han," said Enya, her voice excitably upset. "You told Shane that she wouldn't be harmed."

Maxie had a point to make as well. "If that was the INLA you were talking to, then I am as good as dead when they get here."

Maeve stood up, and demonstrating that she was still listening to them, she walked across the kitchen and started rooting around in one of the drawers.

"You told me that you were reuniting her with her son," said Enya.

"You need to let me go now, or I am dead," said Maxie.

She had found what she was looking for. It was a roll of parcel tape, and she was peeling back the corners as she walked back over to them. Enya guessed first, "Oh no you better not be thinking of…" Her impassioned plea was terminated abruptly by a liberal application of tape over her mouth.

Maxie was next, and he swung his head from side to side in a bid to maintain a voice but, the tape soon sealed his lips too. Then Maeve used the rest of the tape to wind it several times around them at waist level managing to trap both of their free arms which were now firmly bound to the chairs and their bodies.

Now Maeve took the opportunity to address their fears.

"Firstly, I have no intention of letting them have Huong Han. I don't even have her, but I still wouldn't hand her over to those Bogmen. Secondly, I cannot free you yet, Maxie, but I promise you that they will not be allowed anywhere near you. Thirdly, I will be keeping my word and reuniting Huong Han with her son, if I ever get to see her. And lastly, you guys need to be quiet now, because I have an important phone call to make".

Then turning to Maxie, she said, "This number better be the right one, Sunshine, or I might just change my mind and let them have you for supper."

Maeve dialled the number written down in her pocket journal. It connected to the room above the public bar in the Ship Inn in Quay St, Sligo. Feargal picked up the phone.

"I have one of your men, but he might be dead," she said adopting her most heartless tone, as well as being economical with the truth.

"He better not be, or you have just signed your own death warrant."

"Ooh; should I be frightened?"

"We know where you are," said Feargal trying to sound threatening.

"Obviously; seeing as you sent this big heifer out to get me. But consider it this way, now I know where you guys live," replied Maeve in a much more practised sinister voice.

"Seriously have you killed Maxie Jinx?"

"Let me check…"

She stamped on his foot, and he moaned through his gag.

"Nah, I don't think so. Maybe you should just come and get him. We can do a swap."

"Maxie for who," asked Feargal.

"Who do you have?"

"I don't understand," and he really didn't.

"Then you better just come and get him now, before I change my mind."

When Maeve hung up on Feargal, she was smiling. A plan was coming together.

As far as their respective organisations were concerned, the ongoing truce between the Officials and the Provisionals was pretty fragile. She couldn't rely on the cooperation of OIRA, but she could yank their chain a little, and goad them into action. What she had gleaned from Maxie, was that there were three others in the unit, and she reckoned that they were probably tooled up and on their way to Raghly Point already. She had no intention of talking to them or even meeting them. Being aware of their notorious rivalry and mutual hatred, her intention was for them to take on the INLA when they got here.

Her actions were fast, efficient, and a mystery to her two guests. She had to quickly clean the house, which meant taking with her, or else destroying anything which could identify her, Kav, or Aden. She packed everything worth taking into a large carry-all which she loaded into the trunk of her car. Then lastly, she collected all the ammunition, explosive charges, and every gun including Maxie's and placed them into a smaller carry-all which she carried over her shoulder.

34 Mullaghmore (Sunday)

They were the only customers in the hotel's saloon bar, and even the barman had deserted the place whilst he went to help his brother with some lobster pots. He had set them up with a few drinks and told them to either tell any new customer that they were closed or if they were locals, to go ahead and serve themselves.

After the phone call to Maeve, Li returned to their table and to the double set of pints waiting to be drunk. He was concerned that his mother wasn't available for him to talk with her, but he accepted that Kav's wife would phone them as soon as she was delivered to Raghly Point by the man called Aden.

"Well I think that went well," said Kav genuinely pleased that Maeve was on board.

"Is your wife a farmer?" asked Li with a perplexed expression on his face.

"Ex-wife," he corrected. "No, she is not, why do you ask?"

"She seemed to be talking to a cow when I was on the phone to her."

"Well I don't know what was going on there, but there were definitely no cattle around when I was last in her company."

"I see."

"What do you see?" asked Kav, now more than a little intrigued with Li's obsession about animals and his wife.

"Nothing," said Li, inscrutably.

"So did she say how long it would be before she contacts us again," enquired Kav.

"No, but she said it probably would take a couple of hours."

"Great! That gives us time for another few rounds."

Li Han who had lived through three wars in Vietnam, stared at the big amiable man, now really questioning the professionalism of some of Ireland's paramilitaries.

35 Desperate Measures (Sunday)

Shane couldn't quite comprehend exactly what Enya was saying. He was hearing the words, but they were more akin to some April fools prank, and that type of humour was not part of his girlfriend's makeup.

She was giving him an address out at Raghly Point, not far from Eileen's pub which his sister and brother in law were so fond of frequenting. The whole area seemed backward and bizarre and that public house was a menagerie for sure.

Not that she wanted to meet him there, or any such mercy. No; she wanted him to go fetch Mrs. Han again and deliver her to the address which she had given him. She sounded a bit desperate and unable to answer any of his questions, and he had quite a few.

For instance, how did his peaceful day smoking hash and surveying the beautiful panorama from his viewpoint up in Diarmuid & Grainne's cave turn into a Vietnamese bike taxi service? Why was she not back at home where he'd left her? And who the hell lived out in Raghly Point?

He didn't like it, none of it, and without an explanation, he wasn't prepared to do what she'd asked. Besides, his mother and sister were short-staffed and under pressure and they needed him to stay and help out.

Then that woman came on the phone, her voice so chilling and threatening, and the simple mention of the Provisional IRA sent shivers up his spine. He was dead worried for his girlfriend, and completely unsure what he should do.

His mother was still smiling over at him, and he felt too guilty to even smile back, so he averted his eyes instead to watch the increasingly bizarre antics of Guinness the dog. The miniature Yorkie was dragging his favourite hand puppet backwards and forwards across the floor of the reception trying to satisfy some lust fuelled desire of his.

Can dogs have psychiatrists he wondered? Then upon seeing a big 'hench' Dublin detective crossing from the restaurant into the bar, the man inspired the inception of a cunning plan.

These plain clothes Guards were special detectives whose job was to bring paramilitaries such as the provisional IRA to justice. The recovery of the local guard who had been trussed up and left in the trunk of his patrol car had confirmed that there was an active paramilitary team working in the area, and this retinue of armed Special Branch had been dispatched from Dublin to hunt them down.

Of course, the answer was staring him in the face. What he had to do was fairly obvious, he only had to go and speak to a couple of them, and then steal one of their guns.

It took him less than 15 minutes to achieve his aim. It involved him working ten of those behind the bar, and then five to steal the gun. He seized the opportunity when fetching a tray of drinks over to where most of them were standing around playing six man pool.

The gun was still secured safely in an underarm shoulder holster. The fact that it wasn't presently under that particular guards armpit was a blessing indeed. It meant that Shane could simply throw a bar towel over, to conceal it, and walk away from the table where it had been hidden under a suit jacket.

No heed was paid to him and no one watched as he slipped into the men's room. In there, locked in a cubicle, he took it out and basked in the feeling of danger which felt like cold metal in his hand.

The holster had the name of Sergeant Foster on it, and Shane was pretty sure he could return it to him before he had realised it was gone, at least no later than that night.

He strapped it on and concealed it under his own leather jacket, and then went off to collect Mrs. Han. He had practically solved his problem already. Now that he was armed and dangerous, he could deal with the Provos on a level playing field; man to woman.

36 Special Detectives (Sunday)

It was the other squad sergeant Pat O'Riordan who informed him of its loss. O'Riordan had his back on this, but they wouldn't have much time. Sergeant Mike Foster reckoned they had no more than 5 to six hours to get the gun back, or he would have to report it missing. It didn't bear thinking about what would happen if it went down that path. He was a specialist detective sergeant in the Special Anti-Terrorist Task-Force, and the penalty for losing a weapon through neglect and carelessness would end his days in this job for sure.

Retrieval was the only option, and between them, they had already worked out who had taken the gun. It was outside of licensing hours on a Sunday afternoon, and the bar was closed to everyone except the detective task force. Unless another cop had taken it as some sick prank, it could only have been the barman. He even looked like he was trouble; the peroxide white hair, with the plaits at the back; the stoned look in his eyes; it must have been him for sure and now he had suspiciously left the building.

O'Riordan made some discreet enquiries about him with the other barman. He said that he was his brother in law but couldn't vouch for him at all, and told him all about the interest the local cops had in him. He also told him that he rode a Yamaha motorcycle.

Mike Foster got an even better lead from Margaret the proprietor. She said that he was probably in Grange at the house of his girlfriend and she even supplied her name and address. He hoped he would have his gun back within the hour, especially as this guy was so predictable. A complete stoner and head-banger by all accounts, but predictable nonetheless.

All they had to do now was visit the local Garda station, flash some credentials, and borrow a patrol car. Their search would begin at the home of the barman's girlfriend.

37 All in the Prep (Sunday)

The explosive charges were placed outside both exits, and a third set was placed by an old wooden dinghy down by the water's edge. Then Maeve ran across the small peninsula to reach the small hillock which guarded the narrow isthmus causeway.

Now the wig was covered up with a scarf, and she took out a tub of camouflage paste from her bag. That would be smeared across her face as soon as her baby was put together. This was her old but much prized Remington 700. Always cleaned and always dismantled, she carried it in its own canvas bag which she removed from the larger carry-all. Out came the Armalite 'widow-maker' too; probably her favourite gun, and a Glock pistol which she stuffed in the belt of her skirt.

The Armalite AR18 was already assembled, and the gas powered gun was fully loaded and put aside for potential combat. The Remington was a sniper's rifle, and this she began to quickly and carefully assemble, fixing on the telescopic sight last. She reckoned she could afford to fire two rounds before they got here in order to recalibrate the sight for accuracy. The sound of the weapon's gunshots would be somewhat masked by the sound of the Atlantic waves crashing on the rocks below.

An ammunition belt with the various pouches organised for different calibres was worn over her shoulder and across her body. Lastly, the camouflage cream was smeared across her face, neck and arms. Meticulously prepared, as usual, she was ready.

The Remington's tripod took the burden of the weight of the gun, allowing her to get low down and hidden behind the powerful telescopic sight of the gun. She valued the wide angled scope of vision which it allowed saving her from having to rely on binoculars. Instead, she used the guns scope to view the two alternative access roads that led to the causeway.

38 The Knife (Sunday)

To their credit, both Maxie and Enya had been perfectly behaved hostages. They had, for the most part, remained relaxed and composed throughout. This was down to their own good nature as well as that exhibited by their host.

However, now that she was gone, those gloves were off, albeit hidden under a roll of parcel tape and rope bindings. Now freedom was very much on their minds, although they had distinctly different ideas about how to achieve it.

It wasn't so much because they didn't know or trust each other. It was more likely a general psychological trait resultant from them being tied up on chairs back to back. They could only relate to and trust what was part of their own vision.

Enya saw a knife on a counter in front of her. Maxie saw a knife rack a few feet in front of him. To be fair, the tape wrapped around their mouths made it difficult to speak, but it didn't rule out basic communications.

"See'a knife," she spoke with difficulty, "try'to reach."

"See'it too," Maxie replied in kind.

Perhaps she should have spotted the clue in his answer instead. Enya attempted to pull their combined weight forward, using her strong legs to walk them forward, inch by inch. Maxie did the same, except he was trying to pull them in the opposite direction.

Neither of them realised. And so the knife which was becoming another target oriented goal for the young sportswoman remained always outside of her reach. Maxie, on the other hand, wasn't as driven as his new companion. After a few failed attempts, he had mostly given up the ghost, and only tried to pull towards the cutlery draw when inspired by Enya's two-word enigmatic calls to action. "Come'n," and, "do it," and "try!"

She could nearly reach it with her feet; just a little bit further, she thought. However, she couldn't drag his weight unless aided by Maxie's own efforts. She needed to wake up this sleeping giant with better inspiration.

"Nearly," was followed by "—at pie." She was referring to the rest of the quiche pie that the knife had been used to cut. Maxie's ear pricked up, and his stomach almost growled spontaneously. Pie; he couldn't see any pie beside the rack of knives. Was she making it up, or did she have better eyesight? Then it occurred to him, that her knife was not one of those he was facing.

Frustration hit him hard, and motivated by new resolve, as well as by his insatiable appetite, he got to his feet. Crouching at first, and leaning forward all the time to deftly balance Enya and her chair above him on his back, he turned around and walked towards the pie. Then bracing her weight above him, he squatted on bent knees and used the edge of the counter it was on to push the remnants of his gag aside and then lowered his face into the quiche. The filling was over in a second, but he only managed to eat some of the short crust pastry. It was enough, and feeling much better now, he picked up the knife with his mouth and turned around to sit down.

It was like a fairground ride for Enya. Firstly she was launched into orbit, her vision now limited to the ceiling only. Then he kept her in motion, up down and all around. She could hear the clatter of the chair legs, and of her feet knocking things around and busting the light bulb. She almost felt giddy when Maxie finally allowed her back down on the ground, now with just a blank wall in front of her to inspire her.

It didn't matter, because Maxie had dropped the knife into his lap close enough for his left hand to grasp it, and he was already busy cutting through the tape and the ropes.

39 Raghly Point (Sunday)

Both Ballintrillick and Sligo town were equal distance from Raghly, about 14 miles, and a twenty-minute drive, but just as Maeve had planned, the INLA arrived before OIRA, as she had spoken to them first.

A grey Land Rover approached along the road from Ballyconnell. Using her telescopic sight, she studied both men sitting in the front. She could have probably killed them both with a squeeze from her finger, but a promise was a promise. If Kav said it was alright to wound them, then wound them she would.

From her sniper position on the isthmus height, she had all round vision. The cottage bungalow was oriented in such a way that she had a commanding view of two of its sides, and a partial view to the rear. One of its side walls was completely obscured from her, and if necessary she would flush out anyone hiding there with her Armalite.

She had left her car parked out front on purpose, and despite it offering potential cover from her sniper attacks, it was all part of the honey trap. As callous as it seemed, the hostages inside were the other part.

*

The Land Rover pulled up on the offside of her Ford escort. The INLA were thinking about cover too, which meant that they too were suspicious. She watched two men get out, and when the taller guy opened the tailgate to take out two automatic rifles, she could see inside and clearly Aden wasn't there. Just as she had strategized, they had left him somewhere else as a bargaining chip. They had obviously done this before, but probably separately, because they didn't work well as a team despite their air of professionalism.

One man carried his Armalite slung over his shoulder relying more on his un-holstered pistol as he approached the front entrance. The other walked and carried it like a British soldier. He must have watched them doing so from an early age.

She could not allow them to reach the door, and following strategy, she flicked the remote switch on the explosive charge she'd placed under the wooden boat. It wasn't a lot of explosive, but the hollow of the boat would amplify the sound and provide a wooden sail to cast it aloft into the sky before it splintered into shrapnel. It was purely a distraction but it worked a treat.

The two men alert to danger felt obliged to investigate and jogged twenty paces apart in the direction of the detonation which was on the furthest reach of the three-acre sized Raghly Point.

This diversion provided sufficient time to allow OIRA to arrive in a newish looking brown Vauxhall Astra. The Officials had travelled a slightly shorter distance and arrived along the other road which travelled past Lissadell House, past-time home to Countess Markievicz and WB Yeats.

As they drove across the isthmus causeway, they were probably surprised by the two cars already parked in front of the house. Hopefully, they would be on guard as well. Maeve wanted them to hold the upper hand and was quite happy for them to do her dirty work and take out the INLA gunmen who she wasn't allowed to kill. However obscured from their view on this side of the house, those Bogmen were probably not yet even aware of the arrival of the Stickies.

Only two men got out of the Astra, and this was something unforeseen. Maeve was counting on all three of the Official's unit coming to free their colleague inside the house. She had made an oversight; she had assumed malicious intentions on their behalf, yet they had sent along a negotiation team. Two was not enough to corner those Bogmen, who judging from their movements and demeanour, she could tell were superior gunmen. She was going to have to help out and even the score a little.

Once again, the newcomers were drawn to the front entrance, like cats to a cardboard box. Nor did she have another diversion set, but that didn't matter because she had a fall-back to keep them out of her house. There were small detonator charges rigged up over both exits, and Maeve blew the one above the porch as the Stickies got closer. The blast was sufficient to knock them off their feet but not enough to cause injury or blow in the door. Regardless, it would make them assume that the house was booby-trapped, and deter them from entering.

As was her intention, the sound of the second charge would bring the two INLA gunmen running back to the house, but their approach was from the other side of the building. And as they got closer, Maeve fired a warning shot at the corner of the building, alerting the Officials, and preventing them from being surprised and overrun.

*

Nobody knew where the warning shot had come from, or who had fired it, but no one cared too much once the gunfight had begun in earnest.

Séamus and Mickey were only carrying pistols, so when they spotted the snakes, they took up positions behind the same corner which they had just seen hit with the high calibre bullet and used its cover for their advantage.

The two snakes dropped to the ground also seeking cover; anything that the long grass and rough terrain could provide.

*

Brady thought that he had walked into a trap set by the Provisionals, but gut instinct told McCreadie that it was Séamus Tooley on the other side of that building and that this was personal. He would let his young colleague suppress them with his Armalite whilst he crawled quickly out of range of their pistols and outside their scope of vision. His intention was to scout around the building and flank them from the other side.

*

The drone of a labouring four stroke engine caught Maeve's attention and diverted her gaze from the unfolding battle scene. It was coming from the direction of Sligo along the Lissadell road. She lifted her Remington to her shoulder to use its scope to view the motorcycle more closely.

It was a trials bike with a pillion passenger, no doubt sightseeing on this scenic route. They had better stay on the road because she couldn't let them turn off for Raghly Point. If necessary, she would shoot out their tyres.

Maeve now repositioned the sniper's rifle facing the oncoming bike, ready to take a shot if necessary. What she didn't expect was for the rider to swerve the bike to the left and take it off road before the turn off for the causeway.

The bike was now obscured from her vision hidden in the shadow of the very same height that she commanded. Frantically, she looked around, hearing the whine of its engine, but seeing nothing. Then the bike reappeared on the causeway below.

Maeve did not want civilians getting involved in this, and felt like she was already losing overall control of the situation. She was certainly losing her cool, and strangely feeling anxiety, which was a first for her in a combat situation.

It was a question of pulling it together and stopping the motorcycle before it entered the killing zone. There was no time for her to reposition the rifle, so she would take aim in the kneeling position. It was least accurate, but quickest for targeting. She only had vital seconds to make an accurate shot as the trials bike was fast moving. Those seconds were wasted through shock and confusion.

ANGUS CACTUS

There was an aged woman of oriental appearance hanging on for dear life behind the rider. Crap! This had to be Huong Han being delivered by Enya's boyfriend Shane. Uncharacteristically, she had completely overlooked his impending arrival.

Nor could she understand why, after all, she had invited him under duress. Despite that, she now looked at him down the scope of her rifle and was sorely tempted to shoot him in the head, but restraint took a hold and she fired off two rounds at his wheels.

*

Séamus Tooley couldn't believe his eyes when he saw Margaret's son arriving at the cottage in Raghly Point. It wasn't the open face helmet which identified him. It was that damn nuisance of a bike which many in Sligo had seen doing wheelies around town.

Mickey Donelon considered taking aim even though he knew who the rider was, but Séamus' hand restrained him for the sake of the proprietor of the Bective.

*

Shane knew that something was up as soon as he had crossed the causeway to the point. He wasn't the most observant person, and the men up in front brandishing pistols and Armalites had escaped his notice. Not so the sound of the bullet hitting his beloved XT250. He looked down and saw the damage to the crankcase. There was a small hole ripped in it, and then a shower of dirt was thrown up against it as a mini explosion on the ground in front.

It was only then that he realised that someone was shooting at him, and as he approached Séamus Tooley and Mickey Donelon, he wondered if it was them. They both had pistols in their hands and Donelon didn't like him for sure. The feeling was mutual, so Shane didn't feel like stopping to say hello but circled the building instead.

That was when he noticed the other gunman lying prone in the grass and taking aim. An Armalite AR-18 is an impressive looking gun but kind of scary when it is being pointed at you. Thankfully though it wasn't being fired at him, and he took the next corner as tightly as he could, causing the back wheel to skid out and kick up a lot of loose gravel as the bike dipped down low. Shane looked over his shoulder at Huong Han still tightly holding on to his waist and she was staring back at him with that face you often see on theme park rides. He assumed that she must be enjoying herself.

This place, Raghly Point was way too crazy for him, and it made him wish that he hadn't smoked that last splif. He knew what to do, though, the one thing he was still a master at was getting the hell out of Dodge.

Thus gripping the throttle, he was about to open it up, and speed away, when he saw his girlfriend. She was inside the cottage and furiously waving at him through the window. He had already gone way past her, but love wins every time, and so instead of racing in the direction of the causeway, he cornered two more times intent on making another circuit.

This took him past another man with a bushy moustache whom he had seen once before in the hotel, except on that occasion he hadn't been carrying an Armalite in one hand and a pistol in the other. The man stared back, showing surprise, but no intention of shooting at him.

Shane reached down with his left hand and tugged at Mrs. Han's arm pulling it even tighter around his waist. She understood his gesture and moved up tighter and closer to him. This allowed him more manoeuvrability as well as making space to carry Enya. This time, he skirted in between the two cars using them for cover and gave the one finger salute as he passed Donelon again.

This second circuit was more practised, and he pulled up sharply in front of the back entrance to what looked like the kitchen. The door burst open, and Enya fled out of it. She looked as spooked as Huong Han, but was extremely happy to see him. Using her athletic prowess, she hopped and leaped onto the back of the bike in one fluid and graceful motion, gripping hold of Huong Han's waist as the bike reared up on one wheel as Shane let loose the clutch on full throttle.

They didn't get far because he had to engage both brakes rather than run through the man in front of him pointing a pistol directly at his face. This guy with the moustache, had doubled back from where he had passed him earlier, and now, he didn't look shocked, but he certainly looked intent on shooting him, and Shane raised his hands in the air.

Regardless, a shot rang out, but it wasn't Shane who was hit. The man himself had been spun around by the impact of a bullet which had ripped into his right hand. The pistol now lay on the ground, and the poor man clutched at his hand trying to secure his thumb which was hanging by a strip of skin.

Shane had to choose between reaching for his own gun or attempting to ride away. He chose the path of the gun, very much inspired by the same man raising the Armalite with his left hand and awkwardly seeking the trigger as he aimed it. Billy the kid, he wasn't, and with his lack of dexterity, he allowed Shane to pull out the cop's gun from inside his biker's jacket and squeeze his trigger first.

The man dropped to his knees falling forward towards Shane. His

ANGUS CACTUS

Armalite was now on the ground and his whole left arm useless. He was bleeding profusely from his left shoulder, and Shane looked at the Guard's gun quizzically. He pointed it away from the man and squeezed the trigger again. Nothing happened because the safety was still on.

Passing the gun to Mrs. Han sitting behind him, he opened the throttle once more and sped away, feeling bewildered as to how he had possibly shot that man in the shoulder.

*

It had been a tough choice for Maeve. She needed the Vietnamese woman but had just aided her escape. Frankly, nothing would have made her happier, than letting the Bogman and the barman kill each other. However, Huong Han and Enya would have been hurt too, and so she had intervened. A shoulder shot was a wound he could recover from, and her pledge to her ex-husband still held strong.

She was very tempted to follow her shot with another more precise one to the barman, perhaps a shot to his knee. However, wracked by indecision, she failed to even hit the bike, missing twice again in her attempts to take out his tyres. She could only watch in frustrated resignation as she watched Huong Han ride away across the Raghly's causeway, sandwiched between Enya and her most annoying boyfriend.

*

Terry Brady was another person who would have gladly shot Shane, but his hands were tied with laying down suppressing fire against the two Stickies who were shooting back at him from behind the corner of the house.

He was hoping that McCreadie would outflank them and take out their rear, but now that he was shot, and the Vietnamese woman had been carried away, there was no real cause for him to remain. She was the key to a chest of buried gold, and he deserted his position in the ditch in the long grass to run around the other corner and reach the Land Rover before they could stop him.

He looked down at McCreadie with a blank expression as he ran past. There was no camaraderie for his fallen comrade, and by leaving him he ensured his own rearguard defence from the two Stickies that had broken cover and were running out to chase him.

*

In truth, Mickey Donelon was scared witless. He had never experienced combat before and never come up against 45mm high-velocity rounds, any of which were capable of taking off his head. For most of the gunfight, he was only firing his pistol in the general direction of the INLA gunman. Nor was he even sure exactly where that snake lay until he had got up and ran away.

Buoyed by victory over the enemy, Mickey fully intended to pursue him, except he preferred for Séamus to go on point. After all, the old warhorse had a lot more experience of these things. When he finally followed him, he came across his leader standing over the other INLA gunman who had already been shot and wounded. Séamus's pistol was lowered and he was talking to the fallen man. Mickey rushed to assist and was surprised and elated to see his big friend Maxie exiting the back door of the cottage.

"You two get after him," shouted Séamus, and then gesturing to the wounded snake, he added, "Me and him have private business to attend to."

The two friends did as they were ordered and, as they ran around the corner of the building, they were in time to see the other INLA man driving off and accelerating towards the narrow causeway. Mickey could swear that he saw a distant muzzle flash from the height beside the isthmus, and the following gunshot was distinct although distant too.

"I think there is a sniper up there," said Mickey with anxiety and alarm.

"Where the hell is my car," said Maxie with even greater anxiety."

His car was gone, so Séamus's Astra would have to do, and there was no dispute about who was driving it.

*

The several hits on his vehicle did not kill him or stop the robust Land Rover, though she had hit the fuel tank, as evidenced by the trail of petrol left behind. Then she was wrong-footed by the late exit of Mickey & Maxie. Her attention having been distracted by the Stickie who appeared intent on shooting the Bogman at point blank range. At first, they appeared to be just talking, but now he had raised his pistol and was aiming it at the other man's head.

Maeve had to make a call. Truthfully, she wouldn't have been at all bothered, except for her so far successful, zero kills' policy. But if she wasn't allowed to kill, she wasn't going to let someone else mess up her perfect zero count. Knowing her ex-husband's mindset, she reckoned that he would attribute any fatality here today to her anyway. Therefore, she lined him up in her sights and shot him in his right shoulder, which had the effect of knocking the gun right out of his hand.

ANGUS CACTUS

The shot was a little messy; a little too close to his neck and the man seemed poorly as a result. He had slumped to the ground and he was having difficulty propping himself up on his other elbow.

In the melee, she had let the brown Astra escape without incident. She didn't even bother to shoot, being pragmatic about her chances of hitting them. Besides, she really had no beef with them. Instead, she shouldered her sniper rifle, and carry-all, and headed down to the house on foot with her Armalite and a pistol drawn. Then loading it in her car, she sped away after them in pursuit.

As she navigated the thin causeway, she heard the sound of dual and simultaneous gunfire from behind. It looked like those two enemies had still managed to shoot each other. Making the sign of the cross, she murmured, "Rest in Peace," but at the same time thinking, 'Screw this zero kills policy.'

She headed in the direction of Eileen's country pub and was grateful that fresh petrol stains glistened in the sun telling her which road to take. At the main Bundoran to Sligo road, she followed her intuition and also some trials bike tyre markings which she noticed cutting each and every corner.

These told her that they were not Sligo bound but heading towards Grange. However, before she got there, she took the right turn off in the direction of Ballintrillick. Call it woman's intuition.

40   Geniff Horseshoe   (Sunday)

A Yamaha XT250 is a capable motorcycle, on or off the road, but it is master of neither stratum. When carrying a twenty-year-old couple with a 70-year-old Vietnamese woman sandwiched between them, there were some performance issues.

Cornering was Shane's only advantage over the faster more powerful Land Rover which was in close pursuit. However the added weight, plus Huong Han's inability to lean in the right direction, meant that he nearly lost it a few times going around the bends.

Taking the first exit into the Gleniff horseshoe pass, he hoped that the narrow twisting road which looped around the interior would be to his advantage. He certainly couldn't go off road carrying all this weight, and besides if he did, he reckoned the Land Rover would have more prowess judging by the mud splatters that coated it.

The lead that he had started out with, was slowly being eroded by his pursuer who was persistent and driving ruthlessly enough to close the gap. Huong Han still held the Garda issued firearm and Shane hoped that she knew how to operate the thing, because by the time they had coasted past Diarmuid and Grainne's cave, the mean looking gunman was trying to ram his motorcycle. Then a small mercy was granted from above, for the Land Rover started to slow down. Its engine was dying, and it was coasting to a stop.

Shane pulled up about four hundred yards ahead, using a braking sideways skid to enable all three of them to look back and revel in the downfall of their enemy. All three of them gave each other high five slaps as they heard the gunman trying unsuccessfully to turn over the engine. It caught every time, but petered out; his engine wasn't flooded, it was out of petrol.

"So long sucker," said Shane before using the kick start to fire up his engine. However, there was no reassuring purr from it, just a terrible ratchety sound coming from the crankcase. Shane recalled the earlier bullet that it had taken, and his fingers now explored the damage, and it was nearly bone dry. All the oil had slowly leaked out, the engine had seized, and there was nothing that would make this bike go.

At first, he tried to roll the bike along while holding the clutch in. It was vain attempt to fool his pursuer that all was fine, but the lone INLA gunman exited the car and watched their efforts with interest. He wasn't stupid, or easily fooled, and taking his Armalite along with him, he left his vehicle behind and continued his pursuit on foot.

"Everyone get off," yelled Shane, who after taking the gun off Huong Han, then pushed the bike into a roadside ditch in a pathetic attempt to conceal it. "Hurry, you two go ahead. I will catch you up."

He was genuinely worried about leaving his bike, and he was also concerned for Huong Han. She was 70 and had had an exhausting day. Being pursued by a homicidal paramilitary must be a very traumatic experience for someone who couldn't properly communicate with anyone but her son. It angered Shane just thinking about it, and he was tempted to pull out the gun and have another attempt at using it. He wasn't that daft though and so disregarding this temporary lapse of reality, he decided to run as fast as he could to catch up with Enya and Mrs. Han. He was glad he chose that path because Enya had some good news.

"There is a place up here where they will hide us, and where he will never find us. I doubt they will even let him search. We can reach it through the woods if we take this forestry path coming up."

"Whose place?" enquired Shane.

"The Screamers."

"Ah Jeez, I am not sure about that."

"Don't be stupid Shane, or judgemental. I know one of them. We will be safe there."

Amelia had pointed out the pathway to her, but it wasn't clearly marked, or obvious. The pathway was through a dark patch of evergreen pine forest that looked like large Christmas trees. If this was the only entrance, then they really needed to build a service road, or at least cut back the foliage.

After feeling like they were totally lost, a distant large clearing became evident and as they approached, it surprised them all by its complexity and industry. There was a large number of people milling about or working. A large two storey house and four outhouses were being restored as evidenced by the new roofing material and rendered block work. There were also four large old caravans which had obviously found another route in here sometime in the past.

A barn was also in the process of being constructed, and there were fenced off enclosures for roosters and hens. There were also multiple crop farming strips more like an allotment than a farm. All of these were being tended by men, wearing simple brown cassocks that looked hand woven. To all intent and purpose, this appeared like some sort of medieval monastery, except for one thing, and that was the few women who were all wearing white linen and walking amongst the men as overseers. The men folk seemed to be willingly subjugated although some of the women did carry crops or tawses in their hands.

"Where do we go?" asked Shane.

"Up to the big house, I assume."

As the three of them walked an indirect path that skirted around the allotments and past the hen enclosures, they drew a lot of attention from those working nearby. The men bowed their heads respectfully as Enya and Mrs. Han walked past but ignored Shane. The women overseers nodded respectfully too, but more in welcoming acknowledgement. However, this welcome did not extend to Shane who was receiving a lot of disdainful stares as if he was breaking some protocol by being there. It was a very unsettling experience which was making him feel very self-conscious.

No one had yet come over to welcome or even challenge them. Therefore, the house seemed the obvious place for them to introduce themselves. Shane and Enya walked in through the open door first, but an outstretched arm from a man servant barred Shane from entering the main hallway and reception area. He was an older man in his forties wearing what looked like some theatrical cast off made for a roman slave. Shane took exception with his rude gesture and squared up to him, but the man didn't flinch nor lower his arm which formed a barrier barring Shane's entry.

"You have picked the wrong day to pick a fight with me," said Shane, but the man did not reply, nor lower his arm.

"He won't speak to you. He doesn't have permission to, but he will prevent you from entering this sanctuary. Please do not test him." A woman's voice said tersely to Shane. She had just entered the main hallway from a side room. Then turning to address both Huong and Enya, she gave a broad smile and said, "Welcome to the sanctuary of the Sisters of Sardonis. Would you like an audience with our Sister-Superior?"

"I really wanted to see Amelia, if that is at all possible?" replied Enya.

"But of course, but I would advise an audience first because our leader likes to be acquainted with the sanctuaries guests first. I will take you to both of them, but please may I ask that you prepare your male first."

"Prepare him; how in what way?" asked Enya

"The Sister-Superior will wish to inspect him too. He must comply with her wishes if he is to remain within the bounds of our sanctuary."

"I am here you know, said Shane disquietened by being openly discussed. "I can hear you and answer for myself."

"For a start, can you ensure he remains silent unless instructed to talk, and he will need to wait outside on the porch, and he must be on his knees before and during the Sister-Superior's inspection."

"Can you do this Shane, for us?" asked Enya.

"No, not really. I think we should go. We can manage without their help."

"Are you really so stupidly stubborn and proud, Shane. That guy is a terrorist; do you really think he has given up already. He will likely kill you if you leave here now. Just let me go and speak with this Sister-Superior and with Amelia, and I will ask them for temporary sanctuary."

Shane listened to Enya taking charge of the situation. She had hit the nail on the head. He was proud, but he was also no sap and definitely not someone's whipping boy. He crossed his arms and stood his ground.

"Shane!" said Enya. "Just do as I ask for once in your life." She stood facing him with her arms folded as well, looking just as sullen and just as stubborn to get her way. Huong Han stood beside her mirroring her posture and expression, seemingly in total support.

"Oh alright then." He said as he withdrew back onto the porch and got down on his knees. He glared back at all of them with defiant eyes and a pissed off expression.

"Please tell your male that he must look down at the floor when in the presence of the Sister-Superior or any sister here."

"Shane!"

"I heard, you don't need to relay her every word," he said complying with her instructions.

He waited for a good while, alone and embarrassed at his predicament. Therefore, he felt quite relieved when the Sister-Superior finally came outside to look at him. He smiled at her when he realised that she was the Lady that had stayed in the Bective Hotel over the previous fortnight. Then remembering what he was told, he looked down.

"The Goddess obliges me to offer sanctuary to any woman in distress, but a man may only enter her kingdom on his knees, and be obedient and prepared to serve. As you are not a slave or servant to these two women you accompany, they cannot negotiate on your behalf, unless you relinquish your authority to one of them. Are you willing to let Enya speak for you and abide by her decisions? You may answer yes or no."

"Yes, but——"

"Good," said the woman abruptly turning and walking away. He stayed where he was and maintained his kneeling posture although he couldn't quite fathom out why, except that he didn't want to create any more waves for the present.

Enya returned in a short while.

"As much as I like you on your knees before me, you can get up now."

Shane stood up flinching as the blood returned to his legs. "Well?" he said.

"They are preparing a guest room for me and Huong Han. We can stay as long as we like."

"What about me?"

"She said that you can stay in the stable with the horses, or the hen house, take your pick."

"Oh that's nice," said Shane sarcastically. "I think I will go with the horses; they make for better company."

"Come on then, I will walk with you there," she said taking him by the hand and heading in the direction of one of the larger out-houses.

"That is very generous of you, and I am sorry that I am taking you away from your servants and your life of unadulterated luxury," he said taking the mickey.

They had reached the makeshift stables which appeared to be home to only two horses. Shane opened the half wooden door and looked around briefly taking in the ambiance of his first impression.

"At least it's better than the Bective's room no.5."

Enya laughed aloud at his joke. They had used that room to clandestinely sleep with each other for the first time. It was a windowless box room and a tip, which was only rented out for the night to the odd inebriated guest.

"Looks like it is open plan in here for me and the horses," he added with a little concern showing in his voice as he eyed up the size of the horses he had to share with.

"I am going to stay with you silly," said Enya.

"But I thought you had a room being prepared for you?"

"You are my boyfriend, Shane. We stick together, and besides, I am proud of what you did today."

"Which part?"

"All of it stupid. You were reliable, resourceful, and brave."

Shane grinned very much appreciating her acknowledgement.

"I also asked them to go and rescue your motorcycle from the ditch. Amelia is taking out a work crew to retrieve it. They will drag it back here if necessary, and they have a man who was a trained mechanic. He has been instructed to work on it".

"Ah thanks Enya. That was really thoughtful. I appreciate it."

"It's alright Shane. I only negotiated this, but you are going to have to make it up to them."

"What exactly does that mean?"

"Nothing too difficult. Don't worry about it. I will tell you later."

"I don't like being in people's debt."

"Well, you did authorise me to negotiate on your behalf."

"I guess. So how is your friend?"

"Oh she is great, I am sure you two will hit it off. She is really interesting and funny. She is checking in on us after she has retrieved your bike."

"Well, I hope she does. I want to thank her personally."

"I am pretty certain you two will get the opportunity later," said Enya who was smiling as if party to some private joke.

41 The Refuge (Sunday)

They weren't lost, far from it, they were gaining on the Land Rover which they had just seen take the first exit onto the Gleniff horseshoe scenic route. Their intention was to take the 2nd exit and intercept him somewhere in the middle.

Things changed dramatically when Maxie recognised his beloved car parked up on the forecourt of the post office at Ballintrillick. He screeched to a halt beside it and climbed out of the driver's seat immediately.

"I'm driving my own," he shouted back at Mickey. "You go ahead and take the 2nd. I will race down the 1st, and we will catch him in a pincer movement."

"What's that?" said Mickey who was awkwardly clambering over the Astra's gear shift.

"I dunno, something Séamus said before about blocking both exits."

"Right so," said Mickey before accelerating away and disappearing down the second exit which was only about two hundred yards away.

Meanwhile, Maxie was checking his US paratrooper style jacket, patting down all pockets but with disappointing results. He had forgotten that Maeve had taken his gun, and in the excitement, he hadn't asked Mickey for his spare. What he did find, however, was the 2nd set of keys which he always carried. His car was the only thing he couldn't afford to lose.

He didn't even bother to check in with the shop. Instead choosing to climb into his bespoke bucket seat and put the keys in the ignition. Before he turned them, though, there was a sharp tap on his driver's side window. He turned around to find himself looking at two plain clothes officers from Dublin Gardai's Special Detective Unit; at least that is what their warrants pressed against his window said.

Maxie had a strong sense of frustration at having to step out of the car which he had only just recovered. He was annoyed with these Guards, annoyed at himself, and annoyed with Maeve for having left it here. He was hungry and grumpy and annoyed even at the sound of the tyres skidding from a car turning behind him.

The cops stared at it, their interest picqued, but Maxie was forlorn with his head down, which is why he missed Maeve driving like the clappers as she took the first exit thirty yards further back.

*

ANGUS CACTUS

She pulled up cautiously behind the abandoned Land Rover and approached with her Glock in hand. He appeared to be long gone, but she scanned all around seeking any clues to his whereabouts. They were chasing after the same Vietnamese woman, and she preferred to be on his tail rather than vice versa. Maeve was getting back into her car, intending to search further along this route when she saw the first monk.

There were four of them all together as well as a woman, a young woman who appeared to be giving them commands. That was very strange, thought Maeve, and she watched from afar trying to ascertain what they were doing. They were lifting something heavy out of a ditch, and she squinted into the distance trying to identify what it was until the features of Shane's trials bike became clearer and recognition took a hold. If his bike was there and the Bogman's car was here, then the barman and the Vietnamese woman couldn't be that far away. After all, she was at least 70 and probably not fit for walking too great a distance.

Also, these guys weren't stealing the bike; they looked like they were recovering it. They were carrying it, and even though there were four of them, it looked like hard work. Maeve realised that she needed to follow them, because wherever they were taking that bike, she was likely to find Enya's boyfriend, and Huong Han. However, firstly she had to hide her car somewhere; and then she could follow on foot.

There was a narrow slip road nearby which meandered up the side of the sloping mountainside. It didn't appear to head anywhere but more likely provided access to some old quarry. Maeve parked it behind the first turn, which effectively hid it from the main road, then taking her Glock in hand again, she set off in pursuit.

*

Standing two abreast either side of it, the men carried the motorcycle along an overgrown trail through the dense woods. The sunshine could not penetrate the tree canopy of thick pine, which made the pathway all the less obvious to Maeve who followed at a respectable distance.

She always found trees and woodland spooky, probably a legacy from reading Hansel & Gretel as a child. Even now, she felt convinced that she was being watched and followed, despite the fact that she was doing the following.

The men carried the bike into a very large clearing in the forest, some kind of rural settlement with an archaic appearance. There were many more monks working on what appeared to be a small subsistence farm, and there were women here too. They were wearing different variations of hand-made white linen dresses. It seemed impractical dress wear for working outside in a field at first, but then it became apparent that the women did not work. They just supervised the efforts of the men who seemed deferential and quick to pander to the needs of their overseers.

It seemed a bizarre arrangement to Maeve who decided as a result not to follow those monks carrying the motorcycle into this community. Instead, she followed a path around the edge of the large clearing keeping an eye on the bike and seeing where it ended up.

It was taken to one of the smaller outhouses on the periphery of the commune. It was a lot closer to the forest boundary on the other side of the enclosure and exactly where Maeve now stood.

She still had on her camouflage paint, and so made a dash for the same building trying to employ as much stealth as possible. Surprise was always the most effective policy, except, there was no one to surprise in this outhouse, apart from some monk who was closely examining the motorcycle for damage.

Maeve was about to enter and question him when she saw Shane walking over. He looked very pleased to see his bike and started talking animatedly to the monk who seemed more inclined to ignore him. Shane appeared a little deflated from his experience because he now walked back to the larger outhouse close by without the same swagger in his step.

Maeve followed quickly, closing the gap between them with fast nimble steps. By the time he had re-entered the stable, she had entered with him and was standing behind him and holding her gun to his head.

She scanned her new environment quickly, taking in the behaviour of the horses and was satisfied that they were no potential threat.

"Hello again Enya," she said. "I finally got to meet your boyfriend," she said tapping the gun on his head. "So where is the Vietnamese woman right now?"

There was no reply from either of them, and this wasn't a symptom of shock, more pure reluctance to give her up.

"I get it, you are protecting her, but I told you both before, I bear her no malice, and she is in no danger from me. I just want to get her back to her son, so that I can collect my own husband in return."

"I thought he was your ex-husband," said Enya trying to catch her out.

"That's correct, my ex-husband; just a slip of the tongue."

"A Freudian slip," said Shane.

"A What? You keep quiet sunshine," she said, tapping the gun on his head again.

"Why does everyone keep telling me to shut up in this place."

"Because you talk too much, and don't listen. Remember what I just told you, so, 'Suigh síos, stoptar suas agus a bheith ciúin," she said, reiterating her previous point in Irish Gaelic.

"Save it for Mrs. Han, I don't speak Chinese."

Maeve tapped him again and spoke directly to him with a mixture of frustration and aggression, with her face inches from his. "What is your problem, Shane? You always seem to be in the middle of every cock up around here. I wish Kav had never listened to your gossip about Vietnamese gold in the first place. Do you know how many times I have resisted the urge to shoot you today? Perhaps it is better you don't. You are only walking around on two perfectly good knees because I like your girlfriend and because of a promise I made to my husband."

"Wow, you really need to chill out," said Shane being contrary, and feeling in an argumentative mood, he added, "Perhaps you should get some anger management."

Maeve was about to hit his head for the fourth time but chose to look at Enya instead, imploring her to intervene.

"Shut up Shane. She is right. You can be a walking disaster zone sometimes." Then turning to address Maeve, she added "Can I trust you not to kneecap him if I go and get Huong Han and bring her here. We should let her decide."

It wasn't long before Enya returned with Huong Han. She re-entered the stables to find two long faces staring at her, and neither of those belonged to the horses. Something had obviously happened in her absence, and now there was a strained atmosphere.

"What's wrong with you two?" she asked, but stony silence ensued. However, the two of them were trying to tell her something with their eyes. She cottoned on, too late, as Terry Brady closed the stable door after Huong and stood facing his captive audience with Maeve's Glock in one hand, and his own Beretta in the other.

"Now that I have this Vietnamese lady, perhaps you can be so kind to fill me in with the details of the ransom drop. Where is her son for a start?"

Brady was met with four determined expressions of reticence.

"I will shoot each and every one of you, and trust me, it will hurt," he said deliberately grimacing to accentuate his point. "So, one of you better start talking to me, because I haven't got all day."

As if to bring home the reality to them, he pointed his own pistol at each person one at a time, lingering over Maeve, whom he looked like he was contemplating shooting anyway. But in return, he still received three defiant stares and a confused look from Huong Han.

"You obviously are not taking me seriously; let me see what I can do about …"

Thwack!

The hit from the shovel connected solidly with the back of his head. His lights were out before he hit the ground, and his fall was not dignified. Maeve leaned forward attempting to collect both the guns but she backed away when threatened by Amelia still brandishing the long handled shovel. One of her retainers bent down to pick up both guns instead, and her other two lackeys each grabbed hold of one of Brady's legs.

Amelia gave them their instructions. "Take him to the punishment compound, and make sure Sister Agatha is informed. She will know what to do with him." Then turning to her lackey holding both weapons, she said. "You follow them and hit him on the head with one of those if he comes around. You can hand those over to Sister Agatha as well."

"Good shot," said Enya to her friend. "Is he going to be alright? He has got some funny looking ooze on the back of his head."

"Oh that is just muck from the shit shovel," said Amelia. "We will make sure he gets first aid, but Sister-Superior will then decide what to do with him."

"Can I have my gun back," Maeve asked Amelia politely.

"Later, when my friend's business is concluded." Enya had explained the whole escapade to her earlier in the main house. Now she had Enya's back and intended to stay with her until the whole thing was concluded.

Amelia turned to talk to Shane, "I am afraid our mechanic says your bike won't be ready until tomorrow. He has to weld the crankcase or something like that. Will you come and collect it tomorrow."

Shane nodded and said thank you. Amelia did seem to treat him a little more respectfully than the others that lived here, but at the same time, she spoke to him matter of factly, almost curtly, and without the same warmth of tone which she reserved for Enya. It was a start, though, and Shane revised his previous opinion of her.

"I need to get to a phone and call Li Han," pointed out Maeve. "Is there a phone here?"

"No, we have nothing electrical at all," replied Amelia.

"This place is weird," Maeve said as much to herself rather than for the benefit of others.

"There is a telephone box at the post office in Ballintrillick," said Enya trying to be helpful. "It is not far from here, we can walk there."

"I would rather head back and collect my car first," said Maeve. "I am going to need transport to Streedagh, wherever that is."

"WE! are going to need transport to Streedagh," corrected Amelia.

"If you must, but we need to set off now. My car is parked up on the slip road to the quarry."

42 Maxie (Sunday)

Despite his towering presence over the two guards, it was Maxie who was feeling decidedly nervous.

"Are you the owner of this car?" asked detective sergeant O'Riordan.

"Of course," replied Maxie.

"It was driven earlier by a woman with dark hair who was looking for a young man on a Yamaha motorcycle."

"No she was looking for the China-woman," said Maxie correcting his statement.

"So you do know her?"

"Of course, I know both of them."

"Do you know the rider of the Yamaha motorcycle?"

"You mean that fella Shane from the Bective?"

"That's the one," said Sergeant Foster with unabashed enthusiasm.

"So where are they now?" said O'Riordan continuing his line of questioning.

This was a loaded question. If Maxie gave them his best guess, it would invariably lead them into a confrontation involving his best friend. However, if he was to supply another address, he wouldn't just lead them away from Mickey who was carrying a gun, but hopefully, these two cops might be able to get Séamus some urgent medical attention, and screw him over at the same time.

"I think they might be at Raghly Point. If you follow me, I will take you there."

"Not on your nelly, you are coming with us sunshine. When we find them, we will drop you back here."

The Garda patrol car drove off at high speed with Maxie sitting uncomfortably in the back. He wasn't sure whether he was possibly incriminating himself by leading them to the scene of the gunfight, and he also wondered why everyone was so intent on chasing the Bective's barman.

"So what's he done, this barman fella?"

"Best for you, if you mind your own business big man," said O'Riordan from the front passenger seat.

But Maxie couldn't do that. He was far too engrossed at watching the driver who was hurtling around this route with the precision of a rally driver.

"Where did you learn to drive like that?" he asked.

"From the school of chasing fellas like you," was Sergeant Foster's dour reply.

43 Gun (Sunday)

The route back to Maeve's car was quick and uneventful. Amelia had led them along a forest track that joined the Gleniff road a short distance from the quarry.

It was a tight squeeze to fit everybody in the car but Huong Han sat up front and Enya in the middle seat behind, with her friend on one side, and her boyfriend on the other.

Shane who was leaning forward found it difficult to sit back on account of the lack of room. He complained incessantly.

"Well take your jacket off for a start," said Enya mothering him.

Shane did as she said, and as he unzipped his thick biker jacket to the waist, there was a resounding thud on the floor of the car.

"What was that?" asked Maeve turning around with alarm.

"It's another gun," said Amelia with disdain.

"Hand it here," said Maeve, more as a command than a request.

"No, it is my insurance," said Shane quickly picking it up and protectively clutching it in his lap. His actions were noticeably childish as if he was expecting mummy to slap him and take it off him.

"Where did you get it?" Maeve's tone was no less severe or interrogative.

"From one of the Guards at the hotel," he said sheepishly.

"They don't have guns," said Maeve correcting him.

"He was a Special Branch officer from Dublin."

You could have heard a pin drop following Shane's last statement.

"Please tell me you haven't fired it."

"No; I couldn't get it to work."

Maeve now grabbed it from him and started wiping it furiously with a handkerchief.

"That was because the safety was on."

"What's that?"

Maeve shook her head slowly in despair. "I think you should leave guns well alone until a responsible adult is about."

"You're not funny," said Shane glaring at the more experienced woman.

"And you're an idiot."

"Ah come on Maeve, that's a bit harsh," said Enya in his defence.

TO HELL OR SLIGO

"Enya, do you realise how serious the Guards take losing a weapon. They are probably hunting high and low for it. Any of us could do time just for handling it. Can you imagine how serious this could get if they thought for one moment that a member of the provisional IRA had hold of it."

"Well then give it back to me then," said Shane still smarting from her previous insults.

Maeve glared at him, and her expression did all the talking. Shane looked away unable to return her stare.

"First things first, we need to dump this gun quickly," and without seeking any consensus, she turned the ignition and reversed at speed for 50 yards down the narrow access road and back on to the Gleniff road. Then she put it in first and drove the hundred yards to where Brady's Land Rover was still broken down in the middle of the road.

She gave the gun another really good wipe before placing it under the driver's seat. Maeve looked less anxious as she drove away and carried on in the same direction heading for the 2nd exit to the Gleniff loop and turned in the direction of the post office at Ballintrillick.

It was only maybe two hundred yards from the Gleniff road exit, but she was thwarted by a large unruly flock of sheep that was being driven down the road in front of her, and past the post office. She tried blowing the horn, but this only served to scatter the sheep at the rear and further impede her progress. So in utter frustration, she took a handful of change from the well in her driver side door and jogged past the sheep to reach the call box.

She was panting with exertion by the time she dialled the number Li Han had given her and had difficulty hearing him initially because of the bleating of the ewes and rams that were being herded and corralled by the shepherd and his dogs.

44 Reunion (Sunday)

When Maeve phoned up from the Ballintrillick call box, there was the distinct sound of sheep and dogs in background. If it wasn't for the good news she gave him about his mother, he might have developed real concerns about the antics of this woman. Li looked over at his new friend who was standing behind the bar and pulling another four pints of Guinness.

They had talked a lot about Belfast and Vietnam, and both appreciated the other man's view, which was that you had to grow up there, to fully appreciate the respective trials that came along with daily life.

One thing, Li did realise was that Kav was completely in the dark concerning his wife's bestial liaisons with various animals. Sure he suspected that there was something going on between her and the neighbour's dog, but he had no idea about the heifers and the cows, the sheep, and of course the animal farm pornography. He felt sorry for the man but realised that with a western perversion this complex, he was probably better off not knowing.

By the time that the others had arrived at the bar, Michael Kavanagh, and Li Han appeared to all intent to be best buddies with each other. This certainly was a difficult concept for everyone present who had been in gunfights and car chases on their respective behalf. Regardless, those feelings were put aside for later explanation.

Right now the business of the day was reunion, and whilst Li ran over to embrace his mother, Kav let emotion and Guinness override his usual reserve where Maeve was concerned, and he literally swept her off her feet and held her in an even tighter embrace.

Maeve's cold heart had just turned on its central heating, and she returned her ex-husband's kiss with some passion, as she held on to his big head with her hands. It was moving to watch both pairings, and it was also contagious, so Shane and Enya embraced as well. Meanwhile, Amelia looked slightly lost and uncharacteristically somewhat intimidated and shy.

Before they left, everyone stayed for a drink, and Shane helped Kav fill the order behind the bar.

"So where's the barman?" asked Shane.

"He's taken the afternoon off, were good for it, just so long that we stay off the shorts, and put the money in that jar. I suppose he will add it to the till later."

"That looks like his tips jar to me. Anyway, I am fine with that arrangement."

45   Mickey   (Sunday)

After taking the second exit into the Gleniff pass, Mickey was less than a mile in when he caught his first glimpse of the men wearing monk's habits. They were lifting what looked like a motorbike, out of a ditch. He recognised it as Shane's bike and knew that the INLA snake must have been in pursuit.

Therefore, he parked up on the side of the road, got out, and went to find a closer vantage spot in the woods, from where he could spy on them. It was a good judgement on his behalf, because not only did the men carry the bike in his direction, but a woman he had not seen before and who was carrying a gun in her hand, was discreetly following after them.

Mickey reckoned that she had been the mystery sniper firing from the grassy knoll at Raghly Point. She was the person of interest here, so he decided to follow her. He didn't want to get in a gunfight with her so he made sure to follow at the furthest distance possible.

This turned out to be his second incident of good judgement because the intervening gap between himself and the woman became occupied by the very man he was looking for. It was that INLA snake who had been shooting at him earlier on, and he was still carrying his Armalite.

Mickey had a new target to follow, and this guy was not following the others directly. He obviously had a strategy, possibly outflanking them, because he was following the path of a small stream deeper into the woods instead. By the time he had forded it at its most narrow straight, Mickey had lost sight of the monks.

The INLA gunman took a exceptional care stepping onto rocks whilst crossing the stream. He also took a long time and almost appeared to be frightened of the water. In fact, he looked so preoccupied with what he was doing, that Mickey felt brave enough to get closer to him. His own gun was in his hand and he was probably close enough to take a shot.

Two things stopped him. The first was the fact that he had never before, shot directly at a man intending to kill him. The second was fear that his nerves would affect his aim. His hand was shaking and he was unintentionally hyperventilating and taking quick shallow breaths.

This terrible anxiety and over-breathing was creating an urgent need to pass gas and Mickie let out a controlled release as quietly as he could manage. Some farts however, have a mind of their own, and this one just got louder and louder. In fact, as Mickey clamped his cheeks together in a bid to stop it mid flow, it erupted like Krakatau blowing its top.

Turning towards him, the INLA snake immediately spotted him, and raised his Armalite to his shoulder, taking aim. For a full second, Mickey stared back at him in horror, before instinct made him dart for cover behind the nearest tree.

He should have run; he knew that only running for his life could save that same life. However, his legs were gone and his knees had turned to jelly. So instead, he crouched and made himself very small, leaving his defence the responsibility of his now visibly wobbling right hand, which gripped his pistol, and pointed it at anything that moved.

It was difficult to know how long exactly that he stayed rooted to that spot, but when he did look, later on, all trace of the man had gone. To all intent and purpose, it looked like the stream had provided an in-penetrable barrier that kept the snake on the other side.

Good; because he had decided that he wasn't following him anymore. He had just about got his nerves back to a functioning state when he pulled out a pre-rolled splif and lit it up. He hoped that this would help soothe them some more, and it did. In fact so much so, that he drifted off; perhaps not fully asleep, but into a safe haven of a relaxed nirvana.

It must have been quite some time later when he heard voices not too far away and coming in his direction. Mickey didn't move and stayed very quiet, watching from his close vantage point, as five people walked past.

It was the woman from earlier but without a gun in her hand this time. She was in the company of the strangely dressed slim girl, a china woman, and that barman Shane and his girlfriend. Mickey took aim at him, reassuring himself that he could happily pull the trigger, but curiosity told him to follow them instead and just watch.

He watched them get in a car and eventually drive away. He also saw that gun woman stop and stash something under the seat in the abandoned Land Rover belonging to the INLA man. On closer inspection, it turned out to be a shoulder holster with a nice looking gun in it. Mickey put the holster on under his own jacket and accepted this gift as the one of the spoils of war.

Then he walked down the road in the direction of the parked car which he had arrived in. Maxie was obviously long gone, so Mickey decided to drive to Raghly first and see if he had gone back there.

He had smoked way too much today, and it was having a noticeable effect on his driving as he navigated the long thin causeway across into Raghly Point. This still didn't stop him lighting up another splif, but that got tossed out of the window as soon as he saw the Garda patrol car and the man mountain who was his friend standing beside two suited men.

They introduced themselves as detectives, whilst showing him their badges, and Mickey immediately placed his hands in the air in surrender. He was going to have some difficulty explaining why he did that later on after they had explained to him that he wasn't under arrest.

It would have been far better if Mickey had just shut up, but he didn't and proceeded to incriminate himself by virtue of his loose talk and idle chatter.

What is your name; what are you doing here; where are you coming from; they weren't meant to be make or break questions, but even the first one had Mickey on the ropes. The stress of being in a gunfight was much to blame, but not as much to blame as the big fat splif that Mickey had lit up as soon as Maxie had climbed out and put him in the drivers chair. Mickey was more of a part time smoker. He was experimenting with it whilst the town was awash with it. It didn't really sit well with the nationalist cause so Mickey kept his indulgence on the down low.

Managing paranoia wasn't his forte. Sweat was trickling from his brow, but it was a warm summer's day and so he might have got away with this, if only his involuntary convulsing facial expressions hadn't given him away. He was worried about hiding the fact that he was stoned, in fact so stoned, that he had bizarrely forgotten his own name. This in itself was the cause of much of his stress and inner turmoil as he tried to think quickly of some appropriate false name to use. It was probably a mistake to use Maxie's name, seeing as the big man had already used it himself.

"So you are both called Michael 'Maxie' Jinx?"

"Yes," said both of them together.

"And you don't think that that is a tad unusual?"

Maxie answered yes and Mickey answered no.

The Special Branch officer asking the questions was a seasoned professional, and he knew a weak link when he met one. So concentrating his questioning upon Mickey, he asked, "So what is your home address?"

Mickey supplied Maxie's address. At least the records would show a Michael Jinx living there. When asked the same question, Maxie replied, "The same address," but he was looking perplexed and miffed at his friend for having used it already.

"So yous two are both called Michael 'Maxie' Jinx, and you both live at the same address. That is very strange. How do you explain that?"

"Twins?" offered Mickey as an explanation. "We are not identical though."

TO HELL OR SLIGO

"I can see that," said Sergeant Foster looking at the tall big man, and then back at the small weaselly looking fella talking to him. He had already heard enough, and instructed Mickey to spread his legs and place his hands on the squad car whilst he was bodily searched.

As far as Mickey was concerned, the last of the cannabis was in that splif which he had thrown out of the car window. Therefore, there was nothing for them to find. That was except for the police issued firearm sitting in a holster under his shoulder.

46   Aftermath   (Sunday)

Kav showed Li how to start the engine on the Range Rover using the ignition wiring in place of the keys. Li was grateful for the advice, as he was grateful for many things.

"Where shall I park your wife's car when we get to Sligo?"

"Outside the Blue Lagoon should be fine," said Kav thinking it too late to explain the truth now.

"What about the farming magazines. Does she want to take those with her now?" Kav noticed that he emphasised the word farming again.

"No,Li; I am sure she can manage without them. I am sure she will find something to keep herself occupied."

"Don't you mind my friend?" asked Li reaching out to hold his new friend's hand in commiseration.

"Not really Li; it always allows me a little space for myself."

Once Li and mother had driven off, Kav climbed into the front seat of Maeve's car. They too headed off, but in the direction of Grange, as they were giving Enya, Shane and Amelia a lift back to Enya's home.

Arriving a short while later, Maeve declined Enya's invitation to come inside.

"Are you going back to Raghly Point?" she asked Maeve.

"No, we are going back to Belfast. Raghly is too 'hot' for us to return there, and so is Sligo. Then turning to address Amelia, she said, "We can drop you at your commune. I need to collect my gun and question that prisoner you are holding. He can tell me the whereabouts of our friend Aden."

"I don't think that would be a wise move, Maeve. The sister Superior may have already called the Gardai."

"But you don't have a phone," said Maeve.

"She does," lied Amelia. "I will drop the gun back to Enya's house later, and if that man is still our prisoner, we will make sure to find out your friend's whereabouts before we hand him over to the police. I will make sure Enya knows as soon as I do. Is this acceptable to you?"

"It will have to do," said Maeve in reply to Amelia, then in an almost instructional tone to her ex-captive, "Enya, we will speak later; I will phone you when I get home."

Once Maeve and Kav had departed, the remaining threesome all had things on their mind. Enya needed to talk with Amelia in private whilst Shane had to work out exactly who he had to run away from and for how long.

He took the opportunity to use the telephone inside the house to phone his sister, the only person he could rely upon to cover his ass at times when manure was about to hit the windmill.

A random customer answered the phone, but following a brief introduction, he went and got Bernadette.

"You are in a spot of trouble. There are a couple of the Special Detectives want to talk with you. They won't say what it is about, but they seem very upset with you. Did you do anything stupid?"

"What, no," swore Shane down the phone with the utmost sincerity. "I can't come back at the moment, I am in Belfast," he lied. "Can you get Dad or someone else to cover for me for a few days next week?"

"When are you coming back?"

"When are the Special Branch detectives staying until?"

"They are booked in for the week, but I think they should be finished by Friday."

"I will see you next weekend then. Gotta go; bye Bernadette."

Meanwhile, Enya was taking the opportunity to walk with her friend as far as the post office at Ballintrillick. Molly had come along too and the three girls were relieved to be free once again of the accompanying nuisance of men.

"Aren't you worried about holding that gunman prisoner? He seems very dangerous."

"Not really Enya. Sister Agatha knows how to deal with his kind. He will be securely held."

"What do you intend to do with him?"

"Well, I will interrogate him when I get back, and find out what happened to this Aden character. Do you know him?"

"Yes, Amelia; he is a handsome man and very funny."

"Ooh, do I detect a romantic interest here?"

"No, I have a boyfriend. I am loyal to Shane."

"Nonsense, you are a woman; it is your right to be with whom so ever takes your fancy. Shane should only expect leadership and direction from you."

"That does sounds interesting Amelia, but it is not really me. I couldn't pull that off."

"Well, I cannot understand why you take so much crap from him anyway. He never listens to yo" and never does what you ask him or expect him to do."

"Tell me about it. He really drives me up the wall some days."

"So what have you told him?" asked Amelia.

"I told him that he would have to go and report to your Sister-Superior later on and that she expected him to stay the night and that he would have to perform some duty or service in return for the refuge that she had provided and for the mechanical repairs to his bike."

"How long did you tell him he would have to stay?"

"I told him that I had promised at least a whole day's service."

"Okay, I will let him believe that initially, but can you tell him to arrive no later than 8pm this evening."

"Okay I will," said Enya, but appearing to have some reservations about doing so.

"Just remember that I can help you change him, improve him, and make him a better boyfriend for you. Are you worried about what he thinks or what other people think, because I get the general impression that he pisses off most people? You wouldn't be breaking him; you would be fixing him."

"Well, maybe he will pick up some ideas on his stay."

"Of course, he won't; that is naive of you to think so Enya. Nothing ever changes in life, unless you take determined steps to change it. The real question is whether you want him to change."

A long pregnant pause followed, and Amelia felt the need to apologise, "I am sorry if I have offended you, Enya."

"No it's not that. I was just thinking about all that you have said. You wouldn't hurt him would you if you put him on one of your male training programs?"

"Not if you don't want him hurt. In fact, I can get him excused from that training, and release him tomorrow morning if you wish."

Enya looked very pensive as she tried to do the right thing.

"No Amelia, I don't want him excused. Can you train him to listen more to me and be more agreeable with what I want."

"Only if you come over and help me."

"I think that might be embarrassing."

"Doesn't have to be, I will break him first and you can decide what you want to do after you have witnessed him kiss the ground in front of your feet."

"He will do that?"

"Oh yes and much, much more."

"I don't want a slave, and I don't want to beat him."
"I see. You just want him to do what you say and to back down whenever you raise your voice."
"Exactly!"
"Reconditioning him psychologically; I think will need him for a few days at least."
"What else do you want him to do or not to do?"
"I don't want him going to Belfast anymore on his bike. In fact, I want him to sell it and get a car so he can drive me around."
"I see, anything else."
"Yes, I want him to stop looking at other girls and to be more respectful to my mother and sister."
"I'll see what I can do. You leave him with me for the first day, and come down and visit us on the second. Then we can do some exercises together with him. After that, he should be pretty compliant."
"Are you going to hurt him?"
"No I will just recondition him to understand who calls the shots in your relationship. He will be a much better boyfriend, more compliant and happy to follow your instruction. Any problems in the future, you can drop him back to me, and I will fix his attitude again for you."
"You would do all that for me?"
"With pleasure."
"You're a great friend to know."

*

The two men had lost a lot of blood by the time the ambulance arrived. They had also lost a lot of their animosity for each other. Their left-handed duel hadn't been particularly successful, but their terrible shots had broken the ice.

McCreadie had apologised for his poor aim as well as for his part in the loss of Séamus's brother. That had made a real difference to the antagonistic attitude that they had previously exhibited to each other. There was little else they could do but talk. As hardened gunmen and fighters, they realised how important it was to keep each other conscious. Should one of them fall asleep, then medical shock would soon follow as they both slowly bled to death.

They were sitting with their backs against the house walls five foot apart. They thought they would likely die and even though they had both made peace with each other, neither was ready to make their peace with God. So they talked hoping to reach some redemption or compromise and so avoid perdition through listening to each other's experiences. They both had a wealth of stories about their lives and about what had transpired since they had so badly fallen out.

The police car arriving with Maxie sitting sheepishly in the rear was a welcome surprise and the sound of the ambulance which followed later even more so.

Apparently its driver was a local and he craned his neck to chat with them as he raced with his siren blaring on route to the Sligo General Hospital.

"Hello there, Eamon Kennard at your service, I believe you met my daughter," said the ambulance driver.

"I don't think so," said Séamus Tooley.

"Me neither," agreed Chuck McCreadie.

"Sure you did. She has a boyfriend with bleached white hair who rides her around on his motorbike."

"Shane?" they asked each other

"That's the fella. He's a bit of a 'head the ball' as we say in Sligo. I can't say that my wife approves of her choice at all."

"I know his family, lovely folk," said Séamus. "Well; on the women's side that is. Can't say I'm too fond of him, though, or his father. However, I do know your daughter."

"I saw her earlier on today, but I didn't really get a chance to introduce myself or talk," added McCreadie.

"Ah, that's a shame. She's a good girl. A bit headstrong though; likes to get her own way," said the ambulance driver, who was confidently bypassing a line of traffic as he approached a main junction.

"Maybe, she can change him, the blond fella that is," said McCreadie.

"That would be nice. I would like to see her married so; and he comes from a good family."

"I am sure they are sound," said McCreadie

"How long are you planning to stay in town," he asked directly of the Derry man.

"I am not sure Mr. Kennard, maybe just a couple of days; just until the guards are happy enough for me to leave."

"I guess they have to take the bullets out, and let the wounds heal first, though."

"Yeah I am looking forward to that, said McCreadie grimacing with the pain."

*

Maxie was getting a lift back to his beloved car which was still parked outside the post office at Ballintrillick. He didn't mind that he wasn't driving on this occasion. In fact, he was content to sacrifice that honour to his dear friend Mickey who somehow had saved the day once again.

"When he found that gun, I thought we were going to prison for sure. Could you have not hidden it before you got out the car?"

"My mind was a blank Maxie. All I could think about was getting rid of the dope."

"I think they take possession of a loaded firearm a bit more seriously than a cannabis splif," said Maxie.

"It saved our bacon though."

"I know," said Maxie. "Who'd have thought it was his gun. He looked like you had just saved his career."

"When he said that he was going to let us off if we kept 'shtum' about the whole thing, I nearly kissed the dude."

"Yeah, probably better you didn't."

Mickey was so elated and happy and still partially stoned, that he spontaneously broke into song.

"Said he was a Buffalo Soldier, win the war for I.R.A."

And Maxie joined in for the chorus, "Dreadie, woy yoy yoy, woy yoy-yoy yoy."

47 The Next Day (Monday)

It had been a freezing cold night and today's sun had yet to thaw him out. Aden had lost track of how long he had remained bound here and he had literally spent hours trying to work the ropes free, but to no avail.

He was in a disused quarry pit and the only comfort that had been left for him was the pool of water that had collected in the pit below, but that didn't look safe to drink. Most probably, he was going to die of hypothermia out here, especially if he had to survive another night.

The pit was beside a dirt track which meandered up the side of the nearby mountains, and several times yesterday, he had heard vehicles driving up the track, but none of them came up this far. This was an ugly truth which suggested that nobody was going to find him here while he was still alive.

Then the slim girl had appeared. He almost believed that he knew her already. Probably the cold playing games with his mind. She was young and almost a waif, but she had come searching for him with steely determination that betrayed her inner strength. Her name was Amelia and she had helped support his exhausted frame as he walked back with her to some place close by.

It had been a surprise to find out it was a commune and then the penny dropped. He had seen her before on his first day in the Bective and he remembered calling her a 'dyke'. Thankfully, she remained blissfully unaware of their prior connection.

She took him into a large extended cottage and propped him in a comfortable chair in front of a peat fire. A bowl of soup and some bread followed, as well as plenty of water to drink. He felt so content that he dozed off. The sleep was sorely needed and his body fought against his mind attempting to stay awake. He would open his eyes in alertness at every new sound but quickly returned to sleep.

His dreams were strange and bizarre, and often confusing. At one point, he dreamt that he had seen Brady, that INLA bastard who had beaten him, and tried to make him betray Maeve. However in his dream, it was Brady who was now prisoner, and he was cowed and under the cosh. Later he had thought he had heard the voice of that barman from the Bective and when he opened his eyes, it really was him standing in the doorway to the room.

"Mister Clancy, you have to help me."

"What; it's Shane isn't it?"

"Yes. Please, Aden, I can't talk for long, but you have to help me."

"How?"

"You know my girlfriend Enya, she lives nearby at No.8 Yeats Close, near Grange village."

"Which one of your girlfriends is she, the pretty or the plain one?"

"The pretty one. Listen please; they are going to ask you to leave soon. Can you tell her to come here and rescue me?"

"Can't you just leave?"

"These chains," said Shane shaking one of his ankles that was bound loosely to the other.

"Oh, I see, what the hell is going on here?"

A distant voice shouted "Boy?" and Shane almost flinched. "Boy, come here immediately."

"I have to go, or I am in serious trouble. Just visit her and tell her to come here as soon as she can. Only she can save me," said Shane as he scuttled away, quickly and obediently in the direction of the voice.

Aden was much more alert by the time Amelia came back. He now looked at her with suspicion, and this registered in a much less friendly tone as she told him that it really was time for him to leave. Aden had a lot of questions he wanted to ask, but intuition told him it was best just to thank her for her hospitality and leave.

She supplied him with directions to walk towards Grange. It wasn't too far; perhaps a mile and half, and he came across Yeats Close before he reached the main village.

Aden was aware that he was not looking his best as he checked his reflection in the front window of her house. He adjusted his hair and clothes as best he could, determined to make his best impression. He found it hard to believe he was here as he gingerly reached out to ring the doorbell. A few hours ago, he was lying tied up in a quarry ditch and thought he was dead. And now he was about to meet again the woman of his dreams.

Enya looked a little surprised but more than pleased to see him. I knew it. She does like me, he said to himself, settling an argument raging in his mind. She didn't invite him in, yet her body language was openly warm and welcoming. "I hoped I might bump into you again," she said, making Aden's mind go into overdrive looking for hidden meaning.

"Hello, I never got a chance to introduce myself, but I am Aden. Your boyfriend asked me to come here and give you an important message."

"Shane spoke with you?"

"Just briefly. He seemed more than a bit distressed and he said that he really needs you to go to this place a mile or so down the road."

"The commune, I know where it is. Did he say anything else?"

"Yes; he said that only you could save him."

"Ah bless him. I will have to let Amelia know about his little talk with you."

"Are you going to go?"

"Oh, I might head down there later sometime. Don't worry about him, he will be fine. He was probably just being dramatic. I will make sure he contacts you later and lets you know he is okay."

"No, don't bother about asking him to do that."

"How about I contact you later?" said Enya smiling seductively.

"I would like that very much, but I don't think your boyfriend would."

"Oh I am certain that he will be most accommodating on that front"

"Really?"

"I should think so, he chose to be alone in the company of pretty women right now, and I haven't objected. I expect that he won't object to me spending some quality time in the company of a handsome man who wants to take me out."

"Well, I have seen him with another girl in the Bective. So I guess it is only fair and I would really love to go out with you. You are very sexy."

"You are very sweet. Why don't you come inside and use our bathroom to get cleaned up a little."

"That is the very same reason why I cannot. You must excuse me Enya, but I kind of slept in a ditch last night, and right now I want to go and get cleaned up and then go to my bed."

"That's a pity because I thought you could walk with me to the village and have lunch with me. Then maybe stay for a drink this evening, so we can get to know each other."

"That sounds lovely, but shouldn't you be saving him down the road. He was pleading with me to ask you."

"Not really Aden. There is really nothing to save him from. He volunteered two day's service for work on his bike and now he probably wants to back out of the deal. I trust Amelia will take good care of him. So he needs to stop being such a drama queen and fulfil his contract of work."

Enya demonstrated a little too much certainty and confidence in her words as if she was fully aware what was really going on down there. Aden guessed that Enya had no imminent intention of rescuing him, which she practically confirmed next.

"I don't particularly feel like going there today. Maybe tomorrow; I am sure he will still be there and in a much more positive frame of mind. So let's not talk about him anymore if you don't mind."

"Okay, I tell you what I think Enya. How about I go about my business, get some sleep, get cleaned up, and then come back here at 7pm and take you out to dinner. How does that sound."

"That sounds like something that I would be very interested in participating in."

Aden displayed the warmest smile when she said goodbye and closed the door. However, her attitude to her boyfriend, and her propositioning him, none of this sat well with him at all as he thought about it, on route back to Ballintrillick. The car that Kav had stolen on Saturday was parked out back, and he needed to borrow it again, but first, he needed a stiff drink.

48 The Right Thing   (Monday)

The old man was manning the bar today and his hand instinctively began teasing the Guinness pump forward when he saw Aden walk in the rear exit to the pub. Aden surprised him by calling for two double Jameson instead, both on the rocks.

The old man was familiar with the expression but he also knew that there was only one cube left in the ice tray. He popped that directly into one of the glasses and refilled the tray with tap water before returning it to the freezer. Nonetheless, he was aware that some of these Northerners had a taste for slices of frozen carrots in their drinks so he disappeared briefly into the shop and returned with a small bag of them, some of which he poured into a third glass and the rest of which he placed in the small fridge behind the counter.

Aden polished off the first whiskey in two gulps before taking up a seat at the counter. He looked at the glass of frozen carrots accompanying his other glass of Jameson, and then squarely at the bar keeper, thinking that these county Sligomen were totally mad.

He wasn't intending to stay, just long enough to sink a couple of whiskies. It was not his usual tipple, but his needs weren't social, but medicinal instead. He still felt rather traumatised from his close shave with death. It had been a long cold night in which he thought he was surely going to die from exposure. As a result, he had hardly slept and had spent the entire time in deep contemplation.

Laying in a ditch believing that you are going to die soon has a way of focusing the mind on the bigger picture, the pertinent things in life that have been left unresolved. Aden had come out of the experience with a shopping list of aspirations and a to-do list that encompassed everything from revenge to doing the right thing. As much as he would like it to be, taking Enya out later this evening was not on that list.

He still thought she was drop dead gorgeous, and frankly, he was flattered that she was attracted to him in return. Regardless, these considerations were superseded by pending actions from his to-do list of right things to do. The most important being his decision to propose to his long term girlfriend Sheila. Enya was just a pretty distraction, but as his best friend Kav kept choosing to point out, he already had a girlfriend. If he could help get Sheila's inheritance released, then they could move to her father's farm and have a fresh start.

This reminded him that he was going to have to pay that weasel solicitor Walsh a visit in Letterkenny. It was time that he received some payback for all his meddling which had nearly cost him his life.

There was one other thing that remained unresolved from his to-do list and that involved doing the right thing. In all honesty, he was rather taken aback by Enya's attitude towards rescuing her boyfriend from his distressed situation at the commune. Despite the fact that he was exhausted and still tired when he left, he had noted the desperation in Shane's voice and realised that he was not a willing participant to whatever predicament that he had got himself into.

Thus, Aden had decided that if Enya chose not to bust her boyfriend out, then he would do it in her stead. After all, it was the right thing to do which was another reason why he had decided not to go on a date with her whilst her boyfriend remained temporarily incarcerated. This was not an honourable thing to do, and Aden had had enough of doing the wrong things in life. From now on, it was strictly the right way up every time.

Although the red Datsun that Kav had stolen on Saturday was still parked in the car park out back, Aden decided that it was probably best to set off on foot. To reach the commune, he retraced the same route which he had been escorted along earlier.

He didn't attract too much attention as he walked through the grounds towards the main house because many had seen him here earlier today. However, this was not the case when he approached the entrance to the building, where a middle-aged man stood guard outside the front door. The sentry was uninterested in any reason or excuse given by Aden, whom he had earlier witnessed being escorted off the premises.

He told Aden to wait whilst he sought a Sister to decide what to do. Aden however, was having none of it, and he simply banged the man's head back against the wooden pillar he stood beside. Then he dragged his limp body aside and propped it up against the wall of the house.

Aden was in no mood for messing with these idiots, yet he didn't want to leave a trail of unconscious bodies, so he kept a low profile as he searched throughout the ground floor.

Aden found the Enya's boyfriend out the back in a small utility room working on the laundry. He was naked apart from a small utility pouch that covered his genitals and Aden observed him working at a maniacal pace scrubbing white linen tunics clean with bars of handmade soap. He appeared desperate as he encountered difficulties eradicating difficult stains and his expression suggested that he was in deep trouble.

"They have you scared of your own shadow," said Aden by way of introduction.

Shane looked up with some surprise, more at hearing another male voice, as well as one that was familiar.

"You have no idea how strict they are," he replied. "They will punish you, even if you just think bad thoughts about them."

"Go away with yourself and don't talk such nonsense," said Aden in disbelief.

"It's true and they work you so hard; I am always behind schedule on what I am meant to be doing. Has Enya come because I can't stand it here?"

"No she didn't want to come and I need to talk to you about that."

"I can't talk to you," said Shane, suddenly looking very guilty and anxious. "You have to go. I can't talk to you unless Enya or one of the Sisters allows me. They will give me a sound beating if they find out I even spoke with you."

"Relax, just relax will ya. I've come to bust you out. You are coming with me."

"They won't allow you to take me without a Sister's permission."

"With due respect Shane, a bunch of women and their male lackeys is not going to stop me doing what I want to do."

"You don't know them like I do. They're not even human, more like witches, demons, or aliens."

"Jaysus, it's true; you really are a space cadet, aren't you Shane. They are just a bunch of women with high spirits, no different than those you'd find in Belfast city centre watching some male strippers getting their kit off. I should know, I've been a doorman at such events. When women get together, they can get just as boisterous as men, but they are still a bunch of women, and I am a republican soldier after all. I have fought my way out biker pubs, and loyalist dens."

"Have you?" said Shane, openly showing his admiration for Aden's fighting prowess.

"Well, it wasn't quite a den, more like a chip shop on the Shankill Road, but it could have turned real nasty," he said now adopting a more serious 'let's get to business' expression as he stared directly at Shane, hoping to instil courage in him, "So where do we go to find us a key to remove those shackles on your legs and where are your damn clothes."

"I am not sure who has the keys to my shackles, but Sister Agatha put them on me, and she made me strip and took my clothes as well."

"So where do we find her?"

"In the punishment compound, but it is not a place any man would want to go."

"Well we do, so grow a pair and lead the way."

Aden watched Shane use a vintage mangle to quickly dry out the dress he had been previously working on.

"What the hell are you doing?"

"I can't leave it in the soak, it will stain."

"What? No, leave the damn thing! Son, they really have you under manners. Come on, let's go."

"Okay but I need to collect my work permit first," said Shane as he grabbed a small notepad from a hook beside the door.

"Why in heaven's name do you need that?"

"It informs any Sister what I am working on, and allows them to add extra tasks. I need to always present it or have it on show, should a Sister want to inspect my work or make comments about me, or the quality of my work."

"Shane, are you simple or something?"

"No," he said defensively taking some offence from the comment.

"Well, then leave the friggin book here and take me to the punishment complex for Christ-sake."

With Shane's local knowledge and Aden's stealth, they managed to reach the punishment complex without being seen. Just like the laundry room, it was another annex purposely built on to the side of the building. There were no windows which were probably by design.

The two of them approached its main utility room by way of one its two access points. There were two, barred cells along one side which were both empty, but the rest of the room was a veritable dungeon of punishment implements. They didn't see anyone being incarcerated or punished presently, but they did see Sister Agatha, the resident tormentress who was busy writing in some journal. She was massive for a woman, perhaps six feet three, and maybe twenty stone plus; except she wasn't exceptionally fat, more muscular and well built.

I have to say, she's a big angry looking woman," said Aden. "I wouldn't like to meet her down some dark alleyway. However, I am afraid, that you are going to have to go in there and distract her."

"You have got to be joking," replied Shane. "She scares me witless."

"I am serious, Shane. I want to disable her and not hurt her. After all, these women saved my bacon."

"I can't."

"Yes you can, and if you don't. I am going to kick you in your balls.

ANGUS CACTUS

So stop caving into your fear, and start living by tackling it straight on. This is your problem Shane, you seem to always be running away from something, someone, and sometimes just from your responsibilities. I want you to learn through strength. So you are going to damn well go in there, start talking to the woman, and make sure that she turns around so I can sneak up on her."

Shane stepped forward and entered the room, head downcast and looking very penitent. This would not be sufficient to save him, because, part of Sister Agatha's responsibilities, was to dispense correction to anyone unfortunate enough to have been sent here.

"Sister Amelia sent me here because she found my attitude unsatisfactory," said Shane amazed that he could find the words, let alone incriminate himself.

The big woman looked annoyed to be interrupted in her private business but seemingly took her disciplinarian role very seriously. She gestured for him to assume a position in the nearby stocks which he was already all too familiar with. Then following a cursory inspection that he was fully secured, she went to select a cane from the large array collected in a nearby wicker basket.

Shane waited in trepidation, but his expectation was to hear Aden overpowering the woman from behind. Instead, he felt his ass set alight with intense pain and then felt two more follow up strikes hit targets less than half an inch apart, as the air left his lungs and he screamed out in pain.

When it stopped, he restrained his curiosity from turning around until he saw Aden in front of him releasing his hands from the restraints of the stock. He was a welcome sight, but insufficient evidence to convince Shane's brain that a fourth strike wasn't incoming and he tentatively turned around to check on Sister Agatha. Reassuringly for him, she now had a canvas hood covering her head and her hands were secured above her head and attached to a chain of manacles that ringed the wall.

"You didn't tell me that you were going to let her cane me three times," he said with a release of tension and frustration.

"I didn't. She only hit you twice."

"But I felt a third strike," said Shane rubbing his bare backside with both hands.

"No, the third strike was mine," said Aden with a hangdog expression.

"Why did you do that for heaven's sake?"

"I wanted to have a go too. You know for the purpose of testing the cane."

"Well thanks a bunch, but don't bother rescuing me again."

TO HELL OR SLIGO

"Ah don't go all moody on me; you friggin deserve a good beating anyway."

"What's your problem with me?" said Shane becoming argumentative.

"You are my friggin problem, Shane. You go about your business without a care for the mayhem and disaster you are spreading about. For once, I wish you would stop feeling so conceited that you always know all the answers and maybe ask the advice of others. They will tell you, your mother, your family, your friends and Enya that you are always doing the wrong thing."

He listened intently to Aden's words, surprised that a near stranger had such an understanding from his casual observations. He had no comment to come back at him because he knew that his words were partially true. Instead, he stood vacantly staring at the Amazonian figure of fear that now appeared quiet and helpless whilst bound and secured to the wall.

Both of his hands were still rubbing his own backside, still the source of throbbing pain, but concern was also etched upon his face. This was fuelled by fear of the woman, and his worry was that she might break free; but Aden mistook Shane's worry for concern.

"She's okay; I made sure not to hurt her," said Aden, looking almost embarrassed that he had fought and restrained a woman. "I am grateful for them helping me, but this one is better secured until we leave. Grab those keys from her belt and see if you can unlock those shackles on your ankles. Meanwhile, I will scout around and look for your clothes."

Shane silently and almost anonymously tried to release the keys, still afraid that the big woman would hold him culpable for their loss. There appeared to be no way that he could release the heavy key ring without unthreading the wide leather belt that secured it. Therefore, Shane undid the big buckle and yanked and pulled on the heavy belt until he had nearly freed it. He didn't realise that it was connected at two points to a smaller leather sash that crossed over her shoulder. That smaller belt was threaded through lapels on her shoulder and placket.

One overly aggressive tug removed that belt as well as the larger one around her waist. Then as Shane held them like a weapon in his right hand, the heavy key ring fell to the floor and it was momentarily followed by Sister Agatha's white linen skirt. She was wearing just a loose pair of knickers underneath, and the removal of the shoulder sash had ripped open her white tunic top at the front. This revealed an exceptionally large vintage style conical bra fully encasing Sister Agatha's enormous breasts. She seemed aware of this fact as she struggled against the overhead chain which secured her.

The sight of her near nakedness had almost mortified Shane as much as it did to Sister Agatha; thank god for the hood which prevented her from speaking or seeing his petrified face. Shane looked again at the two belts in his hand and wondered how this was even possible. Then, in order to make amends, he tried to adjust her clothing using one hand to try and hold both sides of her tunic together to hide her bosom. His other hand reached down to get a secure hold on her knickers so that he could adjust them and pull them up properly.

Shane tried to be as non-invasive as possible as he pulled them up over her hips. Yet as he did so, his hand brushed against something very unfeminine. Curiosity got the better of him, and his hand made a cursory movement to cup her groin. It was very small, but nonetheless, there was no mistaking the feeling of something akin to two small walnuts and a small sausage. At this point, he tentatively peeled back her knickers by the weakened elastic to reveal that Sister Agatha was really a brother. A look of shock and horror began to take shape on Shane's face.

At the same time, Aden had walked back into the room, holding a pile of men's clothes in his arms. He took exception to Shane peering down the front of the poor woman's underwear.

"What in the life of Jayzus are you up to?" he demanded.

Shane thought it a fair question, well deserving of a reply, except he really had no sensible answer to provide. He was well aware that what he was doing probably didn't look good. His efforts to secure Agatha's modesty had only made things worse, he had accidentally snapped the knickers' elastic, and if he let go now, they would fall and everything would be on show. Agatha was now gyrating and thrashing about, trying to turn around or break free.

The revelation of Agatha's genitals confused Shane, but regardless, he decided it best to hide the man's private parts like a true guardian of his real identity, even though he was flailing about and resisting his attempts to help.

"You need psychological help Shane; now let her go before I knock you out and leave you here," said Aden having lost all patience.

"It's not what it looks like," said Shane with a measure of desperation as he removed his hands from Agatha and stepped away. "Trust me, it just sought of happened."

But Aden didn't really trust him, nor listen to him. Instead, he watched mesmerised from the sidelines looking at Sister Agatha's powerfully built naked body thrashing about against the wall, and the tiny wiener which he now saw for the first time.

Neither was he the only one to be doing so. Two male flunkies stood at the other doorway. They hadn't yet seen Sister Agatha's wedding tackle, but they were witnessing with some horror, an assault on one of their senior mistresses.

These two men, dressed in short thin tunics similar to a Roman servant's, launched a desperate attack on Shane shouting as they ran towards him with flailing fists. Shane managed to sidestep the first, whom he tripped and after unbalancing him, pushed him into the wall head first. The man was dazed by the impact and slumped to the floor between the feet of Sister Agatha who now used them to grip him firmly around the throat, probably thinking it was Shane. The expression on the man's face showed that she was squeezing his head with some considerable anger and strength.

The other assailant had slammed his fist into Shane's face and drawn blood. The impact on his nose had caused it to bleed and disoriented his vision and balance. He too slipped slowly to the floor, and a follow-up kick from his assailant winded him and shoved him hard against Sister Agatha's legs. These were opened partially and closed around his face, holding Shane in a powerful vice grip at her knees. Shane maintained a horrified expression on his face, well aware of what dangled inches above his face. Agatha already held the other man in a secure hold with her feet and didn't seem to know or care which person to now release. In fact, Agatha squeezed so hard that his intention seemed to be either complete submission or unconsciousness, whichever came first.

Shane's hands tried to pull the female impersonator's thighs apart, but his efforts were in vain because he could not match the strength of this large powerfully built man. All he could manage with his entire strength was to relieve the suffocating pressure as he was stuck and immobilised in between a pair of muscular thighs.

He could hear the sound of fighting from behind him and felt someone trip over his legs. Then he became aware of someone pulling him by the legs, and after a minute of struggle, he had been freed from Agatha's vice like grip.

Aden dropped Shane's legs as soon as he heard Amelia's voice.

"Would you bite the hand that fed you?"

"No I wouldn't raise a finger against you darling, but I will fight my way out of here if necessary, and I am taking Shane with me."

"You can leave whenever you want, but I may have a problem with you taking Shane without my permission. I also take exception to your threats, your assault upon Sister Agatha and you beating up two of my servants. If I wanted to stop you, I could. After all, you are just one man, up against many."

"I am not threatening you, Amelia, I am just stating my business, and besides, it's not just me, there are two of us."

"Oh yeah, who else then," she said in challenge.

"Shane as well…" said Aden turning around to make sure that the younger man had his back. However, Shane was currently grovelling on his knees and in supplicant position cowed in the presence of Sister Amelia. Agatha had released the other flunky and he had also assumed a similar grovelling position beside Shane.

"What the feck are you doing Shane?" said Aden losing his rag. At first, Shane didn't look up or acknowledge him. "For feck sake man, get up now and grow a pair," insisted Aden with some aggression showing in his voice.

Shane sheepishly got to his feet and apologised," Sorry Aden, old habits die hard."

"What do you mean; old habits? You've only been incarcerated here for less than a day."

Shane shrugged but made a point of lowering his head as he addressed Amelia. "I am sorry Sister Amelia for all this trouble."

"So you should be, Shane. For your sake, I hope that Sister Agatha is forgiving after you release her and take off that…"

Sister Amelia was literally staring open mouth with shock now that she had just witnessed the little package dangling above Agatha's fallen knickers. "What the freaking hell is that on her?"

"On him," corrected Aden.

Shane had picked up the set of keys from the floor and was reaching up to open the clasps on the overhead manacles.

"What are you doing Shane?" said Amelia almost in rebuke.

"I'm releasing Sister Agatha."

"Don't! That thing is not a sister of mine," Amelia walked over for a closer inspection of the female impersonator formerly known as Agatha. A cursory inspection of his genitals was followed by Amelia delving deep inside Agatha's large bra. Out came several pairs of woollen socks.

Amelia scowled as she instructed her two servants, "Leave it tied up there until I consult the Sister Superior. She is probably going to want to conduct a thorough check through our ranks after this deception."

"Sister Amelia?" said Shane, seeking permission to talk.

"What, Shane?"

"Please, may I have your permission to leave?"

"Alright, I guess you can. Anyway, it looks like I will have my hands full here and be too busy to mentor you. You may leave, but first, I want you to recall our little chat yesterday evening and remember all the promises I elicited from you and how you swore you were telling me the truth."

"I do and I was."

"Good boy Shane. Then I will be checking with my friend Enya later and also with you, to make sure that you are not lying to me and that you remain in our good books."

Aden stared at Shane astounded by his deferential attitude to Amelia. However, he chose not to challenge it, but instead changed the subject.

"So Amelia; are you going to help show us out?"

"Yes Aden, I will as soon as Shane has removed his shackles and put his clothes on," Then turning to Agatha, "Boy, you are in some serious trouble."

Amelia instructed her two servants to remain with the new prisoner formerly known as Sister Agatha, whilst Shane fumbled to get ready as quickly as possible. It felt really empowering to be wearing his own clothes again and he nodded that he was ready even before he had even got his shoes on, mainly because he was so keen to depart this place.

Amelia set off back in the direction that she had come from and Aden fell into step beside her. Shane ran after the both of them, still trying to insert his heel fully in his boot. She was leading them through a set of rooms that neither had had access to before. These were the Sister Superior's private set of rooms, except today they were not so private. The furniture had been cleared away in a large reception room, and the room was now occupied by probably the majority of the sorority that lived in this commune. There were about 15 women, all Screamers, in three rows, all exercising and moving in unison, demonstrating gentle moves with flowing hand movements. They didn't notice the teacher at first because her small stature was hidden amongst the others. Yet during a break in the exercises, they saw a familiar face, except it belonged now to a body that was spinning gracefully in the air demonstrating one of Bruce Lee's famous roundhouse flying kicks.

Aden and Shane stopped dead in their tracks astounded and amazed by what they had just seen.

"That is Sister Huong," said Amelia in explanation. "She was grateful for our help yesterday and she likes our commune, so she has agreed to come here and train us Ladies in the arts of Tai Chi and Kung fu—"

"I knew it," said Aden interrupting her in excitement. "I knew that she was a Kung fu legend. I just knew it all along."

Both men walked with craned necks, looking backwards, still watching Huong Han as they left the room and entered a smaller adjoining room. It was the personal office of the Sister-Superior, and she sat in a heavy cumbersome throne-like chair, with a male guard beside her, and with a naked man tethered at the base and kneeling face down in a supplicant position.

"Aden and Shane are leaving us now and have requested an audience to pay their respects. May we approach?" asked Amelia.

Meanwhile, Shane and Aden stared at each other knowing full well that they had not requested anything of the kind.

"No stay there, I am coming over," said the Sister Superior and she accompanied this statement by giving her naked attendant a sharp crack with her whip.

He immediately sprang into action and seemed to be using considerable effort to drag the heavy chair forward. It was actually bound to his body through leads connected to grip attachments made to sensitive areas of his body.

Both men stared at him fully appreciating his extreme discomfort. However, there was only full recognition showing in Aden's eyes. He would never forget that mean face of the man who had abducted him. The same man who beat him senseless before leaving him alone in a ditch to die.

Aden couldn't resist his curiosity and he walked towards the chair for a closer look. As he did so, there were shocked expressions on everyone's faces in the room.

"Oh I'm sorry," he said to the Sister-Superior, "May I approach and talk to your manservant here."

The Sister Superior nodded in acceptance and Aden leant in closer to talk to the man.

"You deserve everything you get, you mean bast'rd."

"Help me, Clancy," said Terrance Brady. "Please Aden; get me some help to escape from here."

"Hmm. Now, is that plan-A or plan-B? Because I am opting for plan-B myself, which is to go away and forget I ever saw you."

Brady's eyes appeared cold and menacing as if he was allowed his one aggressive stare of the day, and Aden decided he couldn't let him get away with any more attempts at intimidation. Turning to the Sister Superior, he asked, "May I chastise him for his rudeness?"

"Be my guest," was her reply.

Aden followed through with a solid knee in his groin and watched the man drop to the floor clutching his genitals. That was more than sufficient to satisfy Aden, and he turned and walked away.

Before they left the compound, Amelia took Shane and Aden to collect his motorcycle from one of the outhouses. It was only partially welded, but it required oil and a full service before it could be ridden. Amelia offered to keep it in the outhouse, but Shane wanted to get his precious steed far away from this place where he cared never to set foot in again. He decided to wheel it as far as the post office at Ballintrillick and leave it there temporarily.

Amelia also handed Aden a gun wrapped in white linen cloth. It was an immaculate Glock and he had recognised it as Maeve's gun before she had even confirmed this fact. As expected, there was no ammunition provided.

Amelia then took them down a hidden path that led almost directly to the post office before saying farewell. Both men said goodbye, but with different thoughts on their mind. Aden hoped to meet up sometime again with this young woman who had saved his life; Shane on the other hand sincerely wished that he would never see her again.

The two men had the opportunity to talk frankly as the wheeled the motorcycle between them.

"What did Amelia mean when she said that she wanted you to keep your promises to her? What did you promise her?"

"A lot of personal stuff," said Shane, "about me and Enya."

"Such as?"

"You know how it was back there. They have a way of making men say whatever they want them to say."

"So what promises did you make?" enquired Aden more insistently this time.

"Well, I promised not to make any decisions without consulting Enya first, and I promised to be pleasant and friendly to her mother and sister. I also promised to sell the bike and instead jointly buy a car with Enya. Apparently, she is fed up with putting on helmets and messing up her hair, and Amelia says that if we share a car, I won't be able to take it up to Belfast without her coming along, or without her permission."

"So, are you going to fulfil those promises?"

"No, why should I? I'm free now thanks to you."

They had reached the main road at this point, and the Post Office/Pub was only 50 yards away on the other side.

"Shane, I think you should consider keeping your word. Some of those are reasonable requests, and frankly if I was you, I would be happy that my girlfriend wanted to vet my decisions," Aden stopped walking and changed his tone to one with extra gravitas. "Because, Shane, your decision making is probably the most screwed up I have ever encountered. You are your own worst enemy and as an enemy to yourself, you are pretty deadly."

ANGUS CACTUS

"You don't have a very good impression of me," said Shane feeling dejected.

"Far from it, Shane; you are a likable guy, and Kav really thinks your great, but you are also a walking disaster, waiting to happen and being blown around through life by happenstance. You don't appreciate what you have and you don't know how to keep it."

"Like what? I don't really understand what you are referring to."

"I am referring to your mother and your family. They are carrying you, and you are not really supporting them." Aden watched Shane closely, to see if he had taken offence. He wanted to advise him, rather than lecture. "I am also referring to Enya. She propositioned me today and she probably did that because she is fed up with your shenanigans. You have a beautiful girlfriend and you are not treating her right. If you kept her in the loop, rather than trying to get away with stuff behind her back, she would trust you more. You need to take her up to Belfast and introduce her to your friends, properly."

They had entered the pubs car park now behind the Post Office & Bar, and they continued pushing the bike towards the rear hedgerow.

"I know you are only trying to help me and I appreciate what you did for me today, as well as what you are saying now. Okay, thanks, Aden; I will bear in mind everything you said."

Shane's Yamaha motorcycle was pushed through a gap in the hedge. It could remain hidden there until such time that Shane could organise a trailer to come and collect it.

Once that was done, Shane made ready to part ways, but Aden begged to differ and held open the passenger door of the old red Datsun that Kav had stolen and left behind here on Saturday.

"Oh we are not finished yet," said Aden. "You are coming with me because I have a plan in mind."

*

It was early evening, and Aden had collected Enya from her home in Grange and driven her to one of the town's finest restaurants which was actually a few miles outside of Sligo, in a place called Rosses Point.

Aden had earlier showered and changed in the Bective, and then he and Shane had shared a pint with Bernadette and Jimmy before he had set off for Grange.

Enya was looking fantastic this evening and she was wearing a beautiful dress and was looking probably the most glamorous he had ever seen her.

They had only just ordered, starters and mains and in the meantime, Aden was making sure that their wine glasses remained topped up.

"Did I tell you that you look very pretty tonight," said Aden.

"Yes, only about three times already," replied Enya.

"Well, you do. I think a man would have to be crazy to give up the opportunity of being your date."

"Well, you didn't and you're here now, so let's make the best of it."

"I know Enya, trust me, I am. I am filming you right now with my mind's eye so that I can always return to this evening again and revisit how pretty you look."

"Ah you're so sweet; thank you, Aden."

Aden was being genuine, but he also felt awkwardly short of conversation. He barely knew anything about Enya, and this evening was not the best opportunity for him to find out more.

He seemed distracted and was checking his watch a lot, and now he wanted to go to the bathroom for the second time. Enya appreciated that he was probably nervous being that it was a first date and she cut him some slack. She was very fond of him, of his confidence as much as his looks, though she was disappointed that they had so little in common.

One thing that annoyed her about him was the length of time he was prone to spending in the bathroom, but seemingly not this time, as she felt a reassuring touch on her shoulder.

Then she noticed the Claddagh ring. It was more than familiar to her, seeing as she had bought it. It was Shane's hand and she nearly jumped out of her skin, feeling instantly guilty and caught in the act.

Shane took advantage of her discomposure, to sit down in Aden's seat. Then he reached out to hold her hand. Enya flinched at first and nearly withdrew it, before allowing Shane to hold it.

"What are you doing here Shane and why are you dressed so nicely. Are you seeing someone here; are you seeing some girl?"

"Yes Enya, I am. I am seeing you, probably clearly for the first time. Aden and Amelia have explained some things to me and I have decided that I want to be a better boyfriend to you. I have not been told or coerced to say this, just advised and this time, I listened. That Aden is a really good guy, and I can see why you were attracted to him."

"I, I wasn't, I mean I didn't—"

"It's okay, I know you guys didn't do anything, but I want to know if you are prepared to continue being my girlfriend; with a fresh start and a lot more commitment this time around."

"Yes, Shane; yes I am."

That was all that Shane wanted to hear and he leant forward across the table, but held back an inch from her, allowing Enya to close the gap, and seal the deal with a kiss.

ANGUS CACTUS

"Where is he, Aden?" she asked.
"He should be on route to Letterkenny by now."
"So, how will I get home to Grange?"
"Don't worry, he left me his car."
"And what is he driving?"
Shane looked around and smiled, "Probably, one of these other diner's vehicles."

49 Repercussions

The suit he was wearing was helping him fill the shoes of the person he was impersonating. Aden was standing in the porch of Kevin Walsh's home in one of the plusher suburbs of Letterkenny. Kathleen Walsh met him at the door wearing an apron and had seemingly been baking. She was a gentle woman and apparently the perfect hostess, which made Aden a little uneasy about his current deception.

"Oh I am sorry that I am early, Kevin did say six o'clock though."

"I guess you should come in Mr Stevens and wait for him."

"Please call me Roger," said Aden.

"Can I get you a cup of tea?"

"Only if it is no bother for you, Kathleen."

"No bother at all Roger. I am going to tell Kevin off when he gets home for leaving his guest waiting, and for hiding away such a charming man."

"Oh Kathleen, you are making me blush. And to be fair to him, we haven't seen each other for ages; since school days really."

"Oh, then he is going to be so pleased to see you."

When Kevin Walsh opened his front door, he was met by his excited wife; and a ghost from his recent past. The shock was almost palpable on his face as it turned a whiter shade of pale. His clammy hand was met by the determined grip of Aden Clancy, saying, "You do remember me, don't you Kevin. I am Roger Stevens from school," said Aden whilst winking at Walsh.

There was no reply from the man. Walsh still remained mute with horror etched on his face.

"Ah Kathleen, look, he is in near shock. You are right, he must have forgotten all about me coming over." Then Aden, looking him squarely in the eye, said, "Didn't you Kevin?"

"Yes, I did. I thought you had gone away!"

"With those other mutual school friends of ours?" said Aden. "No; they won't be able to make it. Both McCreadie and Brady send their apologies."

Kathleen was still excited to have company over for the evening, and she headed back to the kitchen to see what snacks she could muster together. Some relief showed on Walsh's face, but he still needed to get the Provo out of his home.

"Um, Roger isn't it. Could you come outside so we can speak privately?"

"Kathleen!" Aden called out. "Lovely to meet you, hopefully, see you again soon."

"Oh sure," Kathleen shouted from the kitchen. "I will look forward to it," she said rushing out to the hall to say goodbye, but Kevin Walsh had already closed the door.

Once outside, the fake smiles disappeared from both men's faces.

"What do you want from me?" demanded Kevin Walsh.

"An apology for sending those INLA gunmen after me would be nice."

"I'm sorry; that was a misunderstanding. I only wanted them to protect my house"

"That is not their kind of thing," said Aden.

"So what do you want now?"

"The same as I wanted before plus a little extra compensation this time."

Walsh pulled out his wallet and removed all the cash from it.

"That's nearly four hundred; is that enough?"

"For trying to get me murdered? Perhaps if you make a compensatory payment of 5000 punts, when you release your sequester on the probate. I want that paid to Sheila the beneficiary, along with a written apology to her claiming the money is for her compensation."

"What! I won't do that."

"Do you really want me to mess with you?" asked Aden calmly.

"Okay, okay, will you go away and leave me alone if I do."

"Certainly Kevin and with no hard feelings."

"Then consider it done tomorrow first thing."

*

"That is the most amazing story I have ever been told Aden."

"Really Kav, I thought the tale about the fighting monk, his mother and the gold was a better one."

The two friends were sitting in a beer garden located not far from Belfast city centre.

"So you think that INLA gunman, the mean fellow, is still there at the commune."

"If he is, it serves him right. I am not going to fret over him."

"It's true. You reap what you sow," said Kav studying the bottom of his near empty glass.

"Yep, those ladies are probably keeping him busy in the sewing department; and the laundry and cleaning departments too."

Aden's reply caught Kav off-guard as he was sipping the dregs of his pint, he spluttered through laughing and sprayed traces of Guinness on the bench table in front of him. For some reason the thought of the twisted INLA gunman ironing their smalls amused him. In fact, he took a few minutes to settle down. Sunny days like this, sitting in pub gardens, talking to his friend Aden was what it was all about for him.

"And what about the girl?" asked Kav purposely changing the subject.

"Which one?"

"Sweet tits, I think you called her."

"Enya," said Aden reminiscently as if he was reflecting on a good book. "I am going to have to chalk her up as one of the greatest sacrifices in my life."

"Well, I for one am proud of you Aden. You already have a girlfriend who is a wonderful woman. You did the right thing there with Enya; you left no loose ends that might, later on, unravel your relationship with Sheila."

"I did it for Shane too."

"Who? That crazy barman? I rue the day I clapped eyes upon him in the Andersonstown Republican Club."

"No! You don't really mean that. He was a good sort and I think Enya will help him change for the better. I certainly didn't give up on him."

"He should watch the nonsense that comes out of his mouth. You could have lost your life."

"Maybe you shouldn't have been earwigging on his conversation in Andersonstown. Perhaps you shouldn't have taken him so seriously."

"And perhaps you shouldn't have made enemies with the INLA. Let's not play the blame game here Aden, because you messed up too."

The banter was just playful, but the points were well made. Their ability to accept rebukes from each other was one of the cornerstones of their friendship.

"I suppose you are right Kav. He did start the whole fiasco with his loose talk, but we did have quite an adventure down there."

"Yes, you nearly died."

"And somehow, you got kidnapped by the very person we went down to kidnap," said Aden openly laughing at his friend.

"It makes you re-evaluate your life, doesn't it?"

"It does, that is why Shelia and I are going to get married. We might even move into her father's old farm and give it a go."

ANGUS CACTUS

"I don't see you as a farmer."

"Well, then we can always sell it, or rent it."

Both men were smiling at each other, as recollection of events brought fresh thoughts to mind.

"I wonder what they are doing now, Li and his mother?" asked Kav.

"I am sure they are doing just fine," said Aden. "Is it not strange though, how Huong turned out to be a Kung fu master?"

"I have to agree with you there. That must have been a strange sight."

"And the gold? Do you think it is possible that they lied to us?" and by 'us', Aden really meant Kav.

"A classic Sligonian story," explained Kav. "He told me that when he arrived, the locals told him a similar story about some Germans that lived in the county."

"The sons of U-boat men and the hidden Nazi gold; sure you can get that story anywhere in Ireland," pointed out Aden, "probably started in Sligo though."

"Crazy town full of the maddest kind of people," said Kav confirming Aden's premise.

"So how are you and Maeve getting on? I hear you moved back in together."

"We are giving it a go. It's different this time. She has changed for real and I think perhaps I still love her."

"You never stopped loving her Kav. You two are made for each other."

*

It was a windy blustery day, which guaranteed that the strand would be empty of anyone other than the most determined dog walkers. Sideways rain was being blown in from the sea, but the weatherproof Macs which Li and his mother wore kept them dry on the inside.

The endless dunes of Streedagh strand offered protection from the wind, but once they had crested the top, this protection was lost, and they had to walk side-on to the incoming wind.

Li carried the pointed shovel over his shoulder now that he was in no danger of being seen by any others. He appeared lost in concentration, as if counting ridges in the dunes or correlating land marks. Finding the correct set of markers, he started digging. His shovel wasn't ideal for clearing sand away, but it was ideal for going deeper.

"That is where I took him," said Li pointing to another spot about twelve feet away.

"I can still see the hollow where he dug. He must have been pretty surprised when he found nothing," said Huong.

"I overpowered him soon after that."

"So why did you dig so close to here?"

"I was worried for you Mum. I couldn't decide initially whether I should comply or fight back."

"We didn't…" Huong was interrupted by the sound of metal thumping wood. It was a welcome and reassuring sound for both of them, and they grinned at each other.

She continued. "We didn't defend this and carry it through the jungles of Cambodia just to give it away to a man who was frightened of his own wife," said Huong disparagingly about Li's new friend, Kav.

"It wasn't personal Mum. He is a nice fella when you get to know him."

Huong maintained a stony silence, but the expression on her face and her glare spoke volumes. Then a warmer expression took hold.

"Li, I think we should reward the young man who rode me to safety on his motorcycle."

"Maybe we should buy him a brand new one, Mother," said Li.

Shane had saved the day for them, and much, much more. However, the real truth of exactly how much more, was going to remain buried in Sligo.

V23

I hope you enjoyed reading this book.
Moreover, if you did, please don't keep this a secret.
Consider leaving me a review on the Amazon page for this book.
Reviews help independent authors like me reach more people.
I always value any feedback on the story as well as the writing.
At **http://anguscactus.wix.com/author** : you'll find extras that might be helpful or interesting to have when reading To Hell or Sligo. Photos of places featured in the novel, explanations of concepts and ideas referred to in the storyline, and other background information.

Sincerely
Angus Cactus

Printed in Great Britain
by Amazon

Gorgeous Gyno Book Excerpt

in families. Trying to help the parents learn to budget and get the kids in school and learning. A joint effort to give the next generation a fighting chance of living the life they dream about.

Maybe if I call the CEO, they'll have someone who has been through the program or somehow associated with the mentoring that can give a firsthand account of what it means to the families. Next email on my list. Another skill I have learned: Delegation makes things happen. I can't do it all, and even with Fleur, we need to coordinate with others to make things proceed quickly.

As usual, Thursday morning traffic is slow even at this time of the day. We are crawling at a snail's pace. I could get out and walk faster than this. I contemplate it, but with the summer heat, I know even at this time of the morning, I'd end up a sweaty mess. That is not the look I need when I'm trying to present like the woman in charge. Even if you have no idea what you're doing, you need people to believe you do. Smoke and mirrors, the illusion is part of the performance.

My phone is pinging constantly as I approach the front of the office building. We chose the location in the beginning because it was central to all the big function spaces in the city. Being new to the city, we didn't factor in how busy it is here. Yet the convenience of being so close far outweighs the traffic hassles.

Hustling down the hall, I push open the door of our office. 'FLEURTILLY.'

It still gives me goosebumps seeing our dream name on the door. The one we thought of all those years ago in that hammock. Even more exciting is that it's all ours. No answering to anyone else. We have worked hard, and this is our reward.

The noise in the office tells me Fleur already has everything turned on and is yelling down the phone at someone. Surely, we can't have another disaster even before my first morning coffee.

"What the hell, Scott, I warned you not to go out and party too hard yesterday. Have you even been to bed yet? What the hell are you thinking, or have the drugs just stopped that peanut brain from even working?' You were already on your last warning. Find someone who will put up with your crap. Your job here is termi-

337

Gorgeous Gyno Book Excerpt

nated, effective immediately." Fleur's office phone bangs down on her desk loud enough I can hear her from across the hall.

"Well, you told him, didn't you? Now who the hell is going to run the waiters tonight?" I ask, walking in to find her sitting at her desk, leaning back in her chair, eyes closed and hands behind her head.

"I know, I know. I should have made him get his sorry ass in and work tonight and then fired him. My bad. I'll fix it, don't worry. Maybe it's time to promote TJ. He's been doing a great job, and I'm sure he's been pretty much doing Scott's job for him anyway."

To be honest, I think she's right. We've suspected for a while that Scott, one of our managers, has been partying harder than just a few drinks with friends. He's become unreliable which is unlike him. Even when he's at work, he's not himself. I tried to talk to him about it and was shut down. Unfortunately, our reputation is too important to risk him screwing up a job because he's high. He's had enough warnings. His loss.

"You fix that, and I'll find a new speaker. Oh, and 900 stupid mint-green napkins. Seriously. Let's hope the morning improves." I turn to walk out of her office and call over my shoulder, "By the way, good morning. Let today be awesome." I smile, waiting for her response.

"As awesome as we are. I see your Good Morning and I raise you a peaceful day and a drama-free evening. Your turn for coffee, woman." And so, our average workday swings into action.

By eleven-thirty, our day is still sliding towards the shit end of the scale. We have had two staff call in sick with the stupid vomiting bug. Lucia has called me a total of thirty-seven times with stupid questions. While I talk through my teeth trying to be polite, I wonder why she's hired event planners when she wants to micro-manage everything.

My phone pressed to my ear, Fleur comes in and puts her hand up to high-five me. Thank god, that means she has solved her issues and we are staffed ready to go tonight. It's just my speaker problem, and then we will have jumped the shit pile and be back on our way to the flowers and sunshine.

Gorgeous Gyno Book Excerpt

"Fleurtilly, you are speaking with Matilda." I pause momentarily.

"Hello, Mr. Drummond, how are you this morning?" I have my sweet business voice on, looking at Fleur holding her breath for my answer.

"That's great, yes, I'm having a good day too." I roll my eyes at my partner standing in front of me making stupid faces. "Thank you for calling me back. I was just wondering how you went with finding another speaker for this evening's event." I pause while he responds. I try not to show any reaction to keep Fleur guessing what he's saying. "Okay, thank you for looking into it for me. I hope you enjoy tonight. Goodbye." Slowly I put the phone down.

"Tilly, for god's sake, tell me!" She is yelling at me as I slowly stand up and then start the happy dance and high-five her back.

"We have ourselves a pilot who mentors the boys and girls in the program. He was happy to step in last-minute. Mr. Drummond is going to confirm with him now that he has let us know." We both reach out for a hug, still carrying on when Deven interrupts with his normal gusto.

"Is he single, how old, height, and which team is he batting for?" He stands leaning against the doorway, waiting for us to settle down and pay him any attention.

"I already called dibs, Dev. If he is hot, single, and in his thirties then back off, pretty boy. Even if he bats for your team, I bet I can persuade him to change sides." Fleur walks towards him and wraps him in a hug. "Morning, sunshine. How was last night?"

"Let's just say there won't be a second date. He turned up late, kept looking at his phone the whole time, and doesn't drink. Like, not at all. No alcohol. Who even does that? That's a no from me!" We're all laughing now while I start shutting down my computer and pack my briefcase, ready to head over to the function at McCormick Place.

"While I'd love to stay and chat with you girls," I say, making Deven roll his eyes at me, "I have to get moving. Things to do, a function to get finished, so I can go home and put my feet up." I pick up my phone and bag, giving them both a peck on the cheek. "See you both over there later. On my phone if needed." I start

339

Gorgeous Gyno Book Excerpt

hurrying down the corridor to the elevator. I debated calling a car but figured a taxi will be quicker at this time of the day. Just before the lunchtime rush, the doorman should be able to flag one down for me.

Rushing out of the elevator, I see a taxi pulled up to the curb letting someone off. I want to grab it before it takes off again. Cecil the doorman sees me in full high-heeled jog and opens the door knowing what I'm trying to do. He's calling out to the taxi to wait as I come past him, focused on the open door the previous passenger is closing.

"Wait, please...." I call as I run straight into a solid wall of chest. Arms grab me as I'm stumbling sideways. Shit. Please don't let this hurt.

Just as my world is tilting sideways, I'm coming back upright to a white tank top, tight and wet with sweat. So close to my face I can smell the male pheromones and feel the heat on my cheeks radiating from his body.

"Christ, I'm so sorry. Are you okay, gorgeous?" That voice, low, breathy, and a little startled. I'm not game to look up and see the face of this wall of solid abs. "You just came out that door like there's someone chasing you. I couldn't stop in time." His hands start to push me backwards a little so he can see more of me. "Talk to me, please. Are you okay? I'm so sorry I frightened you. Luckily I stopped you from hitting the deck."

Taking a big breath to pull myself back in control, I slowly follow up his sweaty chest to look at the man the voice is coming from. The sun is behind him so I can't make his face out from the glare. I want to step back to take a better look when I hear the taxi driver yelling at me.

"Are you getting in, lady, or not?" he barks out of the driver's seat.

Damn, I need to get moving.

"Thank you. I'm sorry I ran in front of you. Sorry, I have to go."

I start to turn to move to the taxi, yet he hasn't let me go.

"I'm the one who's sorry. Just glad you're okay. Have a good day, gorgeous." He guides me to the back seat of the taxi and

340

Gorgeous Gyno Book Excerpt

closes the door for me after I slide in, then taps the roof to let the driver know he's good to go. As we pull away from the curb, I see his smile of beautiful white teeth as he turns and keeps jogging down the sidewalk. My heart is still pounding, my head is still trying to process what the hell just happened. Can today get any crazier?

GRAYSON

'I'm just a hunk, a hunk of burning love
Just a hunk, a hunk of burning love'

Crap!
What the hell!

I reach out to grab her before I bowl her over and smash her to the ground. Stopping my feet dead in the middle of running takes all the strength I have in my legs. We sway slightly, but I manage to pull her back towards me to stand her back up. Where did this woman come from? Looking down at the top of her head, I can't tell if she's okay or not.

She's not moving or saying anything. It's like she's frozen still. I think I've scared her so much she's in shock.

She's not answering me, so I try to pull her out a little more so I can see her face.

Well, hello my little gorgeous one.

The sun is shining brightly on her face that lights her up with a glow. She's squinting, having trouble seeing me. She opens her mouth to finally talk. I'm ready for her to rip into me for running into her. Yet all I get is sorry and she's trying to escape my grasp. The taxi driver gives her the hurry along. I'd love to make sure she's really okay, but I seem to be holding her up. I help her to the taxi and within seconds she's pulling away from me, turning and watching me from the back window of the cab.

Well, that gave today a new interesting twist.

One gorgeous woman almost falling at my feet. Before I could even settle my breathing from running, I blink, and she's gone. Almost like a little figment of my imagination.

341

Gorgeous Gyno Book Excerpt

One part I certainly didn't imagine is how freaking beautiful she looked.

I take off running towards Dunbar Park and the basketball court where the guys are waiting for me. Elvis is pumping out more rock in my earbuds and my feet pound the pavement in time with his hip thrusts. I'm a huge Elvis fan, my music tastes stuck in the sixties. There is nothing like the smooth melodic tones of the King. My mom listened to him on her old vinyl records, and we would dance around the kitchen while Dad was at work. I think she was brainwashing me. It totally worked. Although I love all sorts of music, Elvis will always be at the top of my playlist.

"Oh, here's Doctor Dreamy. What, some damsel in distress you couldn't walk away from?" The basketball lands with a thud in the center of my chest from Tate.

"Like you can talk, oh godly one. The surgeon that every nurse in the hospital is either dreaming about fucking, or how she can stab needles in you after she's been fucked over by you." Smacking him on the back as I join the boys on the court, Lex and Mason burst out laughing.

"Welcome to the game, doctors. Sucks you're on the same team today, doesn't it? Less bitching and more bouncing. Let's get this game started. I'm due in court at three and the judge already hates me, so being late won't go well," Lex yelled as he started backing down the court ready to mark and stop us scoring a basket.

"Let me guess, she hates you because you slept with her?" I yell back.

"Nope, but I may have spent a night with her daughter, who I had no idea lives with her mother the judge."

"Holy shit, that's the funniest thing I've heard today." Mason throws his head back, laughing out loud. "That story is statusworthy."

"You put one word of that on social media and I won't be the one in court trying to get you out on bail. I'll be there defending why I beat you to a pulp, gossip boy. Now get over here and help me whip the asses off these glamour boys." Lex glares at Mason.

342

Gorgeous Gyno Book Excerpt

"Like they even have a chance. Bring it, boys." He waves at me to come at him.

Game on, gentlemen.

My watch starts buzzing to tell us time's up in the game. We're all on such tight work schedules that we squeeze in this basketball game together once a week. These guys are my family, well, the kind of family you love one minute and want to kill the next. We've been friends since meeting at Brother Rice High School for Boys, where we all ended up in the same class on the first day. Not sure what the teachers were thinking after the first week when we had bonded and were already making pains of ourselves. Not sure how many times our parents were requested for a 'talk' with the headmaster, but it was more often than is normal, I'm sure. It didn't matter we all went to separate universities or worked in different professions. We had already formed that lifelong friendship that won't ever break.

Sweat dripping off all of us, I'm gulping down water from the water fountain. Not too much, otherwise I'll end up with a muscle cramp by the time I run back to the hospital.

"Right, who's free tonight?" Mason is reading his phone with a blank look on his face.

"I'm up for a drink, I'm off-shift tonight," Tate pipes up as I grin and second him that I'm off too. It doesn't happen often that we all have a night off together. The joys of being a doctor in a hospital.

"I can't, I'm attending a charity dinner. It's for that charity you mentor for, Mason," Lex replies.

"Well, that's perfect. Gray, you are my plus one, and Tate, your date is Lex. I'm now the guest speaker for the night. So, you can all come and listen to the best talk you have witnessed all year. Prepare to be amazed." He brushes each of his shoulders with his hands, trying to show us how impressive he is.

We all moan simultaneously at him.

"Thanks for the support, cock suckers. My memory is long," He huffs a little as he types away a reply on his phone.

Mason is a pilot who spent four years in the military, before he was discharged, struggling with the things he saw. He started to work in the commercial sector but then was picked up by a private

343

Gorgeous Gyno Book Excerpt

charter company. He's perfect for that sort of role. He has the smoothness, wit, and intelligence to mingle with anyone, no matter who they are. He's had great stories of different passengers over the years and places he's flown.

"Why in god's name would anyone think you were interesting enough to talk for more than five minutes. You can't even make that time limit for sex," I say, waiting for the reaction.

"Oh, you are all so fucking funny, aren't you. I'm talking about my role in mentoring kids to reach for their dream jobs no matter how big that dream is." The look on his face tells me he takes this seriously.

"Jokes aside, man, that's a great thing you do. If you can dream it, you can reach it. If you can make a difference in one kid's life, then it's worth it." We all stop with the ribbing and start to work out tonight's details. We agree to meet at a bar first for a drink and head to the dinner together. My second alarm on my watch starts up. We all know what that means.

Parting ways, Mason yells over his shoulder to us all, "By the way, it's black tie."

I inwardly groan as I pick up my pace into a steady jog again. I hate wearing a tie. It reminds me of high school wearing one every day. If I can avoid it now, I do. Unfortunately, most of these charity dinners you need to dress to impress. You also need to have your wallet full to hand over a donation. I'm lucky, I've never lived without the luxury of money, so I'm happy to help others where I can.

Running down Michigan Avenue, I can see Mercy Hospital in the distance standing tall and proud. It's my home away from home. This is the place I spend the majority of my waking hours, working, along with some of my sleeping hours too. My heart beats happily in this place. Looking after people and saving lives is the highest rush you can experience in life. With that comes rough days, but you just hope the good outweighs the bad most of the time.

That's why I run and try not to miss the workouts with the boys. You need to clear the head to stay focused. The patients need the best of us every single time. Tate works with me at Mercy which

Gorgeous Gyno Book Excerpt

makes for fun days and nights when we're on shift together. He didn't run with me today as he's in his consult rooms and not on shift at the hospital.

I love summer in Chicago, except, just not this heat in the middle of the day when I'm running and sweating my ass off. It also means the hospital struggles with all the extra caseload we get. Heat stroke in the elderly is an issue, especially if they can't afford the cool air at home. The hospital is the best thing they have for relief. My smart watch tells me it's eighty-six degrees Fahrenheit, but it feels hotter with the humidity.

I don't get the extra caseload, since I don't work in emergency. That's Tate's problem. He's a neurosurgeon who takes on the emergency cases as they arrive in the ER. Super intense, high-pressure work. Not my idea of fun. I had my years of that role, and I'm happy where I am now.

Coming through the front doors of the hospital, I feel the cool air hit me, while the eyes of the nursing staff at the check-in desk follow me to the elevator. The single ones are ready to pounce as soon as you give them any indication you might be interested. Tate takes full advantage of that. Me, not so much. When you're an intern, it seems like a candy shop of all these women who want to claim the fresh meat. The men are just as bad with the new female nurses.

We work in a high-pressure environment, working long hours and not seeing much daylight at times. You need to find a release. That's how I justified it, when I was the intern. I remember walking into a storeroom in my first year as an intern, finding my boss at the time, Leanne, and she was naked from the waist down being fucked against the wall by one of the male nurses. Now I am a qualified doctor who should hold an upstanding position in society, so I rarely get involved in the hospital dating scene anymore.

Fuck, who am I kidding? That's not the reason. It's the fact I got burnt a few years ago by a clinger who tried to get me fired when I tried to move on. Not going down that path again. Don't mix work and play, they say—well, I say, Tate hasn't quite learned that lesson

345

Gorgeous Gyno Book Excerpt

yet. Especially the new batch of interns he gets on rotation every six months. He is a regular man-whore.

Am I a little jealous? Maybe just a tad. Both me and my little friend, who's firming up just thinking about getting ready for some action. It's been a bit of a dry spell. I think it's time to fix that. Pity my date for tonight, Mason, is not even close to what I'm thinking about.

My cock totally loses interest now in the conversation again. Can't say I blame him.

Just then the enchanting woman from today comes to mind and my cock is back in the game. I wish I knew who she was. Now this afternoon's rounds could be interesting if my scrubs are tenting with a hard-on.

The joys of being a large man, if you get my drift. There's no place to hide him.

Printed in Great Britain
by Amazon